WICKED TRAP

M.V. KASI

To all of us.

May we emerge stronger in our lives with hope and compassion.

Contents

Contents

Prologue

"Arjun, wake up."

Arjun was in the middle of a nightmare when he heard his mother's sweet voice. She was calling him while gently shaking him awake.

"Arjun, wake up baby."

Arjun opened his eyes. It was still dark inside the room and he could only see the faint outline of his mother. He was a little embarrassed. As an eight-year-old boy, he wasn't supposed to be getting scared or having nightmares. But after the last two shocking days, he couldn't sleep without having them.

"Ma. I was dreaming that P-papa was hanging and they burned him—"

His mother hugged him tightly. "Shh," she said with a slightly trembling voice. "It's okay, baby."

Slowly, his shaking body relaxed.

"You have to keep very quiet, Arjun," his mother instructed. "We are going out."

Even though he was still a bit shaken by the nightmare, he could sense the urgency in his mother's voice. He nodded. He also noticed that his two older brothers were already awake and standing by their beds.

"Let's go," his mother gently instructed before she held his hand and walked them out of the bedroom.

But instead of going out through the mansion corridors, his mother led him and his brothers through the door at the back of their bedroom suite. It led into the garden area at the back of the mansion. The beautiful, vivid-colored garden was dark during the nighttime. It was windy and lightning flashed in the sky.

"Don't turn on the flashlight until I tell you," his mother softly instructed.

Arjun's brothers nodded. Arjun was a bit scared of the storms, but when he clutched his mother's hand tightly, he felt slightly better.

His mother led them outside to the gardens.

"Turn on the flashlight now," she instructed.

The lights from the small flashlights lit the path outside. Everything looked strange and scary at night, especially with the heavy wind and lightning. The tall trees his father had planted using Arjun's and his brothers' help were now swaying with the wind.

They continued walking hurriedly somewhere. The estate was big. He had heard people mentioning that it was five hundred acres. Even though he didn't know what that measurement meant, he knew it must be really big.

They passed through the river, walking beneath the surrounding tall trees. And then, they walked through the vast paddy fields before reaching a narrow road. Arjun noticed a car was parked there.

All their cars had been sold a while ago, and this was their only car left. It was small and old-looking unlike their other big, shiny cars, which he and his brothers had enjoyed riding in the backseat.

"We need to hurry, Mrs. Vardhaman," a familiar man's voice said.

Arjun knew it was their longtime driver. But instead of the usual happy, laughing tone, Mr. Rao's voice sounded grim and urgent.

"Arjun, get in, baby," Arjun's mother instructed.

Arjun did as told and sat in the back seat. His mother sat next to him and then his brother, Bharat. His oldest brother Yashwanth sat in the front seat next to the driver.

Soon, the car began to move. It was very dark, and it had begun raining. Arjun didn't know why the car's lights were turned off. It was only much later when the car drove out of the estate and passed the nearby villages that the car lights were turned on.

There was lighting from the streets that lit the car dimly inside. He could see his mother's face. His mother's beautiful eyes were swollen and puffy like they had been the previous day.

He knew his mother had been crying. His father had died a day ago, and earlier that morning, his oldest brother had lit fire to their father's body. Arjun did not want to believe that his father was dead even though he saw the body burning. But he heard the loud whispers during the funeral.

"So sad that Vardhaman chose a coward's way out."

"Couldn't he think of his wife and young sons?"

"After cheating hundreds of families, maybe he felt he deserved to die."

Arjun hadn't understood what the people were saying. But he understood the word 'coward'. It was the opposite of being brave. He didn't know why they were calling his father as a coward. His father was the bravest man he knew.

Feeling shaken and confused, he rested his head on his mother's side. His mother placed her palm on his cheek reassuringly.

Soon, the lights outside the car turned even brighter. Arjun knew they were in the city because he recognized some of the buildings.

The car stopped at the airport. Arjun had been to the airport many times when they went on family vacations or when he and his brothers received their father when he returned from a business trip.

Why are we going on a vacation now?

He wasn't in the mood to go on a vacation. He missed his father. He wanted to go back home and wait until his father returned from heaven.

"I have placed your passports and tickets in this pouch, Mrs. Vardhaman."

"Thank you, Mr. Rao." Arjun's mother took the pouch and opened it. "Mr. Rao. Why is there so much cash in here?"

There was a pause. "Please keep it, Mrs. Vardhaman. It's the money Mr. Ashok had given me. I'm just returning it. This money will help you and the boys in a strange country."

Arjun's mother shook her head. "I can't take the money, Mr. Rao. Please use it for your granddaughter's education. I'm sure A-ashok gave it for the same purpose."

Arjun noticed the break in his mother's voice and clung to her to offer her comfort.

Mr. Rao hesitated for a moment, but he nodded.

Soon, they got out of the car. Mr. Rao hugged Arjun's brothers, and then he hugged Arjun.

"Take good care of your mother, boys. Be happy, and I know you three will be successful no matter where you are."

Arjun was confused by Mr. Rao's words. Why was Mr. Rao acting as though they would not be seeing him anytime soon?

Arjun's mother smiled at the old man. "Thank you for everything, Mr. Rao."

"You are like a daughter to me, Mrs. Vardhaman. Please take care."

Arjun's mother nodded, and then taking a deep breath, she held Arjun's hand before the four of them walked into the airport terminal.

Arjun couldn't keep quiet anymore. "Where are we going, Ma?" he asked.

"We are going to New York."

Arjun had never been there before. But he knew it was a city in the United States of America. He and his brothers knew the names of many countries and cities since they played games based on the names and visited a few countries during vacations.

"When are we going back home, Ma?" he asked.

His mother looked at him. Her beautiful face looked sad. "We won't be going back, Arjun," she replied. "And from now on... your name will no longer be Arjun. It will be Aryan."

CHAPTER ONE

Fifteen years later...

New York

"We are going back home."

Listening to his oldest brother's words, Aryan Varma vaguely thought about how his eight-year-old self would have been jumping with joy at the news. But now, all he felt was rage.

Aryan no longer felt his birthplace where he spent the first eight years of his life was home anymore. New York was his home now.

Maybe it was the tense atmosphere and the current circumstances that added to his rage. He was inside a boardroom, but the meeting they were having was not related to business.

"We have only four months or at most six months to execute most of our plan."

Aryan knew his other older brother was right. Time was of the essence for what they were planning.

"Aryan? Why aren't you saying anything? Do you agree with our plan?"

At his oldest brother's question, Aryan finally spoke.

"No," he replied.

At his reply, Yash Varma's eyes flashed.

"What part of it don't you agree with?" Bhargav Varma asked calmly.

Aryan looked at both his brothers.

"I don't agree with the part where we should keep the families out of this," he said. "Did the bastards leave our family alone? They came after our mother and us too. They destroyed us and left us homeless."

There was a loaded silence.

All three Varma brothers were known for their cold ruthlessness in the business world. But Aryan's two older brothers barely displayed outer emotions. Yash Varma and Bhargav Varma thought it was a waste of time. They often said that anger or happiness or sadness didn't change the course of a person's life. Feeling such emotions would only make one miserable.

But Aryan was different from his two brothers. He felt it all and showed it back tenfold. He was often considered the wild card, and his rivals in the business world didn't know what to anticipate from him. A genius when it came to computer programming and software, he had made his first billion when he was eighteen. By then, his two brothers were already self-made billionaires. Despite all hardships and tragedies they had faced during childhood, they were successful.

Or so they had thought.

They hadn't realized that success was a state of mind. They had recently discovered the betrayal behind the devastating past loss. Unless they sought retribution and brought justice to the loss, all their successes so far would mean nothing.

"When Ma finds out, she would not be happy about dragging the families into it."

Aryan knew his brother was right. Their sweet and kind mother would be shocked and hurt. But it only made him stick even harder to his path of retribution.

"When you two both quit school and were out working in construction jobs to put food on the table, do you know what I was doing at home? I was with Ma. I might have been only eight or nine at that time, but I recall every damn moment. I watched as Ma broke into pieces even though she tried to put on a brave face." His jaw clenched. "I was the one to wipe her tears when she couldn't control her grief and helplessness."

His brothers no longer remained unmoved. Rage was visible on their faces as they recalled the dark times when their family had to struggle for basic necessities.

"Let's go all in," Aryan stated. "Drag in the damn families or anyone that will help destroy those bastards. I don't care who the fuck needs to be involved. I want every teardrop that Ma shed in the last fifteen years accounted for, even if it cannot ever be compensated."

Aryan's brothers knew he was right. The mental and physical anguish they suffered, especially their mother, could not be atoned.

"All right," said Yash.

Bhargav nodded as well. "Let's go all in."

***

"Here are the files you requested, Mr. Varma."

The private investigator placed the thick folders on Aryan's office desk inside a high-rise building that overlooked Times Square. The investigator looked confused as though wondering why a billionaire chairman of a well-known software company in New York was requesting an investigation on people halfway across the world who had nothing to do with software or business.

"Thank you. You may leave now."

The investigator nodded and left. Aryan picked up the thick file in front of him. It was of a noted criminal lawyer who was now a powerful politician. All of the old man's wealth was put into a trust in the daughter's name who was the man's only child.

Even though there was a file with a detailed investigation on the heiress in a smaller file, Aryan opened his sleek laptop and typed in the woman's name. Several articles and videos mentioned her. He clicked on the video link at the top.

He froze momentarily at the first glimpse of her.

He had expected a glamorous society heiress pouting at the camera while partying with her friends—the kind he was used to dating. But the woman in the video was neither pouting nor was she glamorous.

She wore a plain t-shirt and jeans. Her long hair was tied into a ponytail, and her face was completely devoid of makeup. Her eyes blazed with anger and passion. She was surrounded by a huge crowd which included police personnel. There was tear gas and smoke, which made people around her cough and choke and cry out in agony. But the woman stood rock solid. Her eyes watered, but determination shone though.

Her voice cut through the chaos around her.

"We won't back down!" she shouted into the camera held by a coughing reporter.

"You can break our bones, but you cannot break our spirit!"

"You have no right to poison us!"

The information under the video stated it was a protest led against an industrialist who wanted to build a factory close to the city where thousands of families lived. The water and air would be polluted according to the plan.

The protest was one year ago, and it successfully stopped the factory from being built in the area. It was shifted elsewhere. Tanvi Shetty, the daughter of a top criminal lawyer turned politician, had led the protest.

"Come on, get me first!" she thundered as several cops surrounded her and the crowd.

Aryan felt a strange thrill running through him looking at her. It was a feeling he had never felt before. Along with the strong need for revenge, he also felt the burning need to capture the passionate woman.

Laying out a trap for someone like her would be far from easy, but he was looking forward to it.

"Come on, get me!" she goaded again, looking straight at him towards the camera.

Aryan's mouth slowly twisted. "I'm coming, princess. And I'm going to get you soon."

CHAPTER TWO

Tanvi Shetty crossed the road while giving instructions to her friend on the phone. "Yes, I'm on my way there. Don't worry about my security. Just upload the pictures I send to my social media handle."

She spotted a lone taxi waiting in front of a shop where the driver must have gone to buy something. She had been searching for a taxi for the last thirty minutes. But since there was an ongoing bus strike, most taxis were taken.

She somehow managed to cross the road and not get hit by the two-wheelers that had illegally jumped the red signal.

"Finally," she muttered and stood by the taxi, waiting for the driver to come out from a shop.

Meanwhile, she pulled out her phone and went through her mental checklist.

Placards—check.

Slogans—check.

Location messages on social media—check.

Messages to the media—check.

She had everything ready for a protest she was leading that day in front of a corporate building. It was a protest against an international corporation that was planning to raze out the only green forested area in the middle of the city to build a massive mall.

There were several dozen malls in the city. But the green forested area was one of the last areas remaining. It was more or less the lungs of the densely populated city, and the ruthless billionaire was planning to destroy it.

Never! I won't let them get away with it!

She would have to find more information on the company to dig up dirt, so she could send it to her friend who worked in the media.

She tapped her foot impatiently as she waited for the taxi driver. She took a few steps towards the store to check inside when she saw an old man in a taxi driver's uniform.

"Is this your taxi?" she asked him.

The old man nodded. "Yes, miss."

"Thank God! I need to go to the downtown area urgently."

"Okay, miss," the old man replied.

Offering a thankful prayer again, she turned to go towards the taxi.

Just as she neared, a tall and broad-shouldered man wearing a dark blue checkered formal shirt cut in front of her. Before she could say anything, he opened the taxi door and got inside in a smooth move.

"Hey!" she shouted. "This taxi is mine!"

She stepped closer to the back seat and glared at the man seated inside. He was wearing sunglasses, but she felt his gaze sweeping over her.

"Oh good," he drawled in a deep voice. "I need to go to the downtown area."

Tanvi glared at him harder. "I don't own the taxi. I meant this taxi is mine because I *spotted* it first! I was waiting for the driver to come out of the store. And I've already spoken to him."

The man's thick masculine eyebrow rose at her words. But he didn't make a move to get out. Continuing to look at her, he settled back comfortably against the seat, his broad shoulders taking up most of the space as he stretched an arm on top of the back rest.

"Well, I'm already seated inside the taxi," he said. "Find another one."

"I can't!" she snapped. "I'm sure you know there's a bus strike going on. So *you* will have to find another taxi. I have to urgently go to the downtown area. A lot of people are waiting for me there."

She hurriedly opened her large bag and pulled out a couple of hundred notes and held it to him. "I'm sure this will cover for your taxi fare with some change to spare. Just get another taxi."

The man's mouth twisted. "Sorry, princess," he drawled. "I don't need your money. But I need to go to the downtown area too. Why don't you hop in, and we can go there together and be dropped off at our destinations?"

A bolt of annoyance passed through her when he called her princess. Something about the man rubbed her the wrong way. Maybe it was his sweeping gaze and the cocky smirk on his handsome face. He was good-looking—too good-looking, especially with the dimples. She was sure he knew that fact very well.

She also suspected he must have seen her waiting near the taxi. But still, the ass cut in front of her. He stole her taxi, and now he was more or less bullying her into sharing it with him even though she had unofficially booked it first.

"I don't take rides with strangers! Especially *suspicious* strangers."

The arrogant man didn't look offended. His smirk remained firmly in place.

She continued to glare at him. "Can you stop wasting my time! I'm in a hurry!"

He shrugged. "All right, princess. If you are not joining me, shut the taxi door. I'm in a hurry too, and I need to get going."

The taxi driver looked on uncertainly at their interaction. "Miss, I need to start the ride too."

Tanvi knew she couldn't waste the taxi driver's time. With the bus strike, the old man would make a decent profit with multiple rides all day.

But there was also no guarantee of when the next available taxi might come by. She couldn't afford to be late.

"Fine," she said. "I'll share the ride with this man to downtown."

Gritting her teeth at the arrogant man seated inside, she went around the taxi and got in. Although the man had moved, and there was at least a foot distance between them, he was still way too close for comfort. The man's cologne filled up the inside of the taxi, tingling her nose. The fragrance was subtle yet addicting.

Ignoring his presence, she pulled out her phone and texted that she would be at the protest site in thirty minutes. She also checked her messages. A few protesters had already assembled in front of the corporate building.

"Where exactly in downtown are you going, miss?" the taxi driver asked.

"The Prism building."

"And you, sir?"

"The Prism building," the deep voice drawled.

At the man's reply, Tanvi whipped her head to look at him in shock. "You are going to the protest too?" she asked.

He hardly looked like the protesting kind. In fact, he hardly looked like he would care enough for saving anything, let alone trees or the environment.

But maybe she was being too judgmental because they met in less-than-ideal circumstances.

"I'm going there for a job interview, princess," he drawled. "Some of us have to work to earn money for food and shelter. We don't have time for hobbies."

Once again, anger flared inside her at his answer. She was right about the man the first time. The ass was definitely not the kind to care about the trees or environment.

"Leading a protest is not my hobby!" she gritted. "I graduated recently, and I'm looking for a job too."

"Really?" His eyes swept over her.

She was outraged by his skeptical tone. She was dressed in simple faded jeans and a t-shirt. Her long hair was pulled into a high ponytail, and she only had pale pink moisturizing lipstick as makeup.

What was she supposed to look like? Looking for a job didn't necessarily mean she needed to always dress up for an interview. She wore jeans and a t-shirt and tied her hair because it was practical and comfortable, especially since she was going to be leading the protest for hours.

Judgmental ass!

Annoyed, she turned away to ignore him once again.

A few minutes of silence prevailed, but she couldn't tolerate it. The need to educate the arrogant man next to her and also fish for more information from him grew inside her.

"Did you know that the company you want to work for plans to destroy the City Central Park and build a mall?" she asked.

He raised an eyebrow as though to ask *so?*

She gritted her teeth. "The protest is to stop them! If the mall plan goes ahead, thousands of trees will have to be cut, without which all of us living in the city, including children and animals, will suffer. That's one of the last green patches left in the city."

At her passionate outburst, she sensed his gaze intensifying on her. A strange prickling awareness spread through her, causing her skin to break into goosebumps.

What the hell?

She shook off the awareness. Maybe it was simply a strong annoyance because she wasn't the kind to be drawn to strangers—especially arrogant strangers.

She discreetly rubbed her arms so the goosebumps would disappear.

His mouth twisted slightly at her action. "So how are you planning to stop the construction of the mall?" he asked.

"By demanding that Prism Corporation should stop the project right away and go to some other feasible place to build their mall."

"You think they would listen?" There was amusement in his voice.

She raised her chin. "Yes. They would *have* to listen. There's going to be media coverage which will translate into bad publicity. All businesses know how important it is to earn public goodwill and maintain a certain image."

"Not all businesses or businessmen care about their image. A few give a damn about their image. The reason they are on the top is because of their ruthlessness."

She narrowed her eyes. "I know Prism Corporation will stop."

Once again, she saw his mouth twist into a smirking smile. Before she could respond, the taxi pulled over in front of the Prism building, where a small group of people had already gathered.

"Good luck with your protest, princess," the man drawled out.

Tanvi was annoyed by his offhand attitude. She knew not everyone had a similar passion for causes such as saving the environment. But she had hoped the information she provided would at least make him a slightly responsible citizen. Hopefully, if he got the job, he could convince his colleagues and others to help stop the destruction of the environmentally protected park.

The man turned towards her, and she could sense his gaze on her once again. "By the way, since I let you share my ride, you are welcome to pay."

Before she could protest in outrage, he opened the door and slipped out of the taxi before disappearing into the gathering crowd.

Arrogant ass!

She let it slide and didn't argue because there was no time. And also because the man was most likely unemployed since he was going to a job interview.

"How much for the taxi fare?" she asked the driver.

When the driver told her, she hurriedly paid him along with a generous tip before stepping outside.

"Tanvi!" One of her acquaintances she met during protests waved from a short distance.

Tanvi joined the group. "It's almost nine," she said. "The management will start arriving soon. Let's get started."

The placards were distributed. They had already prepared for the slogans. She even got flyers printed for passersby and the employees working in the building to give them information on the level of destruction of the environment and the impact.

Holding a placard in one hand and a speaker phone in another, she led the protest.

"Save City Central Park!"

"Save our lungs!"

"Save our future!"

"Stop Prism Corporation!"

Dozens of people gathered around her and raised slogans along with her. Only a few were her friends and acquaintances. The rest were passionate environmentalists like her. Some of them were aging citizens too, who used the park for their daily walks and fresh air.

It was outrageous that permission was granted to destroy the beautiful park.

Soon, the media vans arrived and began clicking pictures along with taking videos of the protest. One of the reporters she recognized came to ask her questions.

"How long do you plan to protest?" the reporter asked.

"As long as it takes for Prism Corporation to change their mind."

The reporter looked skeptical. Tanvi was reminded of the arrogant man she met a while ago who had looked similarly doubtful. Corporate greed combined with political backing was hard to shake off. But she knew bringing attention to that greed was the only way to stop it.

"What exactly do you plan to do?" another reporter asked.

"We will protest peacefully. But if they go near the park to cut down trees, we'll form a human chain. In fact, each of us will chain ourselves to the trees inside the park."

The reporters looked excited at her aggressive stance. They knew there would be quite a bit of drama to make their news coverage interesting.

"There are some very powerful people involved in the mall construction deal. Do you think you can stand up to them?" a reporter asked.

"Yes," she replied confidently. "No power on earth can stop us from fighting to protect ours and our future generations' health. The mall can be built elsewhere in the city outskirts. There should be a limit to corporate greed."

The reporters continued to ask obvious questions. "Do you think the management of Prism Corporation will listen to your demands and back away?"

She was reminded of the arrogant man she met that morning who thought they wouldn't listen.

"Not all businesses or businessmen care about their image. A few give a damn about their image. The reason they are on the top is because of their ruthlessness."

Shaking away thoughts of the arrogant, handsome man, she replied to the reporter.

"Yes, they will listen to the demands." They will have to.

The crowd began to grow. More and more people who wanted to save the popular park joined the protest. It wasn't that big yet because the awareness wasn't spread that far. But the social media reach for the cause would be tremendous.

While she and the rest of the protestors continued with their slogans, the police personnel got out of their vans and surrounded them.

"You have to clear out," one of the cops instructed. "The management has filed a trespassing complaint."

Tanvi knew they weren't trespassing. "We are outside the company premises. We are on public property, and this is a peaceful protest."

"You are still blocking their way and interrupting the regular operations of the company."

"Then ask a representative of Prism Corporation to speak with us. Ask them to ensure they won't go ahead with destroying the City Central Park. I'm sure most of your families have visited the park too. How can you allow its destruction?"

The cops looked uncomfortable.

One of them spoke to her. "We have to follow orders and clear out the protest."

"I'm sorry, sir. But we can't just walk away without trying to save the trees and fighting for our future health. You are welcome to do what you have to do."

She knew the police were helpless in such situations. They were forced to do their jobs. But at the same time, she couldn't give in.

"Save City Central Park!"

"Save our lungs!"

"Save our future!"

"Stop Prism Corporation!"

The protest continued while the police watched from the sidelines. The crowd was a decent size but not too big. A protester shouted when something hit him on his shoulder.

Tanvi frowned. The protester was standing next to a policeman, and a stone seemed to have hit him.

She turned around quickly to see who had thrown the stone. Most people held placards or were senior citizens. Her eyes fell on a huge man who looked out of place from the protesting crowd. He was maintaining eye contact with a few other men at a distance who appeared huge like him.

They looked more like hired goons she often saw at her father's house. She noticed that those men weren't chanting slogans either. They were watching silently. One of those men raised his hand, and she could see a big stone.

"Hey, stop!" she shouted.

But it was too late. The man threw the stone at someone.

There was a cry of pain. But this time, the stone hit a policeman's head. And it hit hard enough to make him bleed profusely.

Immediately, chaos ensued.

"Charge!"

The silently watching police personnel now became aggressive when one of their own was hurt.

"Wait! It wasn't a protester who threw the stone!" she shouted. "It was those men!" she pointed.

The cops didn't listen. But the men who sabotaged the protest must have heard her and seen her. A huge man charged towards her with a menacing look and with something hidden in his hand behind him.

Is he one of them?

Her heart thudded. Although she wanted to get away towards safety, she couldn't leave the protesters behind.

The man continued to charge towards her. Just as he neared and was about to deliberately crash into her, another tall man came into the path. Tanvi couldn't see who it was. She could only notice the dark blue checkered shirt on a broad back and a somewhat familiar whiff of cologne. Before she could register anything, she was dragged away by a group of policewomen. Her hands were cuffed behind her.

She was then pushed towards a police van where other protesters were being similarly arrested.

***

"You wrongfully arrested us all!" Tanvi stated.

She was held in the nearby police station along with other protesters. The protesters were thankfully placed in separate jail cells that didn't contain any real criminals. And since there were too many, the cops didn't separate them by the sexes and pushed them randomly into two jail cells.

Tanvi didn't get to speak to her jail mates yet. She was still arguing with the police.

"The protest had turned violent, Miss Shetty," a policeman stated. "It wasn't peaceful like you claimed."

"I told you that the men who threw the stones were not protesters," Tanvi argued. "Those men were hired to cause trouble. I'm sure Prism Corporation management sent them."

The policeman frowned, knowing there was a possibility.

"But there's nothing we can do, Miss Shetty. That area is now declared as a protest-free site. There will be security placed there starting tomorrow."

She wasn't shocked by the ruthless corporation's high-handedness. "It's a public road! How can they stop anyone from using it?"

"That's the order, Miss Shetty."

She gritted her teeth in frustration. "Fine. Then we'll just find a different site to protest."

There's no way she was going to allow Prism Corporation to destroy the park to build a mall.

The policeman sighed. "I guess you can do that."

After the policeman left, she sent a few more messages. It was to her father's lawyer she had contacted beforehand. Luckily, her cell phone wasn't seized.

"I suppose your other hobby is to get arrested, princess," a familiar deep voice drawled from behind.

Tanvi turned around, and her eyes clashed with a pair of dark ones that looked amused. His mouth was once again twisted into a smirk, flashing one of his dimples.

It was the arrogant man from that morning who bullied her into sharing the taxi. He was inside the jail cell, standing a few feet away with his hands folded casually and leaning against a wall. He wasn't wearing his sunglasses right then. She was annoyed that without sunglasses, he was all the more handsome.

"What are you doing here?" she demanded.

"I got arrested too," he replied. "After my interview, I thought I'd swing by and watch you protest. Unfortunately, the police thought I was a troublemaker like you too."

She was outraged. "I'm not a troublemaker!"

His mouth twisted into an amused smirk. "Oh yeah? So you are saying normal people get arrested multiple times?"

How did he know she got arrested multiple times?

"It's obvious that you know your way in and out of jail, princess," he drawled. "There's no fear or anxiety on your pretty face, which means someone, most likely your daddy dearest, will come and get you out of this difficult situation as usual."

Her annoyance grew along with her anger because he was calling her an entitled princess. Before she could snap at the arrogant man, the policeman was back.

"Miss Shetty. Your father's lawyer is here with the release papers," he informed.

There was a deep chuckle from behind her, which she knew was the arrogant man. Her cheeks heated despite her anger because his words of her father coming to her rescue were proven true.

She kept her eyes on the policeman. "I hope those release papers include everyone arrested at the protest site. And with the condition that no charges will be filed against any of us."

The policeman nodded. "Yes, Miss Shetty."

"Thank you," she told the policeman.

The jail cells were opened, and the protesters were let out. Tanvi thanked them and apologized for the inconvenience.

A middle-aged woman smiled. "It's not just your fight, child. We care for the park too. I'll come wherever you or others organize another protest to save the City Central Park."

Tanvi felt touched. "Thank you."

Everyone who was arrested felt similarly passionate about the cause. Everyone except the arrogant man.

"Goodbye, princess," he drawled. "And thank your father for helping with the release."

Tanvi was pissed at his words. She was half-tempted to call the policeman and ask to cancel the arrogant man's release papers. A night spent in jail might do him good. He would think twice about stealing a taxi and calling someone an entitled princess.

But she clenched her jaw and ignored him. Her friend Rashmi had come with the lawyer.

"Who is that gorgeous man?" she whispered in excitement.

"No one," Tanvi replied. "Let's go." Before her friend could think of flirting with the arrogant man, she dragged her friend out of the police station.

"Hey!" Rashmi protested. "I wanted to ask his name and give him my phone number!"

"He's an arrogant ass," Tanvi said before pushing her friend into a waiting car. "And we are getting late."

Her friend frowned. "Fine. Maybe he'll come again during your next planned protest. You better ask his name and phone number then."

The last thing Tanvi would do is ask for the arrogant man's phone number. She was also glad that the arrogant man would be the last person to show up at the next protest.

Good riddance.

***

"Are you sure you don't want me to drop you in front of your apartment?"

Tanvi nodded. "At the street corner is fine. I need to pick up dinner on my way."

Rashmi pulled the car to the side of the busy street. "Good night. I'll speak to you later. And I hope you are coming to Kavita's birthday party. Everyone is!"

Tanvi laughed. "Yes. I will come." She had a voluntary event to plant trees along the new highway road that morning. But hoping she would be done around lunch time, she promised her friend. "Good night. Thanks again for the ride."

Waving at her friend, Tanvi got out of the car. It was already dark outside. And the wind had picked up slightly, making it seem like it was about to rain. But the street that led to her apartment complex was still bustling with people. The area was considered safe and mostly consisted of single men and women with occasional old people with caretakers.

"Good evening, Mr. Shankar," she greeted the street vendor outside.

"The usual, Miss Tanvi?" the vendor asked.

Tanvi smiled. "Yes. The usual."

Hot oil sizzled, and the smell of vegetables and sauces being fried with rice filled the air. The vendor packed the fried rice into a container and handed it to her.

"Thank you, Mr. Shankar."

Carrying the takeout from the small mobile restaurant at the end of the street, she walked towards her apartment complex.

It was a four-story building with around fifty flats. Each floor had around twelve flats, and all of them were single-bedroom units.

"H-hello, Tanvi."

Tanvi turned to look at the person who greeted her. He was one of her neighbors who had recently moved into the apartment complex. The guy was cute and the same age as her. He was also painfully and endearingly shy.

"Hello, Sameer," she greeted him.

He smiled shyly. "I heard about the protest. I couldn't join you because I work for Prism Corporation."

Tanvi was surprised. "Oh. I didn't know that. No problem. I understand."

"I think it's great what you are doing, Tanvi."

Tanvi smiled at him. "Thank you. It was a joint effort. And hopefully, it pays off soon."

Normally, she wouldn't mind spending a few more moments chatting, but she was too tired.

"All right. I'll see you later, Sameer."

Waving him goodnight, she went towards the lifts.

Luckily, one of the lifts was on the ground floor. She took it and went to the fourth floor where her apartment was located in the corner.

As she reached it, she noticed that the lights were turned on in the apartment across from hers, and there were men carrying furniture out of the place. Her neighbor usually went to bed by seven thirty. She rarely saw her neighbor, but whenever she did, the older woman always greeted her with a kind smile.

"Hello, Mrs. Vasudev," Tanvi greeted.

The old woman smiled. "Hello, dear. I didn't get a chance to speak to you, but I'm moving tomorrow."

Tanvi's neighbor had been living in the opposite flat for many years. "Oh. That's a surprise."

The woman laughed. "Oh yes. It's a surprise for me too. An investment company bought the entire apartment complex last week. With the profit I made for my flat, I gave an advance to a flat closer to where my daughter lives."

"Wow. That's great."

Tanvi was happy for her neighbor. But she was also quite surprised that the apartment complex was sold. She supposed it made sense that someone would want to buy it since most of the people living there were renters. She also hoped that the new owner of her flat wouldn't expect her to vacate.

"I'm going to miss you, Mrs. Vasudev."

She would miss her sweet neighbor. The old woman had been the best neighbor anyone could have. She was always smiling, quiet and non-interfering.

Tanvi hoped whoever would move into the apartment next would also be the same way.

"I'm going to miss you too, dear. Do come visit me at my new place."

Tanvi smiled. "I will, Mrs. Vasudev. I'll call you once you settle in."

She would definitely visit the sweet woman who rarely had any visitors. Only twice a year, the older woman visited her daughter for a couple of days before returning home to a somewhat lonely life.

"Let me know if you need help with the moving or anything, Mrs. Vasudev."

"No need, dear. The investment company was kind enough to offer complimentary moving services as well."

Tanvi was glad for the generous gesture.

Wishing her neighbor all the best once again, Tanvi went to her apartment. Opening the door, she stepped inside and turned on the lights.

The place was tiny and functional. Despite her father's strong objection, she had moved to the place a couple of years ago. And she had stood her ground since then.

Pictures of her mother adorned the apartment living room walls along with her mother's favorite antique items. They made her feel at home.

Letting out a deep sigh as exhaustion from the day's events was beginning to seep in, she hurriedly took a quick shower. She washed off the dust and grime of the day, especially when she got thrown into the jail cell.

Putting on cotton pajamas, she went into her tiny, mostly unused kitchen and pulled out a plate to serve herself dinner.

"I need to learn to cook," she mumbled to herself as she sat on her couch to eat her meal.

She was getting sick and tired of eating takeout. Once in a while, Mrs. Vasudev sent her delicious homemade food. And a few other times, she had home-cooked meals at her friends' homes. But otherwise, she mostly relied on takeout.

"You should get a boyfriend who can cook."

She recalled Rashmi's teasing words whenever she often complained about not being able to learn cooking or having a homemade meal.

But getting a boyfriend was a bigger nuisance than somehow managing to eat the takeout meals. A boyfriend would mean commitment. She had too many things going on in her life, and she couldn't afford a meddling boyfriend who would question everything she would do.

She already had a father who questioned her and wanted her to change her lifestyle and herself.

Suddenly, a man's face flashed into her mind.

"It's obvious that you know your way in and out of jail, princess," he drawled. "There's no fear or anxiety on your pretty face, which means someone, most likely your daddy dearest, will come and get you out of this difficult situation as usual."

Anger and annoyance filled her as she was reminded of the arrogant handsome man's words.

That man was beyond a nuisance. He riled her in ways no one ever did before. Men were usually intimidated by her, either by her character or when they found out who her father was. Very few men dared to speak to her the way the arrogant man did.

Arrogant ass.

Pushing away thoughts of the arrogant man from her mind, she finished her dinner and cleared up the remnants of it. She then turned off the lights and settled into her small bed in her bedroom.

But she couldn't sleep right away.

She recalled the day's events. Things had gone wrong during the protest, and a hired goon came to attack her. What if the man who came in between and more or less saved her hadn't come there on time?

Would the goon have hurt her badly? She somehow knew he would have. There was a purpose and some kind of recognition on the goon's face.

She shivered slightly even though she had promised herself not to be intimidated by anything or anyone.

Her mind then fell on the man who had saved her. All she recalled was that her savior wore a blue checkered formal shirt and was tall and broad. She also recalled the mild yet familiar cologne.

Another whisper of memory made her frown.

The arrogant man who had stolen her taxi and called her an entitled princess had also worn a blue checkered formal shirt. He was tall and broad too. She also recalled that the cologne he had worn was similarly addicting.

Her frown grew.

No way, the arrogant ass could have saved me.

If anything, the arrogant man would watch from the sidelines and make a smart remark of how she should change her hobby to a less dangerous one.

Yes, it was definitely not him.

Whoever her savior was, she was quite thankful to him. He must be a man who believed in helping people.

Unlike the arrogant men who stole taxis and called strange women entitled.

She felt agitated as the arrogant man's smirk on his handsome face continued to flash in her mind, stealing away her sleep.

"Go away," she commanded.

His smirk only seemed to get wider.

Feeling ridiculous that she was allowing a stranger to affect her, she shut her eyes and commanded herself to sleep.

She also hoped she would never come across the arrogant man again.

CHAPTER THREE

It was just beginning to rain. Aryan took a sip of whiskey while watching lightning flash in the sky.

He was seated by a swimming pool at the outdoor bar of a penthouse.

"Was getting arrested a part of the plan too?"

Bhargav's voice held a hint of amusement. It was close to midnight, and the two of them were having drinks while waiting to visit a gentlemen's club.

Aryan's mouth twisted. "No," he replied.

He wasn't planning on getting arrested. He had intended to only observe the protest from a distance. But when chaos broke, and he saw some suspicious man about to attack Tanvi Shetty, he had intervened.

He didn't particularly care for her. But he needed her safe and sound until the end of his plan.

"So was Shetty's daughter impressed?" Bhargav asked. "Now that you got arrested while protesting with her?"

"Hardly."

Aryan's plan didn't include impressing her in any manner. Ideally, putting on a fake, overly pleasing persona would have helped to get close to his prey. But what he wanted from her was beyond mere acquaintance or friendship. So he chose to be himself. He had mocked her and riled her. He knew she hated him right then, but he also knew she wouldn't forget him easily.

He wouldn't let her.

"When are you meeting Girish Shetty again?" his brother asked.

Rage began to fill him at the name. Controlling his emotions, he twisted his mouth into a dark smile. "He's throwing a party in my honor next week."

"Are you going?"

"No."

"Are you sure he won't start to panic or try to withdraw?"

The old bastard would panic. Aryan wanted to see him suffer.

"He can't withdraw. It's too late."

"That's good," said Bhargav. There was a small pause. "Yash and I are planning to go to the estate and see the mansion tomorrow."

Aryan knew the reason for Bhargav's pause. Aryan hated his childhood home and didn't want to see it. Instead of recalling happy memories from early childhood, all he now recalled were the shocking, devastating circumstances when they were forced to leave.

"Arjun! Where are you?"

Arjun giggled as he ran through the wide corridors of the Vardhaman mansion. He was playing hide and seek with his brothers. Although his two older brothers were much bigger than him in size, he was able to escape easily from their view in the large mansion.

He went towards his parents' bedroom suite. He knew he could hide in one of the closets. Previously those closets were completely filled, but lately, his mother had given away most of her clothes and jewellery.

His father had looked sad that she had given away her favorite things, but his mother said she was happy because she had the best husband and children and didn't need anything else.

Arjun smiled as he recalled the flower jewellery his father had made for her. He had taken Arjun's help for it too. They had spent the entire day in the beautiful garden his father had planted over the years to pluck the best flowers to make the jewellery.

"Arjun!"

He could hear his oldest brother's voice and knew his brother was searching in the music room.

Giggling, he opened the bedroom door and snuck inside. It was surprisingly dark. Although the lights were turned off since it was morning, all the rooms in the mansion were well-lit. Even though he told his mother he was brave, he was still a little scared of the dark.

He quickly turned on the light in the room. He then turned to go towards the closet area when he saw his father. His father was hanging from the ceiling and sleeping.

"Papa?" he called out tentatively.

He didn't want to disturb his father. But he had never seen his father sleep in that way. In fact, he didn't know people could sleep like that.

He had always thought of his father as a superhero, tall with muscles like a superman, his father was the strongest man in the world. His father could pick big trees from the garden and move them around easily within the estate.

His father also picked mother up many times and swung her around until she laughed.

"Papa?" he called again, feeling unsure of why his father was sleeping that way. It looked uncomfortable. And the rope was causing the skin at the neck to turn red.

He didn't like seeing his father getting hurt or in pain. His father always smiled or laughed. But recently, when Ma or anyone wasn't looking, he saw his father looking worried.

"Arjun!" It was his brother, Bharat.

"I-I'm here," Arjun called out. He didn't know why, but his heart began racing. A bad feeling, the kind he felt when he was in trouble, filled his mind.

The door was pushed open, and he heard his two brothers laughing. "We knew you would hide here—" There were shocked gasps. "Papa!"

"Papa!"

Arjun watched as his two older brothers shouted out loud and rushed to their father and held his legs, trying to push him up.

"Arjun, go get help!"

At his brother's order, Arjun ran out to get help.

It was only much later in the night when he saw his mother and brothers crying that he realized his father hadn't been sleeping. His father was gone.

Rage, regret and anguish filled Aryan at those memories.

He regretted that for fifteen long years, he misdirected his anger at his father. He and his brothers had thought their father had committed suicide, leaving his wife and children destitute. But after discovering the truth two months ago, the rage was directed at the people responsible.

Rajesh Mohan. Anand Kashyap. Girish Shetty.

Those were the names of the three enemies. Yash and Bhargav were going after the first two men who had been their father's childhood friends. The so-called childhood friends had betrayed a generous-hearted wealthy man due to sheer jealousy and greed.

Aryan was going after Girish Shetty, the lawyer who was an accomplice and the possible mastermind of the entire debacle. Aryan couldn't wait to destroy that bastard.

Controlling his rage, he turned to his brother. "Let me know if you need help with the negotiation of the estate or if you want me digging up the sales documents of the surrounding lands."

There was a soft buzz on Aryan's phone. He read the message and looked at his brother. "That's the confirmation that Kashyap's son is on his third round of cards."

Bhargav nodded. "Let's go then."

They took the private elevator outside the penthouse and went down to the parking area where an SUV with dark, tinted windows was waiting. As soon as they got in, the SUV sped out of the building and into the crowded streets.

It was raining and yet there was a considerable crowd outside during the night.

The crowd reminded Aryan of the streets of New York. The crowd and traffic in New York were only slightly more organized.

It had been three weeks since he landed in the city for the first time, but he was still getting used to it.

He and Bhargav were on a hunt that night. And the prey was Bhargav's target's son.

Aryan was joining the hunt because he enjoyed the thrill of it. However, the thrill of hunting a weak prey such as their enemy's gambling-addicted son was much lower. Hunting down someone who gave a tough fight was much more satisfying.

Someone like Tanvi Shetty.

Very soon, he was going to be in her life in a way that she would have no choice but to become the pawn who would bring down his enemy.

CHAPTER FOUR

"One moment we were protesting, and then bam! We all got arrested."

Tanvi was at a friend's place attending a birthday party. She had arrived slightly late because the tree-planting event ran a little over. To distract her friends from snapping at her, she began speaking to the group about what had happened at the protest site a few days ago.

Her friends and some of the other girls listened to her with their eyes wide in fascination and horror.

"Did you challenge them to arrest you again?" one of Tanvi's friends asked.

Tanvi grinned. "No. This time, I didn't."

She hadn't challenged the police or resisted arrest. After one of the goons threw a stone at the police, she knew the protest would turn violent. It was safer for the protesters to disperse. And safer if she and the rest of the protesters didn't resist arrest.

Rashmi nudged her. "Get to the interesting part! About a gorgeous, dimpled guy who was protesting along with you and got arrested with you too."

Everyone's eyes widened again but with interest.

"Ooh, who is it?" her friend Kavita, the birthday girl, asked.

Rashmi mock glared at Tanvi. "She doesn't know his name. And neither do I. She ran him away before I could get his name or phone number."

"He wasn't a protester," Tanvi replied. "He was some random arrogant ass who just happened to be there."

"A *gorgeous* arrogant ass," Rashmi said dreamily.

Tanvi let out a scoff. "More like an *annoying* arrogant ass."

Everyone laughed.

"You find all men annoying, Tanvi," Kavita reminded. "Either the men are too intimidated by you, or they are scared of your father."

"Yeah," Rashmi added. "The very few ones who try to suck up to you because they are acquainted to your father, you scare the shit out of those too."

Tanvi didn't argue because it was somewhat true.

"I want a boyfriend," Rashmi continued. "Kavita is getting married soon. Even Divya has a boyfriend."

Kavita was engaged to a family friend's son who lived abroad. Divya Mohan's eyes widened in fear. "Shh. Don't say it out loud. If my father finds out about Rahul, he will kill us!"

Although Divya wasn't as a close a friend as Rashmi and Kavita, Tanvi had known Divya for a long time. Divya's father, Rajesh Mohan, was a distant family friend of Tanvi's father. At one point, they used to be good acquaintances. But over the years, since Tanvi's father became active in politics, they had lost touch. The only time they met and spoke recently was when Divya's brother died tragically in a car accident three years ago.

Despite being the same age and having studied in the same schools and colleges, Tanvi and Divya weren't that close. Divya was completely opposite in personality to Tanvi and of a different wave length. Divya didn't socialize much, was mild-mannered, overly cautious and prone to anxiety. She barely interacted with people. But Tanvi tried to be inclusive and friendly with Divya and invited her over for most get-togethers with college friends.

"You should speak to your father about liking someone, Divya," Tanvi said softly.

Divya shook her head. "No way! He won't ever let me step out of the house then. He will also separate Rahul and me!"

Tanvi didn't understand how the other girl planned to be with the man she loved without ever letting her parents know. Tanvi had tried to reason with Divya many times, but her friend wasn't ready to talk to her parents yet. So, Tanvi let it go and decided to respect Divya's decision.

"What about that cute guy you mentioned who moved in downstairs?" Rashmi asked Tanvi, continuing the previous topic about finding boyfriends.

Tanvi knew her friend was talking about Sameer, the guy who tried to chat her up whenever they met. "He apparently works for Prism Corporation. He seems like a nice guy."

"Not boyfriend material?"

Tanvi laughed. "Not for me, for sure." The guy was cute, but he didn't interest her. "I don't have the time or inclination to date or entertain a boyfriend."

There were too many things going on in her life. A boyfriend would not only prove to be a huge distraction, she also didn't think any man would adapt to her lifestyle.

She thrived on working for multiple causes. And once she picked up a cause, she became obsessed until it reached its natural conclusion.

Her current cause was saving City Central Park. Despite having hit a roadblock a few days ago, there was no way she could give it up. She was already planning and coordinating to find alternate site to protest.

Although none of her close friends joined her at protests or felt similarly passionate about a cause, they did support her by listening to her plans and giving her honest feedback. She enjoyed their company because they accepted her the way she was. She didn't think a man would feel the same. He would expect her to change.

"I want to come to your next protest," Rashmi insisted. "I am sure I would run into that gorgeous guy again."

Tanvi laughed. "We are planning the next protest in two days at the street behind the Prism building," she said. "There's a school." Since it would be the weekend, the school would be closed.

Rashmi nodded. "Wherever it is, even if there is a one-percent chance of running into that guy again, I'm going to come."

Tanvi shook her head with a laugh. "I'm telling you we won't ever run into that jerk again. It was a coincidence that he—"

She broke off when her phone began ringing. Looking at the number flashing on the screen, she wanted to ignore it. But she knew the phone wouldn't stop ringing until she took the call. Feeling irritated and resigned, she answered it.

"Miss Shetty," her father's secretary's voice greeted with a hint of urgency. "Your father wants you to come home right now."

Tanvi frowned. "Mr. Prasad. Please tell my father I am busy today, and—"

"Your father said it's important since he wants to discuss the... recent incident."

Tanvi knew the man meant the protest she led and her subsequent arrest. She knew she couldn't avoid the discussion with her father. He wasn't the kind who would let it go easily.

"Fine. Tell my father I'll drop by later today."

She planned to keep the discussion with her father very brief. "Thank you, Mr. Prasad."

She ended the call.

"Will your father shout at you?" Divya's voice sounded anxious.

Tanvi smiled. "Most likely, yes. But I'm not worried."

"What will he say?"

Tanvi sighed. "Same old spiel about family honor and prestige, I guess."

Divya's eyes widened in fascination because Tanvi wasn't scared or worried about her father's scolding.

Rashmi shook her head with a laugh. "You know, one of these days, your father might hire a bodyguard to keep an eye on you."

Tanvi smiled. "Oh. He can hire as many people as he wants. But he already knows that won't help."

Kavita and Rashmi laughed, knowing it was true.

Tanvi spent the next few hours enjoying her time with her friends. But when it was nearly evening time, she got up.

"All right, girls. I'll see you all next week."

"All the best for the meeting your father," Rashmi teased.

Smiling, Tanvi waved them goodbye.

Rashmi was right. She did need all of her best behavior, patience and many other things for meeting her father.

***

"Good evening, Miss Shetty. Your father is waiting for you in his office."

"Thank you, Mr. Prasad," Tanvi said to her father's secretary.

She walked along the long corridors of the huge house. The house was built nearly fifty years ago by a prominent family who used it as their city home where their children attended school. Although a few updates were made over the last fifteen years, it held most of its original décor.

She had always felt out of place in the house when her father purchased it fifteen years ago. It felt as though it still belonged to the family who had built it.

The previous house where she grew up during childhood was a different home. Her heart ached because she had beautiful memories of her mother in that home. It was also the place where her mother instilled the love of nature in her. They had to leave that home because her father's law practice had picked up, and he was beginning to get into politics at that point.

"Good evening, Miss Shetty."

She nodded and greeted a few of her father's party workers, who were waiting outside her father's office. During the mornings, a bigger crowd waited. As a prominent and powerful politician whose eyes were firmly on winning the top seat, Girish Shetty was always surrounded by people.

She knocked on the office door.

"Come in."

Tanvi pushed open the door and saw there was someone with her father in the room.

"Tanvi, come," her father greeted with a smile. He looked at the middle-aged man seated across him. "I'm sorry, Mr. Pradhan. My daughter is here to meet me. We'll have to cut short our meeting."

The other man nodded. "No problem, Mr. Shetty. I'll follow up on the discussion later this week."

The man shook hands with her father. He looked at her curiously for a moment before he left.

She knew the man must have heard about the protest and the subsequent arrest too.

As soon as the door closed behind the man and a few moments passed, her father snapped.

"Dammit, Tanvi! How could you get arrested again!" he demanded angrily. "Do you know how humiliating it was for me to receive a call from some lowly reporter and a policeman telling me my daughter got arrested for causing a nuisance on the damn streets!"

Tanvi didn't react to her father's outburst. "I was leading a protest to save the City Central Park. I wouldn't have to do that if men who were supposed to serve people didn't grant permission to companies like Prism Corporation to destroy our environment."

Her father's jaw clenched at her statement. "You are still young and have no idea how politics or bureaucracy works."

Tanvi let out a humorless laugh at her father's often-used statement. "I'm old enough, Papa. I'm old enough to know what is right and what is wrong. I've known it for a while."

Her father's jaw clenched harder. "Had your mother been alive, she wouldn't have let you resort to such behavior! It's only because she died when you were too young, and I pampered you too much that you are getting away with doing whatever you want."

At the mention of her mother, Tanvi's jaw clenched as well. "Mamma would have understood me," she said through gritted teeth. "And besides, don't you always tell people that you don't have a problem with my *public nuisance*? And also how *proud* you are that your daughter is as passionate as you to serve the public?"

Her father's face reddened in anger when she called him out for the statements he made during interviews when reporters questioned him about his daughter.

"Prism Corporation isn't like other companies you protested against," he gritted out. "It's a part of an international conglomerate with billions at stake. The mall is just the beginning of their investments. If the construction of the mall is stopped, they will not proceed with other investments."

Tanvi frowned at her father's statements. Slowly, a doubt crept through.

"You are a part of it too!" she accused. "They must have made a deal with you to give them permission to build the mall."

Her father's face immediately shut down. "Whether or not I made a deal with anyone is not of concern. I want you to stop humiliating me by making a scene and dragging our family name and prestige onto streets."

She shook her head. "It's you who is humiliating me, Papa! Do you know how sick it is that I'm leading a protest to save those trees and our city's health and future when my own father is part of the problem!"

"Just stop, Tanvi. Next time I'll tell Bhushan not to get you released from the jail."

Mr. Bhushan was their family lawyer who had helped with the jail release.

At her father's threat, her back straightened. "Do it, then," she challenged. "I will rot in jail, but I will not stop fighting for the cause."

Her father looked angry, but he seemingly controlled himself.

Taking a deep breath, he sat back and drew out some papers from the desk. He pushed them across the table towards her.

"Let's not argue further," he said. "You barely come home as it is."

"I don't live here, Papa. My home is elsewhere."

Her father's jaw clenched once again. "Krishna Ranganath's son has come from the United States for a short visit. He wants to meet you. I want you to come home for lunch tomorrow."

Tanvi frowned. "I don't know who that is. Why would he want to meet me?" she asked.

There was a pause. "His father and I work closely together in politics and in businesses. By marrying Krishna's son, you will help strengthen the relationship."

Her reply was immediate. "No. I'm not interested."

"You haven't even met him," her father said angrily. "How can you say no?"

"I don't have to meet him to know I won't ever marry a stranger."

"He's not a stranger. I know his father very well."

"He's a stranger to me," she said. "And if I want to get married, I will introduce you to that man rather than the other way around."

There was an ominous pause.

"Who is the man you want to marry?" her father demanded.

"No one. I'm telling you that I will let you know when I am ready to marry someone."

Her father gritted his teeth.

"Fine," he said. "Let's talk about this later. I need your signatures on a few documents."

Her eyes fell on the papers. She saw the trust name on the top.

"What are they for?" she asked.

Her father frowned in irritation at her questioning. He wasn't a man who got questioned by anyone. She hadn't questioned him too for the first two decades of her life. It was only the last few years that she began asking him for an explanation for everything.

"These are documents granting me permission to use one of our properties as collateral. The trust board has already agreed."

"Which properties?" she asked.

His jaw clenched at her questioning. "The lands surrounding the Vardhaman Estate."

The estate had belonged to the same family whose city house her father had purchased.

"Collateral for what?" she asked.

Her father let out an angry breath. "You are my only child! All the properties and the money I earn will eventually belong to you. This is for your future. So stop questioning me as though I have some ulterior motive!"

She didn't respond to his statements. "I will speak with Mr. Munshi and sign these papers." Mr. Munshi was the lawyer in charge of the trust.

Her father opened his mouth to argue, but there was a knock on the door. It was his secretary.

"Mr. Bhoopal Yadav has arrived."

Frowning, her father nodded. "Ask him to come inside."

Tanvi got up from the chair. Her father thrived on politics. Anything that would help push him towards winning the top seat, he wouldn't let the smallest of opportunities go. He would also not let anything distract him. Not even his only daughter.

Bidding him good night, she left her father's home.

***

Later that night, Tanvi went straight home. She didn't bother picking up any food for dinner. And neither did she want to place an order for dinner to be delivered. The confrontation with her father left her with a heavy heart, killing her appetite.

With a sigh, she slowed down at her apartment mail boxes of to check her mail.

"Hi, Tanvi."

It was Sameer, the cute neighbor guy. Tanvi wasn't in the mood to chat with anyone, so she stepped away from the mail boxes, deciding to check it later. But not wanting to be rude, she pasted a polite smile. "Hello, Sameer," she greeted before continuing to walk towards the lifts.

Briefly, she wondered what her father would do if she dated someone like Sameer.

Her father would definitely be super pissed that Sameer didn't come from a rich, prominent family who would help his political career.

Just for that reason, she was half-tempted to date Sameer. But she knew someone like Sameer wouldn't dare to stand up against her father. Her father would easily bully him.

Ugh. I don't want to date anyone.

She was fine as she was. She wasn't lying to her friends or herself when she said there were too many things going on in her life for her to think of dating anyone.

With a sigh, she stepped out of the lift when it reached the top floor. She walked towards her flat when a delicious aroma filled the air, making her stomach rumble.

It was coming from her opposite neighbor's flat.

Mrs. Vasudev had vacated the place a day ago to go to her newer flat nearer to her daughter.

Did she change her mind?

There was classical music playing in the background inside the flat. In the few years that Tanvi had lived in her flat, she never heard Mrs. Vasudev playing classical music. It must be the new tenants.

So soon?

Expecting another old lady or an older couple, Tanvi decided to greet her new neighbors and ask if they needed any help. Even though the door was kept open, she rang the bell and knocked. While she waited, she looked inside.

Mrs. Vasudev used to have a rocking chair along with an oversized sofa set and several rugs on the floor. Pictures of her family had filled the walls along with several show pieces on small tables and stools. Compared to that décor, the current décor was shockingly minimalistic.

There was only a single dark brown couch, a matching brown wooden coffee table and a large television set. The walls were completely bare, and there were no knick knacks. She could see a king-sized bed with white bedding from the partially open bedroom door.

Maybe the old lady or couple were going to bring in the rest of the furniture later.

The music continued while sounds of cooking could be heard from the kitchen. She knocked on the door once again and called out. "Hello?"

When no one came, she decided to pay a visit the next day. She turned and was just about to leave when she heard footsteps approaching.

Putting on a pleasant smile, she turned to greet her new neighbor. But her smile froze.

Instead of an old woman, her eyes met with a bare muscular chest of a tall man with an impressive, tanned and sculpted chest. She quickly raised her eyes to the man's face, only to be shell-shocked.

"You!" she shouted.

The man's lips slowly twisted into a familiar smirk, flashing his dimple.

"Hello, princess," he greeted.

***

Tanvi tried to make sense of what she was seeing. Even though she blinked a couple of times, the handsome face with a familiar smirk and dimples remained the same.

The arrogant man she hated was standing in front of her in the opposite apartment.

"What are you doing here?" she demanded.

He raised an eyebrow. "I stay here, princess."

She couldn't believe it.

"Staying with whom?" she asked. She clung to the hope he was just helping his parents or grandparents move and would leave soon.

"I'm not staying with anyone."

The small hope that he might be the visiting son or grandson of her new neighbor also faded.

His smirk grew. "I'm not married. And I also don't have a girlfriend."

Her cheeks heated. "That's not why I was asking you those questions!"

The arrogant ass thought she was grilling him to know if he was single. As if she would be interested in someone like him.

"Oh yeah?" he drawled. "Your earlier gaze indicated otherwise."

Her cheeks heated even more, knowing he had caught her staring and admiring his muscular chest.

"I was just shocked that someone was parading nearly naked in public."

He barked out a short laugh at her ridiculous statement. He was in the privacy of his home, and he was wearing shorts.

She felt angry and flustered by the situation. "Why did you move here?" she demanded.

"Affordable rent. I also heard that my neighbors are very charming and pleasant."

Her face heated at his amused and sarcastic comment.

"Any other questions?" he asked. "In case you aren't done questioning me, you are welcome to join me for dinner. I have to get back to the kitchen before the dinner begins to burn."

Her stomach once again rumbled at the delicious smell from the kitchen.

"No thanks," she gritted.

With that ungracious statement, she rejected his offer to join him for dinner and turned away to walk towards her apartment.

She heard his amused chuckle as she opened the door and slammed it shut behind her.

Oh God.

The arrogant man she hated and never thought she would see again in her lifetime was her new neighbor.

CHAPTER FIVE

Aryan's mouth twisted when Tanvi Shetty slammed her apartment door shut.

Stepping inside his new apartment, he went back to the tiny kitchen to check on his dinner. The entire kitchen was the size of the kitchen pantry of his Manhattan penthouse.

His brothers thought he wouldn't be able to survive the tiny apartment since he was used to the finer things in life. Anyone who had known him in the recent years would also think the same. They wouldn't believe he was willingly living in the tiny place.

Until two months ago, he had been leading a carefree life. And then, everything changed drastically.

***

Two months ago...

New York

Someone was banging a hammer on his head along with blasting a loud sound into his eardrums. He cracked open an eye, only to groan aloud when bright sunlight filtered through his penthouse bedroom window and fell on his face. His head throbbed.

The annoying sound continued, adding to his agony.

What the fuck is that sound?

He realized it was his phone ringing. He frowned for a moment before it hit him.

"Oh shit!"

It was morning already, and he was running late. He sat up with a jerk. Despite the throbbing headache, he pushed the thick bedcovers away and went into his bathroom. He turned on the shower and set the temperature on the panel to hot, allowing steam to fill the glass cubicle. Meanwhile, he brushed his teeth. When he caught his reflection in the large wall-to-wall mirror, he grimaced. His eyes looked bloodshot, his hair was a wild mess and there were a couple of bruises on his neck and chest.

He looked exactly like a man would appear after having a wild, drunken night filled with partying and sex and with barely three hours of sleep. He normally spent most weekend nights similarly. But that particular Sunday morning was important. Very important.

It was his mother's birthday. And he always spent the entire day with her that day.

Stepping into the steam-filled cubicle, he hurried with his shower. He finished rinsing off the soap and then turned on the temperature setting to cool until the icy cold water woke him up and dulled the throbbing headache somewhat. He stepped out wet and dripping and grabbed a towel on his way.

He got ready in five minutes. Even though he was meeting his mother, he wore a three-piece business suit. Ever since he graduated from Harvard and began his own software company, his default attire was business suits. He was more comfortable in them.

He finger-combed his hair before grabbing his wallet and the keys to his sports car. His mother didn't like any of his sports cars. Not that she was too happy with him driving his bikes either. She thought he drove too fast, and there was no need for a car or a bike when New York had good public transportation.

He grinned. He and his two brothers were officially declared billionaires, but in his mother's eyes, they would always remain her boys who grew up in a modest home in the New York suburbs.

Shaking his head with a smile, he went towards the bed to pick up his phone. There were five missed calls. And all of them were from his brothers. He knew the two of them were going to ride his ass for running late.

Grinning again, he slipped his phone into his pocket. His eyes then fell on the naked woman on his bed whose face was covered by her hair.

Shit.

He couldn't recall who he had spent the night with. He had been too drunk to care. Hoping it wasn't a woman who worked for him or any of his mother's acquaintances' daughters, he pushed the woman's hair aside to look at her face.

He let out an internal sigh of relief. It was a familiar woman he had met before a few times in social gatherings. He recalled meeting her at the previous night's party at his business partner's house. She had come with another man. But as soon as she saw him, she ditched the other man and had come onto him pretty strongly. She kept whispering filthy, suggestive words into his ear. And since she didn't have a wedding ring on her finger, he took her up on the offer.

He grinned, recalling how she had lived up to her wild promises.

"Goodbye, sweetheart."

He knew he wouldn't spend another night with her. He didn't date the same woman more than once. Luckily, New York had a big enough population of hot women to keep him going for decades. Hoping the woman would be gone by the time he returned, he stepped out of his penthouse to visit his mother.

He drove out of Manhattan. Thirty minutes later, he drove into a small gated community of a suburban neighborhood. He stopped his shiny red sports car in front of a modest house where two sleek black luxury SUVs with tinted windows were parked.

His brothers were already inside.

Grinning and knowing his brothers would be quite annoyed, he stepped out of his car.

Before he could ring the bell, the door was opened by a middle-aged woman whose beautiful face was lit up in a bright smile.

"Aryan!"

"Happy birthday, Ma."

He hugged his mother. His petite mother hugged him back before pulling his cheeks lower and placing a sweet kiss on his forehead.

He scowled mockingly. "Ma, I told you so many times. You've got to stop pulling my cheeks in public. I'm not a child anymore."

She grinned as usual. "Well, you are my youngest son and will always remain my baby."

Laughing at their usual banter, he kissed his mother's cheek before leading her inside the house.

Just like his mother, the home's décor was bright and cheerful with several pictures and knickknacks of sentimental value. A photo frame with his late father's picture was placed on the coffee table. Aryan knew his mother must have placed it there that morning like she usually did on her birthdays. She wanted her late husband to be a part of the celebration.

"Something smells delicious, Ma. Has the food arrived already?"

He had ordered breakfast and the rest of the meals for the day from her mother's favorite restaurants.

"No. I made Bhargav cancel the breakfast order. I already made breakfast. Your favorite."

Aryan shook his head. "Ma, it's your birthday. You are supposed to relax and have fun."

His mother laughed. "Well, cooking and gardening make me relax and have fun."

He smiled, knowing it was true. He followed her into the small open kitchen and dining area that led to the outside garden. His brothers were seated at the breakfast counter.

"Grab a plate, baby, and start having breakfast. I'm plucking the fresh berries. I'll be right back."

Aryan's mother stepped out to the small garden while he joined his brothers and served himself some of the delicious breakfast.

"Where the fuck were you?" his oldest brother asked with a frown.

Yash Varma was a stickler for time and punctuality.

Aryan grinned. "I had a busy night, bro," he replied.

His other brother raised a brow. "I'm sure you were very busy," Bhargav said drily as his gaze fell on the neck bruise.

Nothing escaped Bhargav Varma's notice.

Aryan threw up his hands mockingly before taking the empty chair next to them at the breakfast counter. "Bros, relax. I'm only a few minutes late. Let's enjoy the day. And by the way, I checked with Ma's school. The summer holidays are starting a week earlier. The cruise dates won't clash."

They were gifting a two-month-long vacation cruise for their mother and her group of friends. He knew his mother had been planning one for a while, and her small group of friends was saving up money for the same. He had checked with all her friends, and they were more than excited to be offered a fully paid vacation.

"Send me the dates," Bhargav said. "I'll ensure the cruise checks into one of our hotels at each destination."

"Ensure the security is airtight during those days," Yash added.

There was no security threat to their mother. But having three billionaire sons who had plenty of business rivals, they didn't want to take chances.

"Yup," Aryan replied. "I'll check on the security."

He went to grab a plate. And on his way, he stuck a small envelope on the refrigerator.

"By the way, I heard murmurs that the Conagra crisis has reached the tipping point," he said. "The brother who had a falling out wants to get rid of his and his wife's shares."

The company was one of the oldest and biggest hospitality industry companies. Although the company was old, it wasn't as big as Yash and Bhargav's companies. However, adding the old established company to their profile would benefit them.

Yash frowned. "How do you know that?"

Aryan smirked. "I just do, bro."

Bhargav shook his head. "Doesn't Conagra's estranged brother happen to have a socialite daughter who parties in your circles?"

The beautiful heiress was currently in his bed back in the penthouse. He recalled their previous night's conversation where the socialite was quite chatty.

"Yup. Apparently, daddy is eager to sell and retire."

Yash frowned. "He won't sell the shares to us for sure."

Aryan laughed. Thanks to their cutthroat reputation, most of their business rivals hated them as much as they feared them.

"They won't sell it to us," he said. "But they will sell it to an upcoming family-oriented company."

It was their usual business tactic to use one of their subsidiary companies as a friendly front to make acquisitions.

"The old board of Futura is still intact," Bhargav added. "I'll use them to buy out the shares."

Right after they made plans to takeover yet another company, Aryan saw his mother return from the garden.

"I was planning to bake a cake," she said while holding a basket filled with freshly plucked berries. "But since you boys are fitness freaks and into that six-pack mumbo jumbo, I decided to serve it with freshly whipped cream."

Aryan laughed. "Ma, whipped cream is hardly low in fat or calories. And when did we ever turn down your homemade food?"

Thanks to their family genes, despite their mother's delicious home-cooked calorie-rich food he and his brothers often gorged on, they remained fit.

"You got those genes from your father. And thanks to him, I enjoy gardening. When I was newly married, I was scared to go near the plants because I was terrified of worms." She laughed as memories brightened her eyes. "I was a silly girl then. Your father taught me how important those worms are along with the importance of freshly harvested food."

Aryan felt a bolt of irritation passing through him as always at the mention of his late father. Unlike during his early childhood, he no longer thought of his father as some sort of brave superhero. He now knew the truth and reality of the man who chose to abandon his family. Ashok Vardhaman was the opposite of brave.

Aryan didn't ever say those words aloud near his mother, though. His mother was as much in love with her late husband as she was when the man was alive.

Pushing away the past memories, Aryan followed his mother to the kitchen.

"Ma, you should upgrade your appliances."

His mother still had the appliances from when she purchased the house five years ago.

She laughed. "These are fine."

He shook his head. "My company stocks increased a couple more hundred since last week."

His mother simply smiled and didn't say anything. His mother invested most of her savings into his company before it became public. Technically, she was a millionaire on her own without her sons' money. But she still chose to live modestly.

Money is the root cause of all evils.

Aryan knew his mother believed that statement strongly. But after the life they had led over the last fifteen years, he and his brothers spent most of their waking moments earning more money and the power and influence that came with it.

As one of the biggest software companies, Aryan had the power to influence companies across the world. His brothers owned several real estate buildings and hotels worldwide. Together, the three of them were a force to be reckoned with. But according to their mother, all of it meant nothing if they couldn't give back to the world.

He and his brothers did donate to charities to get tax breaks. But it was their mother, who even with her meager salary, gave a lot back to society.

She worked as a teacher in an underprivileged neighborhood. She chose to do that even though she could easily quit her job and live a life of luxury.

"Oh my God!" his mother shrieked with excitement.

She had just gone to the refrigerator to get the whipped cream out and discovered her birthday gift stuck on the door with the magnets.

Aryan smiled. "From the three of us. Happy birthday, Ma."

She hugged him. "Thank you, baby!" She then called her other sons. "Group hug!" she said.

Aryan laughed as his brothers joined them, and she pulled them into a group hug. He and his brothers were careful while hugging her. All three were six feet plus. They didn't want to crush their petite mother.

"Thank you, boys. This is the best gift I could have ever imagined!"

When they stepped away from her, she looked at the tickets closely.

"Oh my God. These are not just tickets for me, but they are for my friends too!"

The entire cruise ship was booked to ensure her safety. But Aryan knew his mother would not like the fact. She would think it was a waste of money.

"You can invite more people if you want, Ma. The tickets are at a discounted price."

She looked all the more excited. "That's great! I think I'll invite Mrs. Gerald and Mrs. Kumar too."

Aryan smiled.

"It was so sweet of you to offer the cruise to my friends. The three of you got that from your father as well. He was always taking care of people. He was a true hero."

Maybe it was the lack of sleep. Or maybe it was years of suppressed rage. But Aryan finally spoke out his irritation.

"Stop calling him a hero, Ma," he said carelessly. "Ashok Vardhaman was a damn coward who killed himself. He left you and us because he couldn't bear the harsh reality. I don't know why you keep hanging on to his memories. You should forget him and—"

A slap cracked on his cheek.

Aryan was stunned for a moment and then clenched his jaw. It was the first time his mother ever struck him. She wasn't the kind to ever slap her children.

He looked at his mother's hurt and angry face.

"Never call your father that word again," she said in a shaking tone.

He fell quiet. He knew his mother loved her late husband. And she would continue to love him until her dying days. Facts and reality didn't matter to her.

"You are wrong," she said in anguish. "Your father isn't a coward. He didn't choose to leave us by killing himself. He was snatched from us."

Aryan nearly expected his mother to follow that up by saying her husband was snatched from them by the act of God. But her next words shook his whole world.

"Your father was murdered. And the people responsible were the ones he trusted."

***

Present...

Rage and pain filled him at the memory of discovering the truth. Right from that moment on that fateful morning on his mother's birthday, his life changed drastically.

From partying, dating beautiful women and winning over business deals, his only burning desire was to hunt down the people responsible for his father's murder. He would do anything to bring out the complete truth.

He didn't resent his current circumstances either. Eating a quiet dinner in a cramped apartment in a different country and continent altogether was barely noticeable to him.

And it wasn't the first time he lived in small, cramped spaces. He, his mother and two brothers had lived in places much smaller than the current apartment. It was the only size places they could afford. At that time, food and survival were much more important than the size of the place to sleep.

Dark anger filled him again, recalling those days. For his mother and his brothers.

It filled him with more determination to finish what he and his brothers started—to set right a devastating wrong.

He was in step two of the plan. He had purchased the entire rundown apartment complex for the very reason. He now lived right across from his beautiful, fiery pawn.

CHAPTER SIX

"How dare they!"

It was the day of her planned protest. At Tanvi's heated declaration, her friends looked at her with concern and sympathy. Rashmi had just picked her up from the protest site.

"What happened?" Kavita asked.

"The Prism Corporation has been blocking every attempt at organizing a protest!"

She had organized a protest near the school behind the Prism Corporation. It was the weekend, and it wouldn't interrupt normal school operations. But before anyone could assemble and begin the protest, the cops came in and blocked the street leading to the place. She still had not given up and tried to continue organizing a protest in the nearby streets of the Prism building. But each time, her attempts were once again blocked, and protesters were forced to clear out.

"I'm so pissed they think they can come to our country and destroy our environment without any thought."

"How do you know it is an international company?" Rashmi asked.

"I did some research on Prism Corporation. Until a few months ago, Prism Corporation was actually an old mid-size real estate company. It was recently acquired by some international real estate corporation who is looking to establish real estate presence here." The last part of the information was given to her accidentally by her father.

Kavita nodded. "Maybe it was a hostile takeover."

Tanvi frowned. Although she didn't have a corporate job, she knew what a hostile takeover was. "I don't know whether the Prism Corporation takeover was hostile or not, but the ruthless corporation cannot get away with this."

She had searched the web to see who headed the parent corporation. But there wasn't enough information on who took over Prism. There was a generic company name that was registered recently, most likely some shell company. Ridiculous.

"What are you planning to do?" Kavita asked.

At her friend's question, Tanvi's frown grew. "I will have to meet the person who purchased Prism Corporation."

"How do you know if the owner is even in the country? You said it's an international company."

"Oh the owner is definitely here and involved in day-to-day decisions. The profit made from the mall and subsequent construction in the city is too big for anyone to ignore. If the mall doesn't get built, the company will lose the goodwill with bureaucrats and politicians."

Her father was one of the politicians involved. So she knew it was a high-profile project.

"Why would the owner agree to meet you?" Rashmi asked. "Especially if the person knows you are leading the protests?"

Tanvi knew that problem would arise. She had a plan to bypass it. It would be underhanded, but she had to do it. She had to meet the owner and present her cause and possible alternatives for the mall. And if the person didn't listen, she would give the person a piece of her mind about how she and the rest of the people in the city would not only stop the mall construction but also ensure the company gets defamed and driven out of India.

"I'm planning to use my mother's name," she said. Her mind began to plan the next steps. She would have to come up with a fake reason for her meeting with the owner. "I'm going to dress up differently too with makeup."

"Oh my God! Are you going in disguise?" Rashmi asked.

Tanvi nodded.

"What if you get arrested!" Kavita asked.

Tanvi smiled. "I guess I'll call my father again."

Her friends shook their heads. "Tanvi!"

She always dropped her father's name in situations that would help her cause. Even though she rejected everything else her father had to offer—money, status and a chance to live a luxurious life as his daughter.

Rashmi grinned. "I know I should probably be talking you out of doing something so risky, but knowing you, it's impossible to stop you when you set your mind to something. So instead, I'll lend you my formal wear for the meeting."

Tanvi smiled. "Thanks."

She was beyond grateful for having such good friends.

"So, you didn't come across that hot hunk again during the protest?" Rashmi asked.

Tanvi's heart raced. She had come across that arrogant jerk her friend wanted to badly meet, but not during the protest. That jerk lived right across from her apartment.

"No. He wasn't at the protest site, and you should forget him. He wasn't that special either. Good-looking guys like him are self-centered and arrogant."

For the past week, Tanvi was badly hoping her new neighbor would somehow mess up, and she could complain to the new property management and have him vacate the place. But the arrogant man so far was a damn perfect tenant.

No loud music. No parties at his home. Not even bringing his dates back to his place.

But it had only been a week. So, she kept her hopes up that he would somehow mess up, and she could have him kicked out.

Rashmi laughed. "You are right that most good-looking guys are arrogant. But then, such bad boys make the best boyfriends if not husbands. They are so much more exciting."

Tanvi shook her head at her friend's outrageous statement. "Please! I prefer a sweet guy rather than an arrogant ass. You should too!"

Her friend only grinned.

Tanvi was all the more determined not to tell her friend about her new neighbor. The arrogant jerk might take advantage of her friend.

"So when are you making the appointment to meet the Prism owner?" Kavita asked.

"Monday."

She didn't want to waste any time. She was going to corner the Prism owner as soon as possible.

***

She returned to her apartment complex holding the bags with borrowed clothes and makeup. Her mind was preoccupied with what she was going to present to the Prism owner on Monday. She knew she wouldn't have much time during the appointment, but whatever few minutes she had, she had to maximize them by presenting all the critical information.

"Hi, Tanvi," a man's voice greeted.

Tanvi turned. "Oh hello, Sameer." She smiled at the cute neighbor.

Once again, the man blushed. He was about to say something when a group of giggling girls suddenly approached them. She recognized some of the girls who studied in a nearby engineering college.

Tanvi smiled and greeted them. "Hello, girls. How are you all?"

"Uh... Tanvi," one of the girls began hesitantly. "Can we come by your flat sometime?"

Tanvi was surprised. "Sure. Do you need my help with anything?"

The girls looked at each other and exchanged weird glances. "Uh no. We don't need help. We just thought we'd hang out at your place because we are neighbors."

Tanvi frowned for a moment, finding it strange. The girls had been her neighbors for well over a year. But apart from greeting each other, they didn't really talk much to think they had anything in common.

"Uh... do you often talk to Arjun?" one of the girls asked. "We wanted to introduce ourselves to him."

Who the hell is Arjun?

Tanvi then realized who Arjun was. And she was annoyed. Not with the girls, but with the man who the girls seemed to be interested in.

Ugh.

It had been a week since the arrogant man moved into the apartment across from hers. Since then, he only managed to get on to her nerves even more. They had come across each other only a few times, but the arrogant smirk on his face when he greeted her with a "Hello, princess," was enough to raise her blood pressure.

She had ignored his greetings. The man was an arrogant jerk.

First, it was her friend Rashmi, and now it was the young, impressionable college girls being taken in by his handsome face and dimpled smile. If only she could tell them all about what an arrogant jerk he was. But even if she warned them, instead of thinking his arrogance as bad, they might find him all the more attractive.

"Bad boys make the best boyfriends if not husbands."

She recalled her friend's ridiculous statement.

She opened her mouth to tell the girls she didn't speak to her arrogant neighbor. But she paused. She realized she had the perfect opportunity to get back at the jerk.

She pasted a smile. "You girls can come anytime to my place. But you know what is even better? Dropping by... uh... Arjun's home for an introduction. He loves it when people show up at his place. He is also an amazing cook."

She had no idea whether or not the arrogant man was a good cook or not. But each evening, a delicious aroma wafted into her flat while he cooked. And he had offered her to join him for dinner on the first day. So it wasn't entirely a lie that he wanted his neighbors to join him for dinner.

The girls' eyes lit up with excitement. "Oh! That's great! We'll all go to Arjun's home tomorrow evening."

Tanvi widened her smile. "Yes, please do that. I'll let... Arjun know you girls will drop by tomorrow night for dinner. Make sure to invite other girls too. He will be very excited and cook something extra special for you all."

There was an excited buzz of conversation as they left.

"I didn't know your new neighbor is that friendly."

Tanvi turned to Sameer with a wide smile. "Oh, he is very friendly. You should join for dinner too and introduce yourself."

Sameer nodded, but there was a small frown.

"Good night, Sameer."

She picked up her mail and went towards the lifts.

Stepping inside one, she grinned, hoping at least a dozen girls showed up at her arrogant neighbor's home for dinner the next day. It was a silly trick to play. But it was good enough revenge for having her taxi stolen and being called an entitled princess.

When the lift stopped, she stepped into the long corridor. And once again, delicious smells wafted into the air while she neared her flat.

What the hell did that man cook each day? And why does it smell so damn delicious?

Irritated and also slightly jealous that she didn't have the necessary skill to cook such dishes, she was about to pass by his flat.

"Good evening, princess," a deep voice greeted.

He was standing near his front door fixing a damn door knocker—a beautiful, antique door knocker.

How the hell does he have such good taste in everything?

He was once again only in his shorts, baring his chest and wide shoulders. Although it was damn hard, she kept her eyes on his face and not on the tanned muscles.

"Don't you have clothes to wear?" she snapped.

The weather had been hot and humid lately. And with no air conditioning in any of the flats, most male tenants were dressed sparingly like him. But none of them looked anything close to him or had a ripped body like him.

"You seem obsessed with how I dress, princess."

Her cheeks heated. "I'm not obsessed with anything relating to you. I just mentioned your lack of clothing because many tenants have been complaining about spotting you roaming half-naked in the apartment corridors. The residents are expected to abide by basic rules of decency."

She knew she just sounded like some cranky, old conservative lady. In fact, most old ladies in the apartment complex were sweet and didn't care. And the young female tenants would most likely be thrilled and excited if they ever saw him showing off his ripped muscles.

The arrogant ass knew it as well. He smirked at her lie. "Is that so?" he drawled.

She quickly changed the topic. She looked into his flat and frowned. It was still barely furnished with a single couch, coffee table and a large television set.

"Are you here only until you find a job?" she asked with a hopeful tone.

"I already have a job, princess. So, I'll be here for quite a while."

Once again, her hope died. Even as she frowned, her stomach rumbled loudly at the delicious aroma of whatever he was cooking. The sound was loud enough for him to hear.

He looked amused. "Why don't you come in, and we can continue this conversation? I'm making fish curry in a pot for dinner."

Her mouth nearly drooled at the thought of having scrumptious fish curry for dinner. But she controlled herself.

"No, thanks," she once again said, refusing to be lured by food by an arrogant man she hated.

"Why not?" he asked. "Are you scared of me?"

She scoffed. "I'm not scared of you. And for your information, I'm trained in martial arts."

He seemed amused by that. "Is that so?" he drawled. "Are you saying if anyone were to attack you, you can actually defend yourself?"

Her eyes narrowed. "Not just defend myself but also cause serious damage."

She had only gone for a few weeks of classes and attended them on and off. The jerk didn't have to know that.

"I see," he said.

One moment he was standing by his door talking to her, and the next moment, he grabbed her by her arms. She gasped in shock as her back hit the wall next to his door and his hard body covered hers. Her arms were held above her head using just one of his hands.

"What the hell are you doing!" she gasped.

She was shocked, and fear shot up inside her. His eyes were hooded and dead serious as he looked at her.

"I thought you were trained in martial arts, princess. Let's see you escape my trap."

Her racing heart jerked, realizing he was calling her bluff. And then, anger shot up inside her, replacing the fear.

How dare he!

She tried to raise her knee to kick him in the balls, but his muscular thigh trapped both her legs. She tried to yank her hands down to scratch his face, but the grip of his fingers around her wrists was unshakeable.

She struggled using all her strength, but she could barely budge him.

She was taller than average, but he was at least half a foot taller than her and built of solid muscle. Her struggling movements only made her aware of his hard body pressed against hers. She could even feel the heat of his tanned skin.

Despite her anger, her stomach quivered. Her breathing turned fast due to her struggles and awareness towards him, but his breaths barely changed. The arrogant jerk smirked, flashing his dimples.

"You need to brush up on your combat skills, princess," he drawled.

She glared at him. "How dare you—"

"When the goon was attacking you during the protest, you hardly looked like you were about to tackle him. And you asking him how dare he attack wouldn't have helped."

She stopped struggling as she was shocked by his words. "What? How do you know about the goon?" she demanded.

"I was there."

She looked up at him with widened eyes. She recalled that her savior had worn a blue checkered formal shirt too.

She frowned. There was no way her savior was the arrogant jerk in front of her.

He didn't say anything either. She was sure he would have rubbed it in her face if he were the one to save her.

"Let me go," she snapped.

His hands dropped from her, and he took a step back with the annoying dimpled smirk.

"I can protect myself just fine," she said, glaring at him while rubbing her wrists where he had held them. "I was just tired, and so my reflexes were slow to escape your trap."

"I see." It was obvious he didn't believe her. "So if I trap you in the morning, you will be able to escape?"

Annoyance shot through her at his deliberate taunting. "Do that, and you might have your nose broken by my fist."

He grinned. "Thanks for the warning, princess."

He hardly looked like he was taking her warning seriously. And the bastard had a perfect nose too, which she wouldn't mind breaking to teach him a lesson.

Not wanting to get riled further, she decided to ignore him. She picked up the clothes bags she had dropped and turned away from him. She unlocked her door. But just before she shut it close, she looked up. He was leaning by his apartment door and watching her with a dimpled smirk.

"By the way," she said with a smirk of her own. "You should cook a bigger meal for tomorrow's dinner. Who knows, you might have quite a few surprise guests."

She slammed the door shut with a victorious smile.

Take that, you arrogant jerk.

CHAPTER SEVEN

Aryan shook his head at the dramatic loud bang from Tanvi Shetty's apartment door.

He turned to his apartment door and tightened the door knob before stepping inside. He then checked the coverage on his phone. A small camera was installed inside the doorknob, and he could now clearly see Tanvi Shetty's apartment door and also hear the sounds outside.

Not that he really needed special cameras. He more or less knew her schedule. He knew what she did, whom she met and even what she planned.

And now, he also knew how she felt in his arms.

Touching her was a mistake. And he hadn't expected his body to react to mere touching. The soft swell of her breasts, the sweet smell of her hair and her eyes flashing fiercely at him aroused him in ways he had never been before. He was only moments away from her discovering the effect her closeness was having on him.

She would have been all the more outraged and pissed and called him a pervert.

He shook his head again.

His brothers would be highly amused too if they ever come to know that he got a damn boner from simply touching a woman. Right from the age when he became aware of the opposite sex, he always had his pick from the vying attentions of beautiful women. He had become jaded early on since he was so used to having sex as a mere bodily function that a simple touch or banter didn't cause an extreme physical reaction like it did a while ago.

Hell. Maybe it's just been too long.

He convinced himself that it had been close to two months since he had sex. Finding out the truth about a devastating loss and betrayal wasn't exactly conducive to wanting to have sex. And the longest dry spell of sex was only the reason why touching or arguing with his pawn was arousing him. Not because he thought she was the hottest and the most passionate woman he met.

Fuck.

It irritated him that his fiery prey who was only meant to be a pawn in his game, fascinated him.

Forcibly pushing away thoughts of his fiery neighbor, he went back to the kitchen where the aromatic fish curry was simmering.

It had been close to five years since he last cooked. He had been relying on his personal chefs or mostly ate out or went to his mother's home to eat her delicious home-cooked meals.

But thanks to the plan which needed him to pretend he came from a modest background, he now had to cook his own food again. But it wasn't that hard. It was easy to get back to cooking since he had plenty of experience during his younger days in New York.

While his mother struggled to make ends meet by working as a nanny while also studying for a teaching degree, he often helped her in the kitchen. He learned how to cook, and she enjoyed teaching him as well. It was the only time she laughed and felt happy. Both his brothers were away from home most of the time because they had quit school and worked as construction labor to help with the household income.

He had wanted to quit school as well to help like his brothers did, but his mother had begged him not to.

"Not only me, but your father would also want you to finish your education and make us proud. Please, baby. Don't drop out of school. You are so smart and intelligent. It's my dream to see you graduate from a reputed college."

He had agreed with his mother, only because he couldn't see her disappointed and heartbroken. And the day he graduated from Harvard, she had broken down and shed tears of happiness.

His degree didn't mean much to him beyond his mother's happiness. By then, he had already been earning in the millions. And both his brothers who had no formal education were billionaires.

The only reason he did it was because he would do anything for his mother's happiness.

But Ma wouldn't want you to choose the path of revenge.

He frowned as a voice from a deep, forgotten conscience whispered inside his mind.

He knew his sweet mother was the kind to forgive everyone, including the people responsible for the cold-blooded murder of her husband. But he wasn't willing to forgive or forget.

He would hunt those bastards down. And he wouldn't rest until the entire truth came out.

And the person who would lead him there was his fiery pawn.

Tanvi Shetty.

CHAPTER EIGHT

"Sorry, Miss Palki. No one is allowed to meet the chairman without a prior appointment."

Tanvi was standing at the huge reception area of the Prism building. She was dressed in her friend's borrowed business suit and had enough makeup to hide her identity or the fact that she was leading a protest in front of the company building only a couple of weeks ago.

Luckily, none of the security seemed to recognize her, and they didn't stop her from entering the building premises. But her biggest roadblock was getting an on-the-spot appointment from a busy chairman.

She smiled at the receptionist. "I understand," she said. "But you see, it's really urgent. I need to speak with the chairman about something confidential. Tell him Mr. Girish Shetty sent me here."

The receptionist seemed to have recognized her father's name. Even though the woman looked uncertain about the protocol, she dialed a number and murmured the information given to her. There was a momentary pause while the other person was speaking.

After what seemed to be the longest two minutes, the receptionist ended the call and looked at Tanvi. "Please go to the fourteenth floor, Miss Palki. Someone will receive you."

Tanvi wanted to do a victory dance, but she smiled at the receptionist. "Thank you."

Her high heels made sounds as she walked on the overly polished marble floor towards the lifts. She had to pause and pass through the automatic barricades that were lifted by the guards at the receptionist's nod.

Stepping into one of the many lifts, she pressed the button for the fourteenth floor. It wasn't the topmost floor. She knew the Prism building had fifteen floors. Which meant there might be additional security to the topmost floor and couldn't be accessed by the general employees.

Tanvi frowned. *Why so much security?*

As soon as the lift stopped on the fourteenth floor, the doors opened to an open area that was heavily carpeted with yet another reception area.

She stepped out of the lift and went to the middle-aged man seated there. "Hello, Miss Palki."

Tanvi pasted on a smile. "Good morning, Mr. Tejpal," she said, reading the man's gleaming nameplate placed at the front of the massive desk.

The man didn't smile back. "I'm sorry, Miss Palki. We do not give direct appointments to the chairman."

Tanvi was stunned. "But I was asked to come up here. I thought I would get to speak with him."

"You can't meet him, but you are welcome to state the purpose of your visit to me. I can check with him."

She used her father's name again. So far, it had never failed. "I am from Mr. Girish Shetty's office. I would like to speak regarding an urgent and confidential matter..."

The man nodded. He then made a phone call and spoke softly.

"All right, sir," he said after a few seconds.

Ending the call, the man looked at her. "He has asked me to pass on the regards to Mr. Girish Shetty. At this time, he cannot meet anyone. He also asked me to convey that if you are here to apply for a job position, then you need to go through the application and interview process like everyone else."

A burst of annoyance along with anger, passed through her at the chairman's comments. But she wasn't the kind to misdirect her anger on the wrong person who was simply the messenger. She was pissed at the arrogant chairman who thought she wanted to meet him to ask for a job.

She opened her mouth to tell the man that she wasn't looking for a job. But she paused.

Suddenly another idea began to form. She wasn't looking for a job. But what if she did get a job in the company?

That way, not only would she get to somehow meet the chairman, she could possibly also dig up some information on the corporation that acquired the company a couple of months ago.

Her heart raced in excitement at the plan.

"How can I apply for a job?" she asked.

The man gave her a polite smile. "You can visit our company website for open positions," he stated. "We give the topmost priority to employee references. So if you know someone working here, their reference will help.

You won't need the chairman's reference."

She stretched her lips further. "Thank you. I will."

While she walked along the polished corridors, her mind began to race further.

She had to look up all the open positions and apply immediately. Sameer, her cute downstairs neighbor, worked at Prism Corporation. She could ask his help to provide her the employee reference. Sameer would help her for sure. He was sweet and helpful.

Unlike *him*.

Suddenly a handsome face with a dimpled smirk flashed into her mind. It was of the arrogant jerk who lived across from her flat.

She shook her head. *Ugh. Why am I thinking of him!*

The man was too exasperating, especially when he crawled into her thoughts lately. She didn't know why she thought of him so often.

Maybe because he's so damn hot and handsome.

She clenched her jaw at her mind's unwanted thought. She didn't want to notice how good-looking the man was. His annoying behavior should have killed the awareness. But her mind somehow always registered his good looks.

Shaking her head again, she left the building.

***

It was late evening when she got back to her apartment building.

She stepped out of the lift at her floor and was walking towards her flat when she could hear loud giggles. A big group of giggling girls was heading her way.

"Oh, hi, Tanvi."

She smiled at them. "Were you looking for me?"

They giggled even more while shaking their heads with dreamy looks as though it was a synchronized dance.

"We just had dinner at Arjun's place. He makes the best biryani! We had to leave early since our exams are starting tomorrow."

Tanvi had forgotten about her prank from two days ago. Her arrogant neighbor must have bought one day's time to arrange for dinner. Suppressing a grin, she put on a friendly smile. "Oh, that's great. I'm glad you girls took up the offer."

They nodded, some of them blushing.

Bidding the girls goodnight and wishing them all the best for their exams, Tanvi broke into a grin while walking towards her flat. She was pulling out her keys to her door when she heard a deep drawl.

"Well, since you asked me to make dinner for a lot of guests, there's still plenty of food left. Want to join me for dinner?"

She looked up from her purse. For a change, he was wearing a shirt. The dark blue collared t-shirt made him look even hotter. Irritated that she noticed his looks once again, she opened her mouth to refuse his offer as usual. But she paused when she saw who was inside his house.

"Oh hi, Tanvi," Sameer greeted from the sofa. He was having dinner as well.

She recalled her plan of asking Sameer to help her get a job at Prism Corporation. Instead of meeting him at his apartment or hers, which he could misinterpret as her interest in him, she could talk to him in a neutral setting—which unfortunately was her arrogant neighbor's apartment.

The delicious smell that filled the air was way too tempting to refuse as well.

"Yes, I'll join you for dinner. Thanks for asking."

Surprise flared in the arrogant man's eyes before he slowly grinned, flashing his dimples. "Well, then come on in, princess," he drawled.

Her stomach fluttered strangely. Pushing away the awareness and attraction towards him, she was determined to accomplish what she needed to and leave the place. She followed him inside.

The small flat was surprisingly clean after nearly a dozen girls had dinner.

"Where did they all sit?" she asked curiously.

"They didn't sit," he replied drily. "They chose to swarm around me while I slaved in the kitchen."

She suppressed a grin. But he must have seen the amusement in her eyes.

"I'm going to get back at you for this, princess," he promised.

"What did I do?" She tried to put on an innocent look.

He didn't buy it. "Oh really?" he drawled. "I was repeatedly and clearly told since yesterday that *Tanvi* told them about my open-dinner invitation."

Her cheeks heated at being caught. "They must have misunderstood."

He didn't buy that explanation either.

Knowing she didn't have to impress him, she suppressed a smile and followed him to the small kitchen. Even though it was the same size as hers, it looked very functional and well-used. Things were arranged neatly, and surprisingly, there was no mess.

"I'm Tanvi Shetty, by the way," she introduced herself belatedly.

"I already know that, princess. I've known it the first day I met you."

Her cheeks heated in annoyance that despite knowing her name, he continued to call her princess.

"I'm Arjun," he added with a smirk. "Not *arrogant ass* like you always mutter when you pass by me."

Her cheeks heated all the more. "Arjun what?" she snapped, asking his last name

His smirk grew. "Does it matter?"

Actually it didn't. She still didn't like him and thought he was an arrogant ass. But she had to tolerate him, at least until she could finish speaking to Sameer.

Arjun served the aromatic rice and pieces of chicken into a plate.

Tall, broad and muscular, he looked too big for the tiny kitchen. But his movements were smooth and efficient. Her cheeks heated when her eyes fell on his muscular arms dusted with dark, masculine hair as he held out her plate. His eyes met hers and remained on her face.

Even though there was at least three feet of distance between them, she felt the buzzing heat and awareness.

Ugh. I hate him. Then why do I keep feeling this way!

"Too hot?" he asked.

She nearly choked at his question. "What?"

He smirked. "I was asking if you were feeling hot. You look flushed, princess."

Embarrassed at being caught ogling him, she glared at him. "I'm fine," she snapped ungraciously. "And stop calling me princess!"

He looked amused. "So, why are you actually here, *princess*?" he asked, ignoring her order to stop calling her by that name. "You look like you are scheming something."

"I'm not scheming!" she snapped even though she was there as a part of a plan.

He smirked. "Oh yeah? I can literally hear you scheme."

She gritted her teeth. "No, you can't."

"I can. You have that same look when you are in your zone."

"What zone?" she demanded, annoyed that he was able to read her body language so easily.

"That fighting, determined go-getter mode. The one which makes you lead protests and wreak havoc on some hapless people."

"I don't target helpless people," she snapped. "And why is fighting, determined go-getter mode a bad thing?"

His amused smirk grew. "I didn't say it was. You are the one being defensive when I said you are scheming."

"That's because I'm not scheming!" she snapped out the lie.

She was scheming. But she wasn't going to let the arrogant man think he could read her easily.

"All right..." he said.

Ignoring him, she went into the living room. She put on a wide smile as she sat on the couch next to Sameer.

Sameer looked happy to see her. "I'm glad you joined, Tanvi. Arjun is an excellent cook. But I guess you already know that since he invited you for dinner before."

Her cheeks heated at the last part. She could sense her arrogant neighbor's gaze on her. He sat on the chair next to the couch.

"Yes. He's definitely a decent cook," she remarked.

She was yet to taste the food. Quickly, she took a bite of the aromatic rice.

She nearly had a food orgasm.

Oh God.

Unable to stop herself, she had a few more bites. It was the best she had ever tasted. None of the restaurants could ever match the rich, flavorful yet complex taste.

"I'm glad you approve and think I'm a *decent* cook," a deep, amused voice remarked.

She didn't realize her eyes had fallen close. Immediately, she shot them open, only to see the annoying yet sexy smirk of her arrogant neighbor.

Annoyed, she dragged her eyes away from him. She turned to Sameer and smiled widely.

"I thought I would come across you at your work today," she said.

Sameer looked surprised.

Smiling, she explained. "I went to the Prism building for an appointment."

"Oh." Sameer smiled. "You should have called me. I would have come and met you."

Tanvi shook her head with a laugh. "I know. But I realized I don't have your phone number. I'm going to have to take it now."

Sameer nodded with a blush.

Her eyes couldn't help but fall to the other man, who was the complete opposite of Sameer. The arrogant jerk was watching her with a lazy, knowing look.

Dragging her eyes away from him, she ignored him again.

"I actually went there looking for a job," she continued to speak with Sameer.

Sameer looked surprised. "That's great! I'm sure you'll get the job."

She laughed. "I hope so. But I haven't applied for a position yet. And I heard the company is quite picky about hiring."

Sameer nodded. "Yes, they are picky. But I can help you. I can forward your resume as an employee referral."

She smiled widely. "Oh. That will be of great help. Thank you so much, Sameer."

"Arjun can send a copy of your resume too. Two referrals could help you even more."

She froze mid-bite.

Sameer smiled. "Since Arjun attended the interview more recently, he can help you with the process."

Suddenly, Tanvi remembered the first time she met the arrogant neighbor. He had been going to an interview at Prism Corporation.

She continued to smile. Although, it became forced. "Yes. I will take... Arjun's help too if needed."

The rest of the dinner continued with light chit-chat about the company. Sameer kept the conversation going while she and Arjun remained mostly quiet. Just when she thought she would have to come up with an excuse to leave, it was Sameer who got up first.

"I have a meeting in a few minutes. I'll speak to you later, Tanvi."

Tanvi nodded with a smile. "Sure. Thank you once again for offering to help."

Sameer blushed. "No problem. I have your phone number. I'll text you my email address."

She was surprised because she didn't recall giving him her phone number.

"I got it from Mrs. Vasudev," he said sheepishly.

She smiled. "Oh. I see."

She didn't mind that the normally shy guy had sneakily gotten her number.

Sameer shook Arjun's hand. "Thank you, Arjun for inviting me over for dinner. I'll see you around."

Wishing them goodnight, Sameer stepped out of the apartment.

Tanvi suddenly found herself alone with her arrogant neighbor who she now knew also worked at Prism.

"Why didn't you tell me you worked at Prism Corporation?" she demanded.

He raised an eyebrow. "You didn't ask, princess."

Her cheeks heated as he was right.

"What do you do there?" she asked.

"I'm a security consultant. I take care of the building security."

She froze for a moment. Excitement built inside her at the thought of him having access to the Prism Corporation building, including the topmost floor.

She put on a blank look on her face. "Oh. That's very interesting."

"Yeah. Very interesting." He sounded amused.

Annoyed by his tone, she got up from the couch. She cleared her plate and took it to the kitchen. She washed her plate and placed it next to the rest of the washed plates.

When she stepped out of the small kitchen, her arrogant neighbor was waiting outside.

"Why not ask for daddy's help for a job?" he asked. "I'm sure he'd find something for you to do to pass the time."

Her teeth clenched at his words. The arrogant ass didn't know she was a freelance writer and volunteered in many organizations. She was also actively involved in activities of her trust. But she didn't want to tell him any of that.

"I prefer to work for an outside company."

He didn't say anything. She was sure he thought she was too spoiled to think of working for her father's businesses.

"Thank you for dinner," she said.

With her stomach filled with delicious food and a possible job offer dangling in the near future, she felt generous enough to ignore the arrogance of her new neighbor.

Until he opened his mouth again.

"You are welcome, princess," he drawled. "By the way, that was great scheming. Oscar worthy. Sameer didn't even know he was being lured into your scheming. Let's hope that when the poor bastard helps you get the job, he won't be in trouble with the plan you are hatching against Prism Corporation."

Anger and annoyance once again shot up inside her at his accurate analysis. Ignoring his smirk, she turned away. She could hear his laughter even when she got into her apartment and slammed the door shut.

Ugh. I hate the arrogant jerk.

CHAPTER NINE

"What do you mean you are going to work at Prism Corporation?"

Rashmi and Kavita looked shocked when Tanvi told them about her plan.

"You have been actively protesting against that company," Kavita stated. "Why do you think they would hire you knowing that?"

"I don't think they know it was me in particular." Hopefully, they won't know either.

"You are crazy!" Rashmi burst out. "If you get caught doing something shady, you will be in serious trouble."

Tanvi nodded. "I know. But according to their schedule, they will begin cutting down trees in two months. So far, they have succeeded in blocking every protest that has been planned. If the Prism Corporation is going to be ruthless that way, I would have to be equally ruthless to stop them."

Rashmi didn't look convinced. Kavita looked doubtful too.

"It's very risky, Tanvi. They are powerful people. You might get arrested or worse, harmed in some way."

Tanvi knew it was a huge risk. But she was willing to take the risk for her cause. "The job won't be for too long. I just want to meet the chairman and see which company is behind the mall construction."

She smiled reassuringly at her friend. "Stop worrying about me, girls. You know my father will bail me out as usual if I get into trouble."

"What if he doesn't?" Rashmi asked.

"He will because he needs a clean reputation, at least until the elections are done."

Kavita frowned. "But how will you get the job there in such a short span?"

"I know a couple of people who work there and will help me. Hopefully, I'll be able to join the company before the two-month time frame."

She was going to meet Sameer and work on the job applications right away. She might be racing against time, but she was determined to win the game against the ruthless corporation.

***

"Oh, Arjun. You are the best cook in the world."

"Yes. I never had such a delicious meal in my whole life!"

"And you cooked so fast!"

Tanvi had just returned to her apartment complex. A big group of giggling girls was surrounding a tall man near the mailboxes.

"The color of the t-shirt suits you so well, Arjun. It makes your eyes and dimples stand out."

A scoff escaped Tanvi as she heard and watched the show while collecting her mail.

Arjun's eyes immediately fell on her, and a smirk formed on his face.

"Thank you, ladies," he drawled. "I'll be sure to let my girlfriend know since she picked out this t-shirt."

"Oh!" There were visibly disappointed faces. "You have a girlfriend?" one of the girls asked.

"Yes. We only got together recently because it took me a while to impress her."

"How can any woman not be impressed by you!" one of the girls asked in an outraged tone.

He shrugged with a smile. "I'll be sure to let her know that. Excuse me, ladies. I better leave now. If I don't call my girlfriend on time, she'll be quite pissed and break up with me. She's a bit short-tempered."

With that excuse, he managed to walk away from the group. Tanvi joined him as they walked to the lifts. She stepped in, and he followed behind her. When the doors closed, a whiff of familiar cologne filled the inside of the small space.

"You owe me a big one, princess," he drawled, pressing the button on the lift to their floor.

Her stomach fluttered at his presence. Once again, she felt the buzzing awareness which she tried to ignore.

"I don't know what you are talking about," she said in a prim tone. "But I do know you don't have a girlfriend."

"Oh yeah? And how do you know that?"

"Because no sane girl would ever want to commit to you. You really are an arrogant ass."

His dimples flashed in amusement. "Most women like arrogant asses."

She rolled her eyes.

He let out a chuckle. The lift stopped at their floor, and she stepped out first while he followed next to her.

"So what mayhem have you caused today?" he asked.

She raised her chin. "Nothing."

Nothing yet.

"I don't believe you, princess. I'm sure there's always something or other hatching inside that interesting mind of yours. And this time, it's against Prism Corporation."

They had reached the end of the corridor and stood in front of their apartments. The corridor wasn't too wide, and so he was barely a couple of feet away.

She threw him a glare. "It's none of your business what I do. And don't you have a proper job other than attacking and harassing women in hallways?"

He slowly grinned. "I do have a job. And I only like attacking and harassing you in the hallway, princess."

"Lucky me," she muttered out loud, even though his closeness was having an unwanted effect on her. Her heart was beginning to race, and her skin broke into goosebumps.

Maybe her irrational attraction was obvious. Because his eyes suddenly hooded as he watched her.

"Want to join me for dinner?" he asked, his deep voice sounding huskier.

Her mouth watered at the thought of having delicious homemade food again.

"I can quickly whip up a dessert," he tempted further. "Hot, sticky sweet apricots with melting ice cream."

He was talking about food, but his voice sounded sinfully sexy, making the words seem dirty. Her breath caught in her throat. She suddenly imagined licking off the hot, sticky sweet apricot and the melting ice cream off his lips.

She sucked in a deep breath.

What the hell is wrong with me?

Must be a lack of proper sleep and anxiousness to get a job quickly at Prism Corporation. Why else would she be attracted to an arrogant jerk she hated?

Why else would she also recall the arrogant jerk's touch and the feel his hard body against hers from a few days ago?

"Sameer," she blurted out. "I'm meeting him to help me with my resume and job application. We... uh... will be busy for a while."

Her neighbor froze, and his eyes flashed momentarily at her explanation. But before she could analyze his reaction, his mouth twisted into a mocking smirk. "Is that so? Well, have fun applying for the jobs, princess. And try not to bully or scare the guy too much with your endless scheming."

Annoyance shot up inside her.

Gritting her teeth, she turned away and went to her apartment door. Once she unlocked and went inside, she slammed the door shut loudly on his mocking face.

I can't believe I find the arrogant jerk attractive. I need my brain checked.

***

"Are you sure you don't want to apply for marketing or sales jobs?"

Tanvi scrolled through the job openings list. "Yes, Sameer. I'm sure. I'm looking for something... a bit less challenging."

"Oh."

Tanvi had been on a phone call with Sameer for a while. They had been going through the lists of jobs in each department.

"Which departments are... uh... on the top most floor?" she asked.

Tanvi crossed her fingers, hoping there was no suspicious pause. Luckily, there wasn't. Sameer answered her right away.

"Oh. There are no departments on the topmost floor. It is reserved for the chairman and the board room meetings."

"And the floor below that?"

"It's mostly the executive assistants who are seated there."

She quickly typed the search words executive assistant and found a few openings.

"I think I want to apply for those positions."

This time there was a pause. "But you have a business degree, Tanvi. Don't you think marketing or sales would suit your career better?"

Tanvi laughed. "I don't think I can keep up with those working hours. My father often needs me to attend and host events. I can't travel much either."

"Oh. That makes sense, then. You should apply for those jobs."

She marked a few of them to apply for later.

Meanwhile, she took a bite of the food she had ordered a while ago. After having had the taste of homemade food, the takeout food tasted like cardboard.

Ugh. That evil bastard is making me hate takeout food.

Suddenly, she was reminded of something. "Where does the security team sit?" she asked.

Sameer paused. "Hmm. I think somewhere on the ground floor."

Thank goodness. If she got a job, then she would be far away from where the arrogant jerk would be working.

"Why?" Sameer asked. "Did you want to apply for jobs within the security team too?"

"No. I was just curious."

Although it would give access to the building and maybe more, she didn't want to work in close proximity with her arrogant neighbor. He would most likely catch her red-handed and report her immediately.

"Thanks a lot, Sameer, for putting aside an hour to help me out. I owe you a treat."

"Oh. There's no need for that."

She could imagine Sameer blushing. She hoped he didn't take her offer to treat him as flirting or some sort of encouragement. He was sweet and cute, but she didn't think of him that way and wasn't attracted to him.

"Oh, I insist. When I come for an interview at Prism, let's have lunch together."

"Sure. We have one of the best cafeterias."

Tanvi smiled. "Good night. I hope I'll hear back from them soon."

"You will. I got an initial call within the same week of applying. And a job offer after two days. They are quick."

She was glad since she didn't have much time to waste.

Thanking Sameer again and bidding him goodnight, she ended the phone call. She also put away her half-eaten dinner which now appeared unappetizing, thanks to her arrogant neighbor.

She then sat and applied for every executive assistant position in the company.

She hoped her plan would succeed.

CHAPTER TEN

Aryan shook his head with a vicious curse. He was supposed to be at his brother's penthouse nearly an hour ago, but instead, he was still inside his damn apartment.

Tanvi Shetty had lied about meeting Sameer. But after waiting for well over an hour, he realized it was a lie. He was both amused and annoyed that his little schemer had lied. He was amused because it meant she was feeling the strong attraction she wanted to fight and deny. He was annoyed because her lie did get a reaction out of him, and he wanted to interrupt them.

After two weeks of moving in as her neighbor, things had finally begun moving according to his plan. Although his prey was still prickly and cautious as a porcupine, he knew he was getting under her skin. Along with anger and annoyance in her eyes whenever he deliberately riled her, he also saw the sparks of attraction she tried too hard to fight—the same strong attraction he felt towards her.

He desired his pawn. There was no damn doubt about it. Each time he was close to her, he resisted pulling her close and kissing the hell out of her. He wanted to taste her lush lips and explore her smart mouth to see if she would return his passion despite her anger and annoyance.

But he held off. It was too soon. And it wasn't a part of his plan.

He knew he should stop wanting her. He had to finish the plan he began. And at the end of it, chances were high that she would hate him even more.

Fuck.

Ignoring his painful arousal which was now becoming a constant thing whenever he thought of her, he pulled out his cell phone and dialed a number.

It was answered in a couple of rings. "Mr. Varma?" the man greeted.

"Tanvi Shetty. I want her reporting to me by next Monday."

With those instructions, he ended the call.

A few days ago, when his fiery prey stormed into the Prism building demanding to meet the owner, he had come up with the idea of her working for him. Not only would he be able to keep a better eye on her, but it would also provide him with the perfect opportunity to get closer to her.

He had deliberately put the idea into her head through his assistant. And knowing how passionate Tanvi was about stopping the mall construction, he knew she would try her best to meet the chairman or at least find out information on him.

What would she do if she ever found out he was the chairman of Prism Corporation?

CHAPTER ELEVEN

Tanvi couldn't believe how fast things were proceeding. Barely three days after she applied for jobs at Prism Corporation, she got a call for an in-person interview. She didn't think her interview would yield such quick results.

"Congratulations, Miss Shetty. We are hoping to see you on Monday."

Seeing the shock on Tanvi's face, one of the interviewers smiled. "We usually make quick decisions at Prism Corporation. And you are definitely well-suited for the junior executive assistant role."

"Thank you," she said.

"As you know the role is to assist Mr. Tejpal, who is currently traveling to the New York head office and will be there for two months. He will speak to you and give you further instructions. You will have to handle the phone calls and emails that he would receive. Some of them would also be on behalf of our chairman."

The shocked excitement grew inside her. She had hoped to get an interview, but she didn't expect to land the position that would give her somewhat direct access to the chairman.

She felt a tinge of guilt. But she promptly pushed it away. She had nothing against the company's employees and wouldn't harm them in any way. It was only their chairman she was targeting because he was trying to earn millions at the cost of harming the environment.

"Our HR Department will send you the paperwork to finish, Miss Shetty. It will include an NDA as well. If you accept the position, Monday will be your orientation day, and you will get an ID card along with building access."

Tanvi nodded with a smile and thanked them again before leaving the place. She barely contained her excitement from showing. Of course, she would accept the job. She didn't think she would land one so quickly.

She called Sameer to thank him and see if he could meet her for lunch. Meeting at the office cafeteria was less intimate than inviting him to her home or going to a restaurant.

He answered the call after a few rings. "Hi, Tanvi."

"Hello, Sameer. I got the job!"

"Oh wow! I knew you would. But I didn't know it would be this quick. Congratulations."

She laughed. "Thanks. Are you free for lunch?"

There was the minutest of pauses. "Yes, definitely. But I'm finishing up something important. Why don't you wait by the cafeteria? I will be downstairs in a few minutes."

"Sure. No problem."

Ending the call, she walked out of the building. She asked someone where the cafeteria was located before following the directions.

It was a bit early for lunch and not many employees were there yet. She waited outside because she wouldn't be allowed in. The place was beautiful with lush greenery dominating the area despite the tall buildings surrounding it. Maybe it wouldn't be that bad to work there for a few weeks.

She checked her phone messages to see if there was any news about the mall construction. So far, there wasn't any change in the schedule. There were quite a few social media messages and articles demanding to stop the mall construction. She boosted and shared those messages, adding a few comments with them.

During the interview process, she discovered that the parent company was based out of New York. Although it wasn't a ground-breaking revelation, she made a note of it. She would search for all real estate companies in New York.

"Hello, princess," a deep, familiar voice greeted.

She whipped her head up to see her arrogant neighbor.

"What are you doing here?" she demanded.

He flashed his dimples with a smirk. "Shouldn't that be my question?" he asked.

She shook her head. "I was here for an interview, and I'm waiting for Sameer to join me for lunch."

His eyes flashed. "You can wait inside."

She wanted to refuse. But it would look silly wanting to wait outside when she had the choice to sit at one of the tables.

"Fine."

He let out a short laugh at her ungracious statement and swiped a card that allowed them inside the large cafeteria. Since the place was empty, she could choose from many tables to sit.

"Let's sit there."

He was leading them to a place near the water feature. There were only a few tables there giving enough privacy from the rest of the cafeteria.

She frowned. She wasn't expecting him to join her and Sameer for lunch. But since he was there and she didn't want to be too rude, she followed him. She supposed she did owe him a meal in return for the delicious dinner she had at his place a few nights ago.

They sat at a table.

She sat opposite him. Even though there was enough distance between them, once again, she felt a strong awareness. His long legs brushed hers slightly under the table, and his direct gaze on her fluttered her stomach.

She was once again annoyed by her body's reaction.

"I got the job," she blurted to cut through the awareness.

His mouth twisted. "Congratulations, princess."

She didn't know why but she felt as though he was expecting that outcome. Even she was shocked about her quick job offer, but the arrogant man in front of her had a knowing look.

Annoyance flared along with awareness. "I'm going to be working for your boss," she said.

"My boss?"

"Well, most likely your boss's boss's boss and even higher. With your chairman."

He looked amused. "Wow. That's really impressive, princess. I heard the Prism chairman doesn't hire anyone that easily."

She could hear his sarcasm. The arrogant ass probably knew it wasn't a permanent job under the chairman but only until his executive assistant returned. After that, she would have to work under a different executive.

"Well, he hired me," she snapped.

"Good luck, princess. If possible, do throw in a good word about me."

Annoyed by his sarcasm, she glared at him. "What exactly do you do?" she demanded. She recalled that he handled building access and security.

"I keep an eye on nosy people like you."

Her cheeks heated. "How dare you—"

He grinned. "Relax. I was joking."

She was outraged and annoyed because he was right in his assessment. She did intend to be nosy and snoop on Prism Corporation and the chairman.

"How does your boss tolerate you?" she demanded. "I'm sure you must have come close to getting fired with your *jokes*."

His grin widened. "Sorry to disappoint you, but I cannot be fired that easily, princess. I guess I'm invaluable."

She scoffed. "No one is invaluable in a corporation. Everyone can be replaced... including the chairman."

"Interesting... is that a threat against the chairman?" he asked.

It was. But she didn't say anything.

She looked around to see if Sameer was coming. She had left a message for him that she was seated in the cafeteria by the small water fall. So far, he hadn't responded back.

A man dressed in white cafeteria clothes approached them with two trays. "Today's specials. Please enjoy, sir and madam."

Tanvi opened her mouth to say she didn't want to have lunch yet, but her stomach growled and her mouth tingled, reminding her that she hadn't had breakfast that morning. She had been in a hurry to get to the interview on time.

"We should wait for Sameer," she said half-heartedly.

Arjun shrugged. "He can join us when he comes."

She nodded and smiled at the man who had got them their food.

"They serve food at the table in the cafeteria?" she asked. She thought it would be more like a buffet system.

"Sometimes," he said.

Not wanting to think too much, she dug into her food.

"Mmm. It's quite good for cafeteria food," she remarked.

Arjun's dimple flashed. "Is that a hint to ask me to invite you for a homemade meal again?"

Her cheeks heated. "No!"

"No?"

"Well... obviously, you are a... decent cook. But I wasn't hinting that you invite me over."

He grinned at her calling him a decent cook. The arrogant jerk knew he was quite good.

"Come over tonight," he said. "Let's celebrate your new job."

She opened her mouth to refuse, but he cut her off. "I'll invite Sameer too, princess. So you should be safe from me."

"I'm not scared of you."

He smiled. "Oh yeah. I remember your threat of breaking my nose if I misbehaved."

She knew he was making fun of her threat because he was easily able to pin her against the wall in their apartment hallway. Instead of getting annoyed, her stomach fluttered as she once again recalled how his hard body felt against hers.

Ugh. You hate him, remember! Stop thinking of him.

She forcibly pushed away thoughts of his body against hers and focused on the food. It was hard to ignore him, though. The man was a nuisance. Ever since he crashed into her life, she felt his presence constantly even when he wasn't around.

"So are you going to tell your father about your new job?" he asked.

Of course, she wasn't going to tell her father. She would keep it a secret until her father discovered her new job on his own. And since he was going to be busy with the upcoming campaigning, she knew she had enough time to face the crisis.

"Why wouldn't I tell my father?" she asked.

"Why indeed."

She frowned. The man in front of her knew way too much about what went on in her mind. The fact that she couldn't read him similarly annoyed her.

"Tell me about the company," she demanded. It was to change the topic from her personal information and also because she did want to know.

He raised his eyebrow at her demand. "Sure. What would you like to know?"

"I would like to know more than what's available on the internet."

His mouth twisted. "I'm just a lowly security guy who knows what everyone knows. You are the one who is going to work for my boss's boss's boss and more. So, I think you would discover quite a bit soon."

She was annoyed by his teasing non-answer. The guy was too arrogantly smart to willingly offer any confidential information. She would have to rely on Sameer and the people she would work with to get the information.

She looked at her phone to check if Sameer had left any messages. She blinked in slight shock when she realized well over an hour had passed since she had been eating lunch with Arjun while exchanging taunts.

"Looks like Sameer won't be able to make it," she said. She could see that the lunch break was nearly over, and most employees were leaving the cafeteria. "I'm going to have to leave. If you see Sameer, tell him I had to leave for a different appointment."

"Sure."

He took her outside from the cafeteria's side entrance, where there were fewer people. He accompanied her to the taxi stand where many taxis were waiting. She got into one.

He looked at her through the window. "Well, I guess I'll see you at my place tonight," he said.

She narrowed her eyes. "I didn't accept the dinner offer at your home."

Slowly, a smirk formed on his face. "Too bad. Then I guess it'll be just Sameer and me having the slow-roasted mutton curry and apricot pudding."

She gritted her teeth. "You are evil! Do you know that I hate you?"

He grinned. "I know, princess. I know."

She turned away from his handsomely arrogant face and let the taxi take her back home. But the strange flutter inside her stomach warned her she might not hate him as much as she thought.

***

"Mr. Munshi. I will not be available to come in person to sign the papers for a few weeks. Can you please email them to me so I can put my electronic signature on them?"

Tanvi was speaking to the lawyer in charge of her trust. The older man looked surprised since he knew she had been very involved in every aspect of the trust since she turned eighteen. She looked into every transaction and questioned anything out of the ordinary. She still intended to do the same, but since she would be starting a job, she couldn't oversee things personally.

"Sure, Tanvi. Are you travelling somewhere for a few weeks?"

She smiled at the older man. "No. I'm just planning to take up a few more freelance writing jobs. So I'll be busy for a few weeks."

Although she trusted the lawyer she had known for nearly two decades, she didn't want to take chances of him mentioning her job at Prism Corporation to her father.

"That's great. All the best, Tanvi."

Thanking the lawyer, she left the lawyer's office and returned home.

It was late evening when delicious aromas once again filled the air outside her apartment.

It was too early for dinner, but she wanted to go and help her arrogant neighbor. Even though he was an ass, she couldn't simply freeload off him.

She went into her apartment and took a quick shower before putting on her usual t-shirt and jeans. The weather was still warm and humid.

Pulling her hair back, she tied it into a ponytail before stepping out of her apartment.

The opposite door was open as usual. Knowing he must be in the kitchen, she went there. She suppressed a grin recalling how he had to 'slave away' the last time a big group of girls turned up unexpectedly for dinner.

She saw him in the kitchen. He was facing the other way, and she could only see his back. Her stomach fluttered hard noticing that he was wearing a sleeveless half-shirt that showed off his tanned skin and impressive muscles. He was chopping vegetables in a smooth motion, which he eventually put into a bubbling pot and stirred it.

She was fascinated to simply watch. She had never thought of cooking as interesting. But looking at the handsome, arrogant man in front of her, she realized how hot and sexy it could look.

"Hello, princess. You are home early," he remarked.

He was still facing the other way and hadn't turned towards her.

"How did you know it was me?" she asked. It could have been Sameer too.

He turned to look at her, and she could see his dimple flashing. "Sandalwood soap," he remarked.

Her heart jerked at his remark. Pushing away the awareness, she twisted her lips into a smirk.

"Do you make it a habit of sniffing your neighbors to recognize them by their scent?" she asked.

He laughed. "Just you, princess. It's something I remember you by when we sat together in the taxi we shared."

Her stomach fluttered. She remembered his subtle cologne too. If she placed her nose against his hard chest, she knew she would smell the musky, citrusy fragrance.

Oh God.

She was shocked by her wicked thought.

What is wrong with you! Stop thinking of sniffing him! You hate him, remember?

She tried to remind herself that she hated him.

Once again, there was a knowing smirk on his face, flashing his dimples. He was so damn hot and annoying. She was torn between wanting to sink her teeth into his dimples and also wanting to slap the arrogant smirk off his handsome face.

"I would love to know what you are thinking, princess," he drawled.

"I was thinking about how my previous neighbor was so sweet and quiet and made me delicious food without being arrogant and annoying."

He laughed. "I'm sorry that I'm not an old lady."

She narrowed her eyes. "How do you know Mrs. Vasudev is an old lady?"

"Sweet and quiet without being arrogant and annoying sounds like an old lady."

"Sameer is sweet and quiet too. He isn't an old lady!"

Once again, there was an arrogant smirk.

"Ugh. You are such a jerk!"

He laughed. "Come help me with the fruits."

"Oh." She was intrigued. She had never cooked or been asked to help in the kitchen.

She went closer. "What should I do?"

"Cut them into small pieces." He handed her the dried fruit pieces.

She noticed that even though his living room was sparsely furnished, his kitchen seemed well-stocked. All the kitchenware looked shiny and well-maintained. Either everything was brand new or he was obsessively clean.

She washed the fruit and carefully cut them into small pieces.

He put them into a saucepan with sugar syrup and a couple of cardamom pieces.

"Keep stirring it," he told her while he took care of the simmering curry next to it.

She held the ladle and carefully stirred the contents of the saucepan.

She could sense his gaze on her all the while.

"I'm quite intrigued by you following my instructions without any arguments," he said.

She threw him a glance. "Don't get used to it," she retorted. "I'm like this only in the kitchen. I'm not going to blindly follow your instructions elsewhere."

There was a slow grin. "I'll remember that, princess."

Her cheeks heated at the suggestive tone. She imagined following his different kinds of instructions in the kitchen.

Ugh. Stop thinking of him that way!

"Does your father have a tough time making you follow his instructions too?" he asked.

She raised an eyebrow. "What do you think?"

He smirked. "I think you give him a hell of a time to keep you out of trouble."

She was annoyed because it was true. But she didn't want to discuss her father or her personal things.

"What about you?" she demanded. "Do you have a family? Or were you born to wolves in a forest?"

He laughed. "I do have a family, princess. Although I would like to think I'm a big bad wolf when it comes to you."

She rolled her eyes even as her stomach fluttered once again.

"Let me guess," she said. "You must be the only child or the youngest."

He raised an eyebrow. "Youngest of three. How did you guess?"

This time, she smirked. "Because you are an arrogant brat who is used to getting away with a lot of things for being the youngest."

He laughed. "Guilty as charged."

Despite herself, she smiled. He was an arrogant jerk, but he didn't give out the vibes of being creepy. Although she was annoyed by him, she didn't find him disgusting. In fact, she had to try hard to fight the strong pull she felt towards him.

"Check to see if the sweetness is enough and turn off the stove," he instructed. He topped the concoction with a generous amount of toasted nuts and apricot seeds.

She nodded and took the small spoon he handed her and tasted the apricot dessert. Her eyes nearly rolled at the taste. It was perfect.

When she opened her eyes, she saw him watching her with a look that had her heart beating faster. The awareness she had always felt with him blazed into a roaring attraction. He was looking at her lips, and she felt them tingling strangely. She wanted to know how it would feel to have his lips on top of hers.

"It's perfect," she whispered, her voice was getting stuck in her throat due to her forbidden thoughts. "You can taste."

One moment, they were standing next to each other, and the next moment their mouths were fused together. She didn't know how it happened, but heat blazed while his tongue tasted her lips.

"Fuck, it is perfect," he growled deeply against her lips.

She was shocked. For a moment she thought she was imagining the kiss since she wanted it moments ago. But the rough feel of his bearded stubble along with his kiss felt too real.

Arjun was kissing her.

She knew she should be outraged and push him away before slapping him for daring to kiss her. But she held his t-shirt and pulled him even closer.

He gripped her hair and tugged her head back before his tongue slid between her lips. Passion blazed as he devoured her mouth, tasting her along with the sticky sweet she just had. Every rough lick of his tongue made her stomach quiver in passion.

Her body felt blazing hot. Her breasts felt swollen and sensitive as the aroused buds brushed against his hard chest. She moaned at the sensations. She wanted to feel more.

Letting go of his t-shirt, she slid her hands underneath it and touched his hair-roughened, hard muscles of his chest. He groaned into her mouth.

She was lost in heated sensations when his mouth suddenly pulled away from hers.

"Fuck," he cursed softly. "We should stop."

"Why?" she demanded even as she grabbed his t-shirt and tried to pull him closer again.

"We have company, princess."

Her eyes opened. She stared at his face. His eyes were hooded, and his lips glistened from their kiss. His signature smirk was gone, and he looked both aroused and pissed.

That's when she heard.

"Hello? Anyone home?" Sameer called from a nearby distance.

Shock ripped through her when she realized what she had done. She had kissed Arjun—her arrogant neighbor and the man she supposedly hated. Her cheeks blazed when she realized that she still had a hand inside his t-shirt. Pulling her hand out and letting go of his t-shirt, she stepped away.

Arjun watched her shocked face. "Stay here and straighten your hair. I'll receive him."

With those instructions, he stepped out of the kitchen.

She realized her ponytail was loose and crooked. With slightly shaking hands, she straightened her hair and retied her ponytail. She wanted to run out of the apartment and go back to hers to hide inside and never come out. She was shocked and embarrassed.

But she took a deep breath and stepped out of the kitchen. She heard the conversation between Arjun and Sameer as they greeted each other.

Sameer saw her coming out of the kitchen. "Oh, hi, Tanvi," he greeted with a shy smile. "Congratulations on getting the job."

She forced out a smile. "Thank you, Sameer. I wouldn't have got it had you not helped me with the applications."

Sameer blushed. "You are welcome," he said. "But I'm sorry that I couldn't meet you this afternoon. I had a last-minute meeting I couldn't decline."

"No problem," she said.

Sameer smiled. "I'm glad that Arjun could keep you company, and we are celebrating at his home."

She nodded.

"So, what are you guys doing in the kitchen?" Sameer asked.

Her cheeks blazed, and she tried not to look at Arjun as she answered. "We were cooking."

Had Sameer walked into the kitchen directly like her, he would have caught Arjun and her kissing. He would have also seen her hands under Arjun's t-shirt.

Oh God.

She hoped her face wasn't too flushed.

Sameer just continued to smile shyly. "It smells delicious, and I'm quite hungry since I had to skip my lunch today."

"Food's ready," Arjun's deep voice drawled. "Let's eat."

Arjun and Sameer went into the kitchen and brought the dishes and plates out, placing them on the coffee table. Tanvi sat on the couch, still fighting the urge to run into her apartment. Her lips still tingled, and she could feel the effect of Arjun's rough stubble on the sensitive skin around her lips.

She avoided eye contact while they served food onto their plates. Luckily, Sameer sat next to her on the couch.

"I still can't believe you are starting your job on Monday," Sameer remarked with a smile. "You must have done really well in the interview for them to confirm on the spot."

Tanvi forced out a smile. "I think they needed someone quickly. I just happen to meet the qualifications."

"But that's great, Tanvi. I'm glad we will be colleagues too, along with neighbors."

Sameer was being sweet and nice, but she couldn't return a genuine smile. She was too aware of her arrogant neighbor, the one whose kiss and touch still lingered on her body.

Luckily, Sameer didn't pick up the sexual-tension vibes from the room. He kept speaking, telling her once again about the company in general. She listened, but only with half an ear. All her senses were focused on the man seated on the chair next to the couch. Even though she didn't look at him directly, her body buzzed with awareness and knew he was watching her.

She shoved a spoonful of curry and rice into her tingling mouth. Despite the awareness and the need to run, she could enjoy the delicate flavors. She continued to eat. Arjun was quiet too.

Like her, he only replied to Sameer's questions, adding a comment or two. Sameer continued to be oblivious. Soon, it was time for dessert.

She wanted to avoid it because it would remind her of what it had led to, but the dish was too tempting. She took one of the bowls it was served in, along with ice cream. It was incredible. She finished it and went for the second serving too.

"Wow," said Sameer. "I can't believe how good this is. It's perfect."

Tanvi almost choked on her bite. Her eyes flew to Arjun. He was watching her with hooded eyes, and when their eyes clashed, his mouth twisted, and his gaze lowered to her lips. Her lips tingled as she recalled their kiss.

Oh God.

I have to get away.

"Excuse me," she said, getting up. "I-I forgot that I told my father I'd call him to tell him more about my job. He'll be busy during the mornings. I will see you later, Sameer."

Sameer looked taken aback by her abrupt departure. "Oh sure. See you tomorrow."

She murmured a thanks and goodnight in the general direction of Arjun before walking out of the apartment. She hurried into her flat, shut the door and leaned against it.

What did I do!

She tried to reason that the kiss was forced on her.

He kissed me first.

But you grabbed him and kissed him right back.

Her cheeks heated, knowing it was true.

I'm never going to face him ever again.

Even as she made the vow to herself, she knew it was impossible to avoid the hot, arrogant jerk since he lived right across from her.

It was well past midnight when Aryan met his brothers. They were seated by the outdoor bar at his oldest brother's penthouse.

Aryan was well into his third drink.

"Easy there," Yash said in amusement. "I don't think you will be in a state to ride your bike back home."

Aryan didn't care. He wanted to forget the incredible fuck-up he had made a while ago.

He had kissed his prey. He now knew how her lush lips and smart mouth tasted. She tasted damn fucking sweet. Like a damn paradise.

And she had not only returned his kiss, but she also matched his passion and hunger.

Fuck.

"Well, looks like our little bro is getting drunk because of a pawn."

Bhargav sounded amused.

"That's shocking," Yash said with a hint of amusement as well. "Considering our little bro was warning us both repeatedly about the perils of getting involved with our pawns, and how our pawns were to be considered as our enemies too."

Aryan was annoyed that both his brothers were amused by him.

"I'm not involved with her," he said irritably.

"Really?" Bhargav asked. "Is that why she's going to start working for you at Prism?"

Fuck.

He should stop sharing every damn aspect of his life with his brothers.

"We warned you, little bro. That beautiful pawns can turn into a maddening obsession. It's impossible to escape the pull."

"Unlike you both, I can escape my enemy's daughter's pull just fine."

Arjun frowned. He sounded like a damn hypocrite considering his tongue was down his enemy's daughter's throat just a few hours ago.

"I have to get closer to her," he reasoned. "It's only a part of my plan."

"No, it isn't," Bhargav said in amusement. "You planted a guy to trap her. You were supposed to push her towards him."

He cursed his brothers' sharp memories because they didn't ever forget a thing. He had hired Sameer to trap Tanvi Shetty. He assumed rich heiresses would fall for simple, modest and sweet guys. But the damn woman barely showed interest in Sameer, prompting an immediate change in the plan.

He had moved opposite to her to taunt and tease her and try to make her see how well-suited Sameer was for her. But the plan backfired.

Even though Sameer had gotten marginally close, it was him who couldn't accept the fact.

He was jealous. He began desiring his prey himself.

Fuck.

"I'm letting her see how well-suited he is to her compared to me."

His brothers didn't buy his explanation entirely. They had knowing smiles which spoke vastly of their own failed attempts not to get obsessed by their beautiful pawns.

No. Tanvi Shetty is just a pawn. I will not let her be more than that.

CHAPTER THIRTEEN

"Welcome to Prism Corporation, Miss Shetty. If you have any questions regarding the training or security access, please reach out to either me or the helpdesk number."

Tanvi smiled at the man who was the coordinator in charge of the new-employee training.

"Thank you, Mr. Goyal."

Thanking the man once again, she headed to the fourteenth floor, where her desk was located. Her heart thudded in excitement as she went up the office lift using the employee keycard.

Will this allow me to go all the way to the top?

She desperately wanted to try it out. But she knew she had to wait until things settled down a bit. There were people waiting for her at her office desk on the first day. And also, there was no guarantee that the chairman was at his office that day.

She reached the floor below the topmost floor where most of the executive assistants were seated. She was received by a middle-aged woman who introduced herself and the rest of the team.

"You are younger than we thought," one of the women said to her.

Tanvi was surprised too. She later learned that most of the executive assistants were retained from the previous takeover of Prism Corporation. The few new ones had at least ten years of experience.

Most of her morning was spent in training. And soon, it was lunchtime. She joined Sameer for a quick lunch at the cafeteria.

Her heart beat faster, expecting to see Arjun as well. But her arrogant neighbor didn't crash the lunch.

She knew she had to face Arjun at some time, and it was silly to avoid him like she had been doing over the past few days. But the very thought of being in his proximity made her want to hide and never leave her house again.

Ugh.

How could I kiss him back!

It's okay. You are an adult, and such things happen between healthy consenting adults. It's no big deal. Just ignore him when you see him.

She decided to play it cool and behave maturely when she came across him either at work or near their apartments.

"How is your first day going so far?" Sameer asked with a smile.

Dragging her mind forcibly away from her arrogant neighbor, she focused on the sweet guy who helped her with the job.

"A bit boring with all the training," she said with a laugh. "Hopefully, I'll begin working on the tasks soon."

"Let me know if you need any help," he offered before he began to blush. "I... uh... can give you a ride back home this evening."

It was sweet of him to offer. But she didn't want to take advantage of Sameer or encourage him in any way. "I'll be fine, Sameer. I'll take the taxi."

He nodded.

Thanking him for joining her for lunch, she headed back to her desk to finish the rest of her training. But when she got into the lift, instead of pressing the button of her floor, she pressed the button for the topmost floor.

She had been planning it during lunch. If anyone asked why she was on the topmost floor, she could pretend to be confused on her first day.

But her plan didn't work when red lights flashed, and the damn lift didn't move.

Dammit!

She had no access to the top floor even though she was the assistant to the chairman. Disappointed, she went to her assigned floor and sat at her desk. She opened her emails and read through them. Most of them were for the initial set up. She had a call with Mr. Tejpal the next morning. He was going to guide her through the rest of the task list of what needed to be done.

Soon, it was close to evening when most of the executive assistants began to leave. When the floor was nearly cleared of people, she began to dig through the documents placed on the shared folder to which she was given access.

She knew she couldn't risk staying too late right on the first day, but she kept scanning through them. When she didn't come across anything significant, she shut her computer and decided to go home.

***

It was dark when she arrived at her apartment building. Although her day began earlier than usual, she was far from tired. Her mind was spinning with the information of her training and also of the folders she began digging through. None of it was useful so far, but she knew it was only a matter of time until she stumbled across something important.

She went towards the lifts. Hoping she could catch up with her writing on one of the articles that was due, she planned to get to sleep before midnight.

The lift doors were about to close when a masculine hand stuck inside to hold it open. Annoyed that she was being delayed, she was frowning when the doors opened completely and revealed who it was.

"Good evening, princess."

Her face heated in a hot blush seeing Arjun's amused face as he stepped into the lift with her. She recalled her decision to ignore him and pretend nothing happened between them.

But her body heated when he stood next to her.

The ride up was tense, and when the doors to the lift finally opened, they stepped out together. The walk along the corridor was also tense.

Why couldn't the jerk walk faster with his long legs? Why did he have to walk next to me?

Is he looking to talk about their kiss?

Hoping to get it over with, she turned to him when they reached the end of the corridor.

"The kiss is a mistake," she snapped. "It was a huge mistake that won't ever happen again."

His mouth twisted into a dimpled smirk. "Okay."

She was annoyed by his attitude. She had been haunted by their kiss day and night, recalling every moment of it and how she had felt and reacted to it. Even now, her senses were hyperaware to his subtle cologne and reacted to his close presence with goosebumps on her skin.

But the jerk in front of her behaved as though it weren't a big deal. The ass probably kissed dozens more women.

I hate him!

"You look quite worked up, princess. Are you okay?" he asked in amusement.

"Go to hell!" she yelled before whirling away from him.

She realized she was hardly behaving in a cool, mature manner as planned.

Taking a deep breath, she ignored her arrogant neighbor. She had a lot to do that night, and she wasn't going to let him annoy her. She placed her key into the lock to open the door. But her key wasn't fitting properly.

Frowning, she tried again.

"What the hell?" she muttered out loud.

She tried for a few more times. But each time ended the same. She let out a vicious curse for not being able to open the damn door. She didn't know what to do. She supposed she had to call a locksmith, but it would take them a while to arrive.

"Your cursing is quite impressive, princess," Arjun's deep voice drawled.

She swung around and saw him leaning against his door with an amused smirk. He had unlocked his door.

"My main door key isn't working," she gritted. "I need to call a locksmith."

He raised an eyebrow. "You can call the new building manager and have a maintenance guy look at it. It would be faster."

She frowned. She didn't know there was a new building manager or a maintenance team. But the new owner who bought the building must have set them up.

"Do you have their number?" she asked.

He nodded. "Come inside and wait while I call them."

Her frown grew at his offer. Before she could refuse, he stepped back into his apartment.

Knowing she would look foolish waiting outside and hoping it would only take a few minutes, she followed him inside.

He made the call and asked for someone to come and unlock the door. When he finished the call, she was standing by his couch.

"They will be up here in five minutes," he said. His eyes swept over her. "Have you eaten? I'm about to reheat dinner. There's plenty, and you can join me if you haven't had yours."

"I'm not hungry," she lied.

She was starving. She realized in her eagerness for snooping on the first day of her job and finishing up her pending article, she forgot to plan her dinner. All she had in her apartment refrigerator were a few apples.

"Have a little," he tempted. When she shook her head, his mouth quirked. "Just a little taste."

Her cheeks heated as she recalled their kiss while they tasted the dessert they made together.

"I told you the kiss was a mistake!" she snapped.

He grinned. "I wasn't talking about the kiss."

"You were! You mentioned tasting, which meant—" She broke off when she saw amusement in his eyes.

Arrogant jerk.

She took another deep breath and waited calmly. Thankfully, a couple of minutes later, the locksmith arrived. She stepped out of Arjun's apartment and looked on while the man checked her key and lock.

"The lock unit will have to be changed, madam."

She was shocked. "What? I used the key just this morning!"

The man nodded. "Sometimes, it happens, madam. You will need to change it."

"Break the lock," she advised. "I can use the tower bolt to lock the door for tonight. And I'll buy a new lock unit tomorrow."

"Okay, madam." The man proceeded to do as she ordered.

"Pizza," her arrogant neighbor said from behind her.

Starving and unable to resist the delicious aroma since he began reheating it, she turned to him.

"It's homemade," he further tempted.

Unable to control herself, she gave in. She followed him inside, where he had already placed the pizza on the table along with two plates. She picked up a plate and then took a piece of pizza before she sat on the couch.

As usual, the jerk's pizza tasted amazing.

"How was your first day?" he asked, taking a bite of his pizza. He was standing opposite to her.

"Good," she replied. "I was in training most of the day."

His mouth quirked. "Did you get to meet my boss's boss's boss?"

Her cheeks heated at his reminder of how she had taunted him about getting a job under the chairman. "Not yet. But I will soon."

Arjun's mouth quirked. "I'm sure you will, princess."

Irritated by his taunting, she ignored him, but she finished her delicious pizza.

She still found it hard to believe the arrogant jerk was such an amazing cook.

Not just an amazing cook but also an amazing kisser.

Her cheeks heated at the unwanted thought.

"Is the pizza too spicy?" he asked in amusement. "Your face looks flushed."

The heat in her cheeks increased at his observation. "No. It's fine."

She hurriedly got up and went to the kitchen to wash the used plate in the sink. She needed to leave right away. She could wait outside her apartment while the locksmith removed the unit.

Finishing the cleanup, she turned to hurry out when she saw Arjun leaning against the kitchen entrance. Her heart began to race. His eyes were hooded, and the normally mocking smirk was missing from his face while he watched her.

"Dessert?" he asked huskily. "It's the same as what we made together."

Her heart began to thud. A loud voice inside her warned her to get the hell away from temptation. And the temptation wasn't just in the form of the sticky, sweet dessert. It was also in the form of the tall, sexy man in front of her.

"I... I..." She wanted to refuse.

He took a step closer. She didn't know if he wanted to go to the refrigerator or whether he was coming to her. Her heart raced, and she stepped towards him as well. It was to go out of the kitchen, she reasoned. But her skin broke out in goosebumps as they neared.

Electricity seemed to buzz around them in the small kitchen as they looked at each other. Once again, she didn't know how it happened. One moment, they were looking at each other, and the next moment, she held his t-shirt and dragged him closer while his long arm wrapped around her waist.

Their mouths met hungrily.

Passion flared, and pleasure sizzled through her body. She felt hot and giddy with an urgent need for more. His mouth devoured hers again, his tongue tasting her and thrusting deep inside. She moaned with her nails digging into his skin through his t-shirt to pull him even closer.

He let out a half-growl and half-groan and dug his fingers into her hips. She felt him lifting her and carrying her somewhere. A moment later, her back hit something hard. It must have been a wall. He held her against it as they continued to kiss. Her body heated and melted against his as she wrapped her legs around him. She gasped and then moaned when she felt his hardness rubbing between her legs. The pleasure that sizzled through her was unlike anything she had ever felt before.

But he suddenly stilled, and a moment later, he dragged his mouth away from hers. "Fuck," he cursed. His hot and heavy breaths fell against her ears.

He spoke out loud. "If you are done, you can leave. We'll pay you in the morning after you finish replacing the lock."

Dazed and still floating in passion, it took her a while to realize he was talking to the locksmith working outside. Soft footsteps could be heard while the locksmith walked away from her apartment.

Slowly, Arjun raised his head and looked at her with hooded eyes. "Too many interruptions," he said huskily. "Next time, we better lock the damn door."

Shock ripped through her, along with embarrassment.

Oh God.

I kissed him. Again.

Her shock grew when she realized how her legs were wrapped around his hips, and she was clutching his t-shirt in a death grip.

She let go of his shirt and tried to push him off her. But he barely moved. His hard body kept her pinned against the wall.

"Let me go!" she said as shock and embarrassment grew.

He slowly stepped away, and her feet landed on the kitchen floor again. With her face flaming, she glared at him.

"Stop kissing me!" she snapped.

He raised an eyebrow. "You kissed me first."

Heat grew in her cheeks. "This was a mistake," she said. "It will never happen again!"

His mouth quirked. "If you say so."

Oh God.

Why couldn't she stay away from the man in front of her? She hated him. And yet, electricity buzzed around them each time they were together, drawing her towards him. His eyes were hooded as he watched her. Her stomach trembled, and a voice inside her screamed to touch him again and kiss him.

"I have a deal, princess," he said as he watched her fight the urge to kiss again. "Since we both can't seem to stay away from each other, I propose a deal to give it a try and date."

That shocked her. "What! I don't even like you! I hate you!"

His eyebrow rose at her outburst. "Well, then channel in all that hate during our dates, princess. Just like you do during our kisses."

Her cheeks heated at his words. She was outraged by his proposal. But at the same time her lips tingled and heat spread through her body at the way he was watching her with a hooded-eyed look.

She was attracted to the jerk. A lot.

She chose not to reply to him right then. Dragging her eyes away and ignoring the live current that continued to buzz at his proximity, she hurried out of the kitchen.

She didn't stop until she was inside her apartment. Shutting the door, which now had a missing lock, she kept it shut using the bolts.

Oh God. What is happening to me?

He must be adding something to the food.

Even though she desperately tried to reason he might have drugged her for her to be unnaturally attracted to him, she knew it was not true. Sameer had dinner at Arjun's place too a few nights ago. But the other man wasn't overcome with uncontrollable passion.

It was all her. She was attracted to her arrogant neighbor. For some reason, she couldn't stay away from the damn man despite her repeated vows to herself.

She shook her head.

No! I have to stay away from him!

Even as she made the vow once again to herself, she knew she wouldn't be able to keep it.

CHAPTER FOURTEEN

"I can't believe you got the job! My God, Tanvi! This is so exciting and scary!"

Tanvi smiled as Rashmi and Kavita looked at her with widened eyes. "I know."

"So you are going to work right under the Prism chairman?"

"Yes. At least until his executive assistant is back from New York."

"Wow! This is incredible!"

Tanvi nodded. "I still can't believe it either."

Rashmi frowned. "But what are the odds that you would land a position right under the chairman? Do you think the chairman somehow knows it's you?"

Tanvi shook her head. "I doubt it. Based on how fast things moved from my job application, interview and confirmation, I doubt if he was even consulted."

The confirmation had happened on the same day as the interview. Unless the chairman went through hundreds of job applications each day and specifically looked for hers, it wasn't possible.

She shook her head, pushing away doubts.

She was on the right path of getting the information she needed to stop City Central Park from being destroyed. She wasn't going to be hung up on some lucky coincidences and think of them as a part of some elaborate plan.

Kavita smiled. "So how did your first day go?"

Tanvi felt the heat of her blush creeping up on her face. Instead of recalling the trainings or the snooping of her first day, all she recalled was the scorching kiss with her arrogant neighbor.

"Oh my God! Why are you blushing! Tell us what happened!" her friend demanded.

Knowing it was hard to keep the secret, and her friends wouldn't let go until the truth was fished out, she told the truth.

"I kissed my neighbor."

Rashmi looked shocked. "Oh my God! You kissed Sameer?"

Tanvi felt her blush intensify. "No. Another guy. An arrogant jerk who lives opposite my apartment. He's... uh... the same guy you saw on the first day of the protest when he was arrested with me."

Her friend shrieked and jumped up. "What! He's your neighbor? Why did you not mention it to me until now!"

"I didn't want you involved because he's an arrogant jerk," Tanvi murmured.

Rashmi laughed. "Well, it looks like you broke your own rule and kissed the arrogant jerk. I'm so glad. How did it feel? Was there tongue involved? What else happened?"

Tanvi shook her head at her friend's questioning. "The kiss was just an accident. We were in his kitchen cooking together because he invited me and Sameer over for dinner."

The kiss wasn't accidental. But it was definitely a mistake.

Rashmi grinned widely. "Oh my God. I can imagine it. This is incredibly exciting. More than your new job! So what did he say after he kissed you?"

"Nothing."

She hadn't met him yet. She had avoided him all weekend by staying out of her home and returning late in the night. But she knew she couldn't avoid him forever.

"Maybe he is the one, Tanvi!" Kavita teased.

Tanvi rolled her eyes. "Stop it! I hate the guy, remember?"

Rashmi laughed. "And yet, you let him kiss you. And I'm sure you liked it!"

Tanvi was embarrassed. She more than just liked it. She didn't dare tell her friends that she had kissed him twice. They would start planning her wedding.

"Let's not speak of this again," she said before getting up from the chair. "I need to get home."

Rashmi grinned. "Ooh, to see your boyfriend again? When am I going to get to meet him?"

"Stop it! I'm going home early to prepare for my day at work. I have forgotten about the kiss and am going to ignore the guy. And so should you."

Her friend continued to grin. Tanvi knew her friend would not forget the topic easily.

"Fine, I'll let you go for now," her friend finally said. "But you better throw us a party for getting the job."

"Yes. I will. Let me get through this week first." She hoped she wouldn't be discovered and fired.

"Don't worry. You'll do great."

Smiling at her friends' confidence, she waved them goodbye. "I'll see you both on Friday night."

Hopefully, she would not only last but also discover something important by then.

CHAPTER FIFTEEN

"Mr. Varma. Thank you so much for agreeing to meet me."

Aryan looked at the distinguished-looking man in front of him. "Well, after receiving dozens of calls and having your people send my office messages, I guess I had to meet you, Mr. Shetty."

The older man's face darkened with embarrassment. "I'm sorry to trouble you, Mr. Varma. But I just wanted to convey that there will not be any issues during the construction of the mall."

Aryan sat back. "That's not what I'm hearing, Mr. Shetty. There's a lot of noise going around where investors and bureaucrats are doubting whether the park will be allowed to be converted into a luxury mall. In fact, I've heard that members of your own family are the ones to strongly oppose it."

There was a look of anger on Girish Shetty's face. "My daughter is a hothead, Mr. Varma. She is young and quite out of touch with reality. I've spoken to her, and she has agreed not to intervene. She strongly regrets her actions."

Aryan was amused. If only the bastard in front of him knew how strongly his daughter regrets her actions by joining the company in an underhanded way and working under the chairman to find defaming information that would stop the mall construction.

"Mere words don't run businesses, Mr. Shetty, especially when it comes to a billion-dollar investment over the next five years. The mall construction will set the precedent of how my company will choose to spend the rest of our money. And I value my company's reputation the most. Your daughter might be a hot head, but her actions and words are damaging."

The older man looked panicked. "Mr. Varma, I will speak to my daughter again. I would like to assure you that things are well on schedule, and there will not be any interruptions. And your company name has not been revealed in any of the news outlets or elsewhere. Prism Corporation is in the forefront. I promise there will not be any negative impact on your company's reputation."

Aryan didn't respond. He let the silence intimidate the older man.

"Mr. Varma, I know it's hard to believe me. But please give me the opportunity to show you how much I and other top politicians and bureaucrats appreciate your investment in our city. Please accept an invitation to throw a party in your honor. I will have my daughter attend it. She will apologize and do anything to convince you she won't interfere."

Aryan's mouth twisted at the not-so-subtle eager and desperate look on the older man's face. "I'll think about it, Mr. Shetty. I have upcoming travel to New York planned. Maybe when I get back, you can show your appreciation as well as provide proof that things are going to go as planned."

"Yes, yes, of course, Mr. Varma. I will be in touch with your personal assistant to keep providing you updates as usual."

Aryan got up from the chair.

Girish Shetty hurried towards him and shook his hand. "Thank you so much again, Mr. Varma. I am looking forward to hosting the party in your honor at my place."

Giving the older man a curt nod, Aryan turned to leave. The older man escorted him outside.

The rage Aryan felt each time he saw Girish Shetty was still bubbling inside him. But knowing how close he was to destroying the cunning old bastard gave him immense satisfaction. The house that Girish Shetty lived in belonged to the Vardhamans.

After the death of Ashok Vardhaman, the banks auctioned all the properties that belonged to the Vardhaman family. Before even an auction could be held for the Vardhaman house in the city, the property was purchased by Girish Shetty.

It not only proved that the crooked lawyer was more than involved.

Even after fifteen years, as he passed through the large open halls of Girish Shetty's house, Aryan's mind filled with the memories of the time his family spent in the same home. He had been too young to recall everything clearly, but his family had used the city home mostly for visiting his brothers who were enrolled in a city school and also when their father had business meetings. The rest of the time was spent in Vardhaman Estate which had been their primary home.

While Bhargav worked on getting back Vardhaman Estate, Aryan was determined to get back the city properties. He knew it was only a matter of time when all of Girish Shetty's properties would be seized.

Aryan wondered how his fiery prey would react after finding out that he was responsible for her father's bankruptcy and arrest.

Will she hate me more? Or will she stand by the truth?

***

Girish Shetty watched as the sleek Aston Martin drove away from his house.

He was fifty-five years old and among the richest and powerful men in the city. But his hunger to be the most powerful man in the entire state made him suck up to a rich man who was less than half his age. He needed Aryan Varma's money to win the upcoming elections.

He hated men like Aryan Varma. He resented their existence.

With a suit that cost more than a car, men like Aryan Varma didn't know what it was to be a middle-class man in a rich man's world. Men like Aryan Varma didn't experience a day-to-day struggle. They didn't experience how it felt to always crave a better life.

And men like Aryan Varma would never lose the women they loved to another man.

"I'm sorry, Girish, I can't marry you. I love someone else."

"How can you say that! You know I have always loved you."

The woman's beautiful face fell. "I didn't know you loved me, Girish. I always thought of us as friends. And even if you did like me, we don't suit well together. We want different things in life."

"How can we not suit well? We are both from middle-class families. I know you want to marry that man because he is very rich!"

She shook her head. "No. I love him because of the man he is. His love for nature. His generous heart and the drive to help the ones in need. His ability to make others laugh and feel good about themselves. He is confident and content. The fact that he has money is just coincidental." She looked at him in regret. "I'm sorry to disappoint you."

He lost the woman he loved to a rich man. But he hadn't given up. He got his revenge on the woman who spurned him. The same qualities the woman he loved had wanted in a man were also that man's downfall. The generous heart and the need to help others bankrupted that man.

Satisfaction passed through him. *I'm the winner now. And that bastard lost everything, including his life. And I'm enjoying his riches.*

The woman he loved would have come running to him had she not lost her life in a fire accident. He regretted losing her. Only because she didn't suffer enough for ditching him and he didn't get to gloat.

But she was right when she said he was not content. It had always been his nature to hunger for more. He wanted to be the Chief Minister of the state by hook or crook. He desperately needed Aryan Varma's money and goodwill.

He frowned as he recalled his promise to have Tanvi apologize to Aryan Varma.

His hotheaded daughter would not listen to him and most likely ruin things even more. But he had to convince and bend her to his will somehow.

Suddenly, a thought entered his mind.

Why the hell haven't I thought of this before?

Right from the time Tanvi was conceived, she was his ticket to wealth and prestige. Indira Palki, a beautiful young woman from a rich, privileged background, married him only because she was two months pregnant.

Tanvi will once again help him trap another person from a rich, privileged background. This time it would be a billionaire from New York who would help him win elections.

CHAPTER SIXTEEN

"Miss Shetty. I'm quite impressed by the work you've accomplished during your first week."

"Thank you, Mr. Tejpal."

A week had passed since Tanvi began the job at Prism. She was attending yet another meeting with her boss on the phone. She had been talking to the older man regularly, where he went over the tasks with her and cleared her doubts if she had any.

So far, the work given to her was simple. It almost bordered on boring too.

She had to schedule meetings and reschedule a few and call some people in person and ensure they were prepared for the meetings. On a few rare occasions, she even had to work on the meeting slides that were to be presented by the chairman.

None of those meeting presentations had information on the upcoming project of the mall. Most of it was surprisingly about new software or regarding companies that were soon to be acquired.

"When can I... uh... meet the chairman?" Tanvi asked. "I wanted to meet him in person to introduce myself to him."

There was a pause. "Our chairman is very private, Miss Shetty. He prefers to deal with only a select trusted few in person. I'm sure you were made aware of it when you signed the Non- Disclosure Agreement about not meeting him or revealing information in case you happen to meet him in the future."

Tanvi frowned with annoyance. She did recall signing the NDA. Why was the chairman so damn secretive?

She had met rich, powerful men in her life. But none of them guarded their privacy to such an extent. Whoever the man was, she knew he must have a lot to hide.

But she was determined to draw out everything and expose the man before he ruthlessly destroyed the precious ecosystem and the health of the people living in the city for his personal gains.

"All right, Miss Shetty. I'll speak to you on Monday around the same time. Have a great weekend."

"Good night, Mr. Tejpal," Tanvi greeted the man, knowing that it was still Thursday night in New York.

After the call ended, she once again set out to finish her tasks quickly, so she could check the rest of the folders on the shared drives, where she would hopefully stumble across some incriminating information she could use against the chairman.

It was close to seven o'clock when her phone began ringing. She glanced at it and saw that it was Rashmi. She answered it, hoping to make it a quick call and get back to her snooping.

"Hello?"

There was loud thumping music in the background.

"Are you ready?" Rashmi's voice asked.

"Ready for what?" Tanvi asked absently, clicking on her desktop screen.

"Oh my God! Don't tell me you forgot!" Rashmi's voice yelled over the music.

Tanvi frowned and then she recalled. *Oh shit.*

"Don't you dare ditch us!" Rashmi threatened. "You promised a party on Friday night for your new job. We are heading to your place. You better get ready soon. We will be there in a few minutes!"

Tanvi knew her friend would lose it if she said she was still at work.

"Okay. Give me thirty minutes."

There was some grumbling, and then the line cut off.

Tanvi suppressed a smile and put her phone away. She stared at the screen for a few seconds before letting out a sigh and shutting down the system. She supposed she needed a break from her snooping. Hopefully, blowing off steam with her friends over the weekend will help her think of a better way.

***

She only had ten minutes remaining to get ready. Closing the lift door, she hurried down the hallway toward her apartment. She heard the giggles followed by a deep drawl.

She couldn't see anyone in the hallway. When she neared her apartment, the sound of giggles grew louder. It was coming from the arrogant neighbor's home.

Is he on a date?

With a dark frown, she turned towards his apartment. She could see the small living room. But what surprised her was to see Rashmi and Kavita seated on the couch. They were blushing and giggling like school girls.

"Tanvi!" Rashmi greeted when she saw her. "We got here ten minutes ago. Since you weren't home yet, Arjun let us wait at his home."

Tanvi's eyes automatically shifted and fell on her arrogant neighbor watching her with his usual amused smirk.

"Since we both can't seem to stay away from each other, I propose a deal to give it a try and date each other."

Her cheeks heated, recalling their last kiss and his outrageous proposal. She had deliberately stayed away from him for the last five days. She had left for work early and returned home late. But although she had avoided the man, his arrogant presence along with the memories of their burning passion remained inside her head to haunt her all week long.

"Thanks," she murmured. Then dragging her eyes away from him, she looked at her friends. "We'll leave in a few minutes."

Rashmi looked excited. "Arjun suggested a new restaurant and bar lounge where one of his friends works as a manager. We can go there. I was just asking Arjun if he can join us too."

"No!" she said immediately. "I'm sure he's busy and has other plans already."

"Actually... I am somewhat free tonight," he drawled.

Her eyes flew to him, and the jerk looked amused. She glared at him, only to see his amusement increase.

"Unless my presence bothers you in some way, I can join you guys later tonight."

Feeling cornered and not wanting to show that his presence affected her in any way, she raised her chin. "No. You don't bother me at all."

His eyes flashed in amusement.

Rashmi clapped excitedly. "That's so awesome!"

Feeling cornered and unable to find an excuse, Tanvi scowled at her friends. "Let's go."

As soon as she stepped out and unlocked her apartment door, her friends burst out with questions and comments.

"Oh my God, he looks so hot!" Rashmi said excitedly. "I thought it was my imagination when I saw him briefly a few weeks ago."

"He's so charming too," Kavita added.

Tanvi was annoyed. "He's not that special," she said, brushing it off, even though she found him hot too.

Rashmi was amused. "Not that hot? Is that why you kissed him a few days ago? I don't blame you. Those dimples and sexy smirk would have any girl leaping on him."

Tanvi's annoyance grew along with embarrassment. She did find the jerk irresistible and had more or less leaped on him and kissed him twice. Her cheeks grew warm. And not just his good looks, the arrogant jerk's cooking skills were unbelievable. That made him all the more damn sexy.

"He's an arrogant jerk," she said forcefully. It was more to convince herself than her friends.

Her friends began giving her knowing looks. Feeling annoyed, she walked away to get ready for the night. She was determined to ignore her arrogant neighbor the entire night.

Suddenly, she had an idea how to compensate for the jerk's presence.

***

"Thank you so much for inviting me to join you, Tanvi."

Tanvi smiled at the sweet man. "There's no need to thank me, Sameer. You helped me get the job. This is my treat."

Sameer smiled shyly. "You are most welcome."

"These are my friends Rashmi and Kavitha." She introduced her friends to him.

Sameer offered to drive since he didn't drink alcohol. They sent away Rashmi's car with the driver and went to the club in Sameer's small car.

"When is Arjun joining us?" Rashmi asked.

"He left already on his bike," Sameer replied. "He said he'll join us later at the restaurant."

Tanvi frowned. She was hoping he would somehow not make it. Pushing away thoughts of him, she once again reminded herself to ignore him that night.

Thirty minutes later, they reached the place which was in the heart of the downtown area and on the top of a tall building.

They took the elevator to the top floor, and when the elevator doors opened, Rashmi let out a gasp.

The entire place had glass walls, and the view outside was breathtaking.

"Wow! This looks awesome!" Rashmi said excitedly.

It was a new place she and her friends had never visited before. It did look awesome. But from the glass walls, it was also obvious that the place was crowded.

"I didn't make a reservation. I think—" Before Tanvi could suggest they might have to go to a different place for dinner, the hostess greeted them near the reception area.

"Welcome to Opium," she said with a smile. "Name, please."

"Tanvi Shetty."

The hostess began to look at the computer screen.

"I don't have a reservation. What would be the wait time for us to get a table?"

The hostess looked surprised. "Oh. But I do see your name, madam. Tanvi Shetty. A party of five."

Tanvi was surprised.

"Arjun must have made the reservations through his manager friend!" Rashmi said excitedly.

Tanvi frowned, feeling unsure how she should feel towards the gesture. She didn't want to be grateful to her arrogant neighbor in any way.

"Please follow me, Miss Shetty."

The hostess led them to a corner booth that overlooked the stunning night view of the city.

"Wow," said Rashmi with a grin. "Looks like your job celebration might cost your first paycheck."

Tanvi hadn't thought about it until then. Although her bank balance did have a considerable amount thanks to her monthly payments from the trust fund, she preferred not to spend money unnecessarily.

"Please don't worry, madam," the hostess said with a smile. "Your table has a note saying you would get the manager's discount. Please enjoy."

Tanvi was once again surprised.

"See! I told you Arjun was awesome!" Rashmi grinned.

Tanvi shook her head.

Soon, they ordered drinks and a few appetizers. Since Sameer was part of the celebration, they stuck to general topics. But not for long.

"So, Sameer," Rashmi said with a smile. "What do you think of Tanvi? Do you like her?"

Tanvi had to kick Rashmi under the table. Poor Sameer's face turned beet red.

"I... do like her," he said shyly.

"Sameer and I are good friends," Tanvi added. "Stop embarrassing him."

Rashmi grinned. "Well, I'm glad you two are good friends. So do you have a girlfriend?"

Sameer continued to blush. "Uh... no."

"That's all the more great. I don't have a boyfriend either."

Tanvi shook her head with an exasperated laugh as her friend shamelessly flirted with the poor shy guy.

The food and drinks were delicious. The conversation was amusing. But something was missing. She felt a strange restlessness, and her eyes kept going towards the restaurant's entrance.

Suddenly, her heart jerked and began to race when she saw a man entering the restaurant. He was wearing a black jacket and was holding his bike helmet.

Quickly, she looked away and pretended to focus on the conversation going on around the table.

A minute later, her friend burst out with excitement.

"Arjun! We almost thought you weren't going to make it!"

A whiff of familiar cologne floated in the air filling Tanvi's senses as he stood next to the booth.

"I always keep my word," he drawled.

"I'm so glad! Come sit next to me," Rashmi suggested and scooted to give him space to sit.

Soon Tanvi's eyes met with her arrogant neighbor's as he sat next to her friend right opposite her.

"What did I miss?" he asked with amusement.

"Oh. You missed a lot," Rashmi continued. "We were asking Sameer if he liked Tanvi. But apparently, they are just good friends. So both Sameer and Tanvi are single and ready to mingle with others."

Tanvi's cheeks heated, and she wanted to kill her friend.

"I see." A dimple flashed as his eyes caught hers during a smirk.

Her stomach fluttered. Taking a deep breath, she pushed away the feeling. "You should place your order now. We are almost done."

"What!" Rashmi shrieked. "We are just getting started. Don't you dare say we have to leave before midnight or that you have to wake up early tomorrow. I know there is no protest planned or any other urgent work that you need to get to."

Tanvi couldn't find an excuse to wind up the night early either.

Arjun looked all the more amused. "Actually, I'm done with my dinner. I'll just get a drink later."

"Woohoo! Then let's get to dancing and partying."

Tanvi didn't resist when she was dragged by her friends to the dance floor at the back of the restaurant.

It was dark enough to forget everything and give in to the thumping music. She had always enjoyed dancing with her friends. But with the man she was attracted to standing near her, heat sizzled through her body. She could sense his presence even through the heavy crowd.

Without turning towards him, she began to dance.

She didn't know how long she danced, laughing and swaying and twirling and dipping along with the music next to her friends. But even as she enjoyed herself, she constantly felt his presence right behind her, the awareness adding to the thrilling enjoyment.

There were only two brief breaks during which they got some drinks. Soon, it was midnight, and the music turned faster until it eventually came to a stop.

"Woohoo!" Everyone cheered and thanked the DJ before heading back to their booths and tables.

"What next?" Rashmi asked with a slur.

Tanvi laughed. "Next is we all go home."

Rashmi grumbled. "Spoiled sport," she said, followed by a yawn.

Tanvi and Kavita held Rashmi's hands and dragged her along. "Come on. Let's go."

They took the elevator and went to the underground parking. Rashmi slept in the back seat while Kavita sat in the front next to Sameer. There was no place for Tanvi to sit in the small car.

She tried to push Rashmi's legs back to sit in the corner, but it was hard.

"Let Sameer drop them," Arjun's deep voice drawled. "I'm heading back home. You can come with me."

Tanvi was about to refuse when he smirked. "Unless you are scared of bikes... or me."

She knew the arrogant ass was deliberately challenging her. "I'm not."

His teeth flashed. "Good. Let's go then."

She frowned when he placed the helmet on her head. She was tired and wanted to get home.

"We'll be fine, Tanvi," Kavita said with a smile. "I'll call you when Rashmi and I get to my place. You go home with Arjun."

Tanvi blushed at her friend's not-so-subtle matchup. Knowing there was nothing she could do, she waved goodnight to her friends and Sameer as the car took off.

"You can trust Sameer, princess," Arjun said with amusement. "He's a nice guy. He will drop your friends at their homes safely."

"I trust Sameer just fine," she snapped. "It's you I don't trust."

He grinned at her taunt. "Really? What do you think I'd do to you? I thought you said you know how to protect yourself from me."

She ignored his taunt and followed him. He stopped near a sleek and well-maintained red bike. She recalled sometimes seeing it parked outside the apartment complex.

He sat on it with a fluid motion. In his biker jacket and a devilish smirk on his face, the man looked like sin personified.

"Hop on, princess," he commanded with amusement. "You can stare at me once we get home."

Her cheeks heated at being caught staring at him.

"I wasn't staring at you," she lied. "I was wondering if you knew how to ride the bike and if I was going reach home in one piece."

He grinned. "Don't worry, princess. I'll take you home safely."

If the arrogant jerk didn't tease her about the effect he had on her, she would have chosen to go back home in a taxi. But instead, she let out an annoyed huff and sat behind him.

An electric sizzle ran through her at the slightest contact. She held him gingerly at first. But when he gave a powerful kick to the bike and started it, her grip tightened on his wide shoulders.

The bike raced out of the semi-darkened underground parking and onto the road. Her heart raced as adrenaline rushed through her. The cool wind fell on her face, and she felt as though she were flying. The roads were nearly empty, and the bike zipped through smoothly.

It must have barely taken them twenty minutes before they reached the apartment complex. When the bike stopped, she felt reluctant to get off. Pulling her hands away from his shoulders, she got down from the bike.

"Thanks," she murmured.

She hurried towards the lifts, hoping she could go up in the lift on her own. But thanks to Arjun's long legs, even with normal strides, he was able to catch up with her.

She stepped to the side and stood against one of the lift walls. But his presence and awareness filled her, enhanced by the charging silence. The few seconds it took to go up to the top floor felt like ages.

When the lift finally stopped and the doors opened, she hurried out.

Once again, he caught up with her. She went to her door and unlocked it immediately. But before she got inside, she paused.

She knew she had to thank him for reserving the table and getting her a huge discount on the bill. "Thank you for reserving the table tonight. And also for getting me the discount. My friends and I enjoyed the place."

He didn't respond.

Frowning, she thought he must have slipped into his apartment quietly, so she turned.

Her breath got stuck in her throat when she saw him watching her quietly. His usual cocky smirk was missing.

"I... I..." She forgot what she was saying.

One moment, they stared at each other, and the next moment their mouths crashed together. She dug her fingers into his leather jacket and dragged him closer. The grip on the back of her hair tightened as he bent her head back and ravaged her mouth.

Heat once again spread through her like liquid fire.

Her back hit the corridor wall with a small thud, but she didn't feel a thing. All she felt was the heat and electricity coursing through her veins as their mouths fused.

Their mouths parted for a moment, and he rasped out against her lips.

"You looked so damn beautiful tonight, princess. I have been waiting to kiss you."

A thrill ran through her at his compliment. Her legs turned weak, and she clung to him as their mouths met again.

"Agree to the deal," he said, licking her bottom lip and causing her to shiver in pleasure. "Come out with me. Let's spend time together."

Despite the pleasure coursing through her body, his words pulled her back to reality.

Gasping out, she pushed him away from her. He didn't move, but his mouth left hers. They stared at each other, drawing in heavy breaths. Hot and heavy tension continued to surround them, making her want to drag him to her once again.

"This is a mistake," she said with panic. "I kissed you again because I'm drunk."

"You are drunk, princess," he said with a smile twisting his mouth. "But not with alcohol." He leaned in slightly bringing his face closer to hers. "You are drunk on me just the way I feel drunk on you."

Annoyance flared because the arrogant jerk was right.

She only had one drink, and that was nearly five hours ago. She had kissed him because she couldn't stop herself. Even now, watching his hooded eyes and sexy smirk, she wanted to drag him close and bite his lips in passion. She wanted him to kiss her again.

She was pissed at how her body didn't care that she hated him.

He could read her easily and was watching her with hooded eyes and an amused smirk.

"Go to hell!" she snapped.

And then, stepping into her apartment, she slammed the door shut and once again leaned against it.

Oh God. Why can't I stop kissing that jerk!

Even as she thought those words, she knew it was impossible to stop kissing him or avoiding him. But there was no way she would agree to the deal of dating him.

CHAPTER SEVENTEEN

The loud sound of her phone ringing woke up Tanvi.

She groaned when she saw the call was from her father. Knowing he would keep calling or even send someone to her apartment if she didn't respond, she answered the call.

"I'm organizing a social event next weekend. I want you to attend it."

Tanvi sighed. "I'm busy next weekend, Papa. I have preplanned voluntary work."

"I don't care. Cancel it! This event is critical to me. I need your presence."

Tanvi frowned. "Why do you need my presence? You are the one who asks me to stay away from politics and your businesses."

Her mind flew to the conversation she had with him a few days after her arrest.

"If you are trying to set me up with some guy for marriage, I'm still not interested."

"Why the hell not?" her father demanded. "The man I want to set you up is a billionaire investor from America. He is eligible in every way."

She knew her father wouldn't stop setting her up with so-called eligible men. So she decided to lie.

"I'm not interested in the man you want me to meet, Papa, because... I'm seeing someone."

There was an ominous silence. "Who!" her father roared.

Arjun's face flashed into her mind. Pushing away the arrogant man's face, she focused on her argument with her father.

"We just started dating, but I like him."

The lie pissed her father off even more.

"You are twenty-two years old. And the trust money makes you the target of all gold-digging men. Stop acting childish and meet the man I want you to marry!"

"Sorry, Papa. I can't. My... boyfriend wouldn't like it."

There was an outraged breath. "Who the hell is he! What does he do?"

"I can't tell you anything right now, Papa. Please stop looking for matches for me."

Before her father could continue to rant, she ended the call.

She hadn't deliberately mentioned anything else about her fictional boyfriend. She knew her father would dig up every fact soon and try to find out who she was seeing.

Frowning, she hoped that poor Sameer didn't get into trouble because she often spoke to him near the mailboxes and met him at the office building.

But what if her father thought her boyfriend was Arjun?

She shook her head with a scoff. If anyone were to see them together, they would know right away that she hated Arjun.

But not if they caught you kissing him.

Ugh.

She tried to go back to sleep. But as soon as she closed her eyes, a handsome face with an arrogant smirk began to haunt her along with their last night's kiss.

Letting out a frustrated sound, she opened her eyes and sat up. She knew she would have to go about her day and keep herself busy so she could forget about the arrogant devil haunting her.

She picked up her laptop next to the bed and began to work on her articles she often published in various magazine portals. Her current article was about City Central Park.

The reach and reaction to her articles on the topic were tremendous. But unfortunately, she and the rest of the people wanting to save park were helpless. Prism Corporation was still going ahead with the plan for the mall.

Her eyes fell on the separate folder she created to add information on the Prism Corporation and the chairman. Unfortunately, she was yet to fill up that folder with any relevant information. There was only one piece of information that said the parent company was from New York.

Suddenly a thought struck her.

Oh God.

Why didn't I think of it before!

Maybe it was a coincidence. But she did not want to take any chances. She immediately called her father. She knew he would be in a pissed-off mood, but she had to try.

"Hello?" her father's angry voice spoke.

"Hello, Papa. I wanted to ask you something about this man you wanted to set me up with."

"What?" he snapped.

"You said he is a billionaire from America. Is he the chairman of Prism Corporation?"

There was silence. "How do you know who I was talking about?"

Her heart jerked with shock and excitement.

"It doesn't matter how I know, but I'm willing to meet him like you wanted."

There was another suspicious pause. "Why do you want to meet him when you claim to have a boyfriend? If it is to harass him to stop building the mall, then—"

"No. No. I won't harass him. I promise."

There was another ominous pause. "If you mess it up for me, I'll make sure you regret it. And so will your boyfriend."

The call was cut. She shivered at the not-so-subtle threat by her father of hurting her fictional boyfriend. Pushing away the threats and fear, she began planning for the event where she would finally be meeting the Prism chairman.

CHAPTER EIGHTEEN

"There is something very odd about Girish Shetty."

At Aryan's statement, both his brothers waited for him to explain. They were at Bhargav's penthouse. Aryan paced the living room which held a lot of paintings and knick knacks from the Vardhaman Mansion.

"I've been to Shetty's place two times now," he continued to say. "I noticed there are still a lot of paintings and collections that Ma had designed."

Bhargav frowned. "Maybe the man is too lazy to redesign. And Ma always had excellent taste."

Aryan shook his head. "Ma does have excellent taste. But there are way too many things that are the same as Ma designed. There is Ma's portrait too. Even though Ma had been nice to Shetty's late wife, I doubt Shetty's wife would want a portrait of Ma in her living room. Just Ma's and none of our portraits. It's just fucking odd."

"What are you saying?" Yash asked.

"How did Girish Shetty have access to the Vardhamans? As far as I know, our father didn't know Shetty before. We never met him except for the last year when he suddenly popped up and visited with his family. Rajesh Mohan and Anand Kashyap even made Shetty their partner during that time. According to the investigation, they didn't know Shetty before either."

"What's your theory?" Bhargav asked.

Aryan frowned. He didn't know what to think either. Girish Shetty was a corrupt, greedy bastard for sure. But something about the man made Aryan feel there was more than greed involved. It seemed personal.

"I have a feeling Ma knew Girish Shetty from before."

"What the fuck, Aryan!" Yash looked pissed at Aryan's speculation.

Aryan shook his head. "Relax, bro. I'm not saying Ma knew that dirtbag in a romantic sense. What I'm saying is she might have been acquainted with him."

Bhargav was silent. "Then we should ask Ma about him."

Aryan shook his head. "No. If we ask her about Girish Shetty, then she will know exactly what we are up to. Ma is too smart not to be able to figure it out."

There was silence.

Aryan knew he was right. Asking their mother about Girish Shetty would make it obvious that her three sons were on a quest to avenge their father's murder. She would immediately insist they abort the revenge and let the past go.

Aryan wasn't willing to stop until his father's murderers were punished and made to suffer. He knew his brothers felt the same.

"So if we are not going to ask Ma, how do you think you can pursue this?" Bhargav asked. "How will we know whether Girish Shetty had a personal grudge against Ma?"

Aryan frowned. "I'll have to chat up the old bastard for that. Maybe I'll accept the invite for him to host a party in my honor."

"Won't Shetty's daughter be at the party?"

Aryan's mouth twisted. "I doubt it."

He knew Girish Shetty would not want his fiery daughter anywhere near the man she openly called ruthless and corrupt. Although the older man said his daughter would apologize, Aryan knew it was an impossible task.

His fiery pawn would rather stab herself than apologize to the man she hated.

"What's going on between Shetty's daughter and you?"

Aryan yanked his mind away from his pawn and focused on Bhargav's question. "Nothing."

His brother raised an eyebrow. "Are you sure? For someone who demanded we shouldn't get directly involved with our pawns, you sure do spend a lot of time with yours."

"Bhargav is right," Yash added. "During our last board meeting, your eyes were glued to the phone with camera feeds of Tanvi Shetty."

Aryan frowned. "I'm only checking to see if she was snooping again."

Tanvi had been playing quite the detective looking through protected shared folders to see if she could get information on him or the mall project. Unfortunately for her, she would never get the information she needed.

Bhargav shook his head in amusement. "You are a software maverick who built a billion-dollar empire in your teens. Are you telling me you need to monitor someone on cameras to see what she's snooping on her computer?"

Aryan knew his brother was right. He could track Tanvi Shetty's digital footprint without having to see her. He could even get signals on his phone when she left her apartment or returned home.

But he wanted to watch her live. He wanted to see every little frown and bite of her lip or her few rare smiles. He enjoyed watching her.

"What about the guy hired to woo her?" Yash asked.

Aryan was still annoyed by how Tanvi had invited Sameer to the restaurant for celebrating her job at Prism. "He's almost getting there."

Yash shook his head. "I doubt if he ever would. You won't allow him or another guy to get anywhere near her."

Aryan's frown grew. "I was the one to hire him. He is being *paid* to do his job of wooing her and making her fall in love with him."

Bhargav and Yash exchanged amused glances.

"Very soon, little brother," Yash said with a small twist of his mouth. "You'll be proof as well to how best-laid plans go awry when obsession takes over."

No. It won't happen to me. I won't let that happen.

He will not be obsessed with his father's murderer's daughter. She would only remain his pawn.

CHAPTER NINETEEN

It was Tanvi's second week working at Prism Corporation.

Letting out yet another frustrated curse, she shut the computer.

Where the hell did the chairman keep the documents of the upcoming new projects? And why the hell is his name not mentioned anywhere.

Her snooping hadn't yielded any results. She knew she needed to find another strategy to get the required information. Time was ticking, and she was nowhere close to stopping the City Central Park demolition that would begin in a few weeks.

She had to meet the chairman. Her father was yet to call her with specific information regarding the event he was planning where the Prism chairman would be in attendance.

What was taking him so long?

Maybe the damn chairman is travelling.

She did schedule a lot of meetings that were held around the midnight hour. Although the wait was frustrating because she was losing a lot of time, she knew her attempt to meet the chairman through her father might be the one to succeed.

With that thought, she felt slightly better as she exited the office.

It was dark and windy with a drizzle of rain. Since it was close to eight o'clock, the building lobby and outside the building was empty. Waving goodnight to the building security, she stepped out.

She frowned when she saw there were no taxis waiting outside. She began walking to see if she could get one on the next street where there was a taxi stand. That's when she saw them.

There were two men standing right outside the building. They were watching her. When she began walking, they started to follow her. Something about those men sent chills down her spine. They looked somewhat familiar.

Oh God. Are they one of them?

With her heart thumping in fear, she broke into a run. The next street was only five minutes away and luckily there were many taxis waiting at the stand. She ran to one.

"Where to, miss?" a taxi driver asked.

She gave him the address and sat inside the vehicle hurriedly.

She turned to see if the men had followed her to the taxi stand. Luckily, they didn't. They stood in the shadows. She could see them and could also sense their gazes.

Controlling a shudder, she asked the taxi driver to hurry home.

As soon as she reached her apartment complex, she let out a sigh of relief that she was home. It began to rain. Feeling thankful that she didn't get wet, she hurried up the stairs instead of taking the elevator.

It was silly, but she was trying to avoid running into Arjun. She didn't want to see him as the arrogant man was too distracting.

Instead of putting all her effort into unearthing the identity of the Prism chairman, her mind was often haunted by her arrogant neighbor and his passionate kisses. She also kept thinking about the deal he offered. When she felt almost tempted to accept it, she knew she had to stay away from the distracting man.

It was ridiculous that she had come close to thinking she could date someone right then, let alone her arrogant neighbor. Letting out a sigh, she hurried to her flat. While she pulled out her key, she threw in a glance sideways.

The opposite door was closed, and she couldn't hear anything. She hadn't come across him all week.

Is he on a date?

As soon as the thought crossed her mind, she became irritated with herself. It was none of her business if Arjun was on a date or meeting some other woman. She had gone out of her way to avoid him and also made it known to him that she wasn't interested in dating him.

But the thought of him on a date and kissing another woman left a sour feeling inside her stomach.

The bastard must have kissed hundreds of women. Why else would he be such a good kisser?

She scowled at the thought. Shaking her head to push away the unwanted jealousy, she stepped inside her apartment.

She reheated the previous day's dinner leftovers. As she sat down to eat, the rain picked up in intensity. She watched with an uneasy feeling as lightning lit up the sky.

She hated the storms. Taking a deep, shuddering breath, she focused on other things to distract herself. She tried to finish her dinner. But each lightning strike followed by rumbling of thunder made her jump and caused her stomach to be queasy.

She left her dinner uneaten. Clearing up the dishes, she hurried to her bedroom. She changed into her nightclothes. Keeping the lights on in the bedroom as well in the living room, she slid into her bed. She closed her eyes and took a deep, shuddering breath. Slowly, she slid into an uneasy sleep.

***

Tanvi woke up to loud shouts.

Rubbing her groggy eyes, she sat up in her bedroom. It was dark and raining heavily outside. Her mother said there was a storm expected that night.

Although Tanvi was scared of the loud noises of the storms, her mother comforted her saying storms were natural, and there was nothing to be scared about.

"Shh, you are safe, my love," her mother soothed her often.

Why isn't Mamma sleeping next to me?

Tanvi's mother always slept next to her during nights when there was a storm. But during the past week, her mother slept next to her instead of with her father. Tanvi loved holding her mother's big stomach where there was a baby inside. Tanvi's little brother or sister was expected to come out in one month.

Tanvi was excited because she would then have someone to play with.

But she didn't know why her mother was suddenly sad and angry. She saw her mother crying a few days ago and shouting at her father. Her father tried to console her mother, but her mother still seemed upset.

Tanvi frowned when she once again heard shouts coming from outside the bedroom.

Suddenly, there was a loud scream.

Tanvi's heart thudded. Apart from the loud thunder outside, it was utterly calm outside her bedroom.

"Mamma?" she called out.

Pushing her blankets away, she got down from her bed. She opened the bedroom door, and it was dark in the hallway. The only light came from the lightning flashing outside the windows.

"Mamma?" she called again.

There was no response. Holding the railing of the staircase, she carefully went down the steps. She jumped as the thunder continued to rumble loudly in the sky.

When she reached the last step, her foot touched something. She didn't know what it was.

It was only when lightning flashed and the living room lit up, she saw what she had stumbled on. It was her mother lying in a pool of blood.

Tanvi woke up with a gasp.

Her vision was blurred, and there were tears in her eyes due to her recurring nightmare.

As her vision cleared, she noticed it was dark inside her room as well as outside. There must have been a power outage due to the storm. Thunder continued to roll while lightning flashed in the sky.

Her heart thudded when she heard something outside her bedroom. It was as though someone was trying to break into her apartment. She knew she might be imagining things. But she heard the sounds of someone standing outside and trying to open the door.

Did those men follow me home?

Maybe she was just imagining things. But she knew she couldn't stay inside her apartment like a sitting duck. With her heart thudding, she reached for the cricket bat she kept next to her bed. Holding it in a firm grip, she got out of her bed.

She slowly walked out of her bedroom and then towards the small living room. She couldn't see much. She jumped as thunder rumbled loudly along with lightning flashes.

The sounds of someone trying to open the door continued.

With her heart thudding, she went to her door. And then with a quick move, she unlocked it and pulled it open. She held the bat up in an attack position, but there was no one outside her door. With her heart thudding, she took a step outside to see if the intruder was running away.

Her heart almost stopped when she saw a shadow in front of her apartment. She automatically swung the bat towards it. But before the bat landed on someone, it was held in a tight grip. She tried to yank it to attack the man.

"Fuck. What the hell are you doing, princess?"

With her heart racing, she stilled. Lightning once again flashed, and she saw that it was Arjun standing in front of his apartment door. He was holding the bat with a frown. He was most likely trying to unlock his apartment door in the dark when she swung the bat towards him.

"T-there's a s-storm," she tried to explain. "The p-power went out, and I-I heard someone. Two men followed me outside the office. I-I thought they came here and were trying to break into my apartment and..." She couldn't continue.

There was a momentary silence. "Come with me."

She felt his warm hand wrapping around her wrist and tugging her towards him. She didn't resist. He held her close to him while he tried unlocking the door. She leaned closer to him, trying to absorb the warmth of his body while chills began in hers.

He managed to unlock the door. Then holding her wrist, he led her inside and stopped near the couch. He sat down and pulled her next to him before wrapping his arms around her. Her head was against his broad chest.

She opened her mouth to protest, but she realized she was trembling hard and her teeth were chattering. It must have been the shock of thinking she was being attacked.

"Shh, you are safe, princess," he said in a soothing tone.

Her eyes welled up because she was reminded of her mother, who used to comfort her during storms using similar words.

"I-I hate the storms," she said.

The image of her mother lying at the bottom of the stairs in a pool of blood flashed in her mind. Her body trembled even harder.

The arms around her tightened. "I don't like the storms either," he said.

She didn't believe him. The normally cocky, arrogant man she knew for the last few weeks hardly looked like the kind to be bothered about silly storms, let alone hate them.

"There was a huge storm on the night of my father's funeral," he said.

She was shocked by the information. It sounded as terrible as her experience with storms.

She took a deep breath. "My mother fell down the stairs on a stormy night. I-I was the one to find her. There was so much blood. She was nine months pregnant at the time."

She didn't know why she was telling him that. Maybe because he shared about losing a parent too. And also because being enclosed in his comforting arms, she felt a strange sense of security that she could share the worst of her nightmares with him.

"How old were you then?" he asked.

"Eight. But I still remember that night clearly and often have nightmares."

There was a momentary silence.

"Is that why you keep the lights on in your apartment during rainy nights?" he asked.

"Yes."

She waited for him to make a sarcastic, arrogant remark about her fear of storms. But he didn't. He just held her in his arms.

The heat from his body seeped into hers, making her feel warm. Her trembling stopped. But as she continued to be held in his arms, she slowly became aware of him.

Thunder rumbled outside, and lightning continued to flash. But she wasn't scared anymore. Her heart slowly picked up speed and began to beat faster. But it wasn't because of the storm. It was because of the man who held her.

She wanted comfort, and she also wanted to feel alive. And the only man who could make her feel alive was him. He made her angry, he made her weak, and he made her feel uncontrollable desire. He made her feel everything.

She dug her nose into his hard chest covered by a thin t-shirt and took a deep inhale. She let his addicting cologne fill her senses. She missed him when she had deliberately avoided him the past week after their kiss.

His arms tightened, and she felt his heartbeat picking up speed under her ears.

Slowly, she raised her face towards him. She didn't know whether he could see her or not in the dark, but she let her desire show on her face.

"Kiss me," she demanded softly.

She felt his body immediately tense.

She knew she would regret her actions later. But right then, she didn't care. She wanted to forget the past tragic memories and feel alive. Placing her palms on his hard chest, she let the hard ridges of his muscles tingle her fingertips as she moved her fingers slowly.

He let out a rough exhale. "What are you doing, princess?"

She bit her lip at his rough tone. But before she lost her nerve, she forged on. "I want you to kiss me... and... and... more."

She gasped when he suddenly slid his hand into her hair and held her face. "More?" he asked in a deep, rough voice.

Her heart raced as desire coursed through her blood. "Yes... more," she confirmed.

There was silence. Apart from the sound of the storm raging outside, the man holding her was completely silent and still.

She held her breath too, not knowing if he would listen to her or push her away.

Just when she thought he would push her away, his mouth crashed against hers.

Heat burst inside her stomach and spread through her body. Moaning out loud, she clutched his hair and kissed him back.

But he pulled away and gritted his teeth. "Fuck. We should stop this now," he said.

"No!" she said, panting out loud, pulling him close again. "Don't stop. I want you. I want more."

There was a pause. "I'll give you more, princess. But I want you agree to our deal."

She was willing to agree to anything as long as she felt the heat of his kiss and more. "Yes, I agree," she said.

He resisted as she tried to pull his head down. "Agree to date me and spend time together."

"Yes. Yes. I agree to date you and whatever you want."

There was a rough exhale, and then his mouth met hers again. She moaned at the feeling of pleasure. She placed her hands under his t-shirt and soaked in the heat of his hard muscles. But she wanted more. She wanted to feel the heat of his skin against hers.

She pulled away from the kiss. Then moving back a few inches, she held the bottom of her t-shirt and pulled it up before throwing it away.

The darkness made her braver, but the lightning that continued to flash did bare her to him.

She heard the sound of his harsh inhale of breath. "Fuck, you are so damn perfect," he growled.

She felt his fingers tighten on her waist before the heat of his mouth enclosed on her breast.

She let out a shocked cry when his tongue swirled around the tip of her breast. "You taste perfect too," he murmured deeply.

Her fingers dug into his hair and clutched him close as he sucked her aroused breast deep into his mouth. Heat pooled in her trembling stomach as he repeated the same with her other breast.

By the time his mouth left her heated sensitive skin on her chest, her entire body was trembling.

"You taste perfect, princess. I want to taste and see if the rest of you is perfect too."

His wicked words made her shiver in anticipation. Wetness pooled between her legs, and she realized he could feel it since she was more or less straddling him.

But he didn't give her the chance to be embarrassed. His hand gripped the back of her neck and dragged her close before kissing her and drugging her mind with more passion.

Her head spun with passion and soon she was falling. She realized a moment later that the feeling of falling was because she was lying on the sofa with him on top of her.

"More," she whispered greedily.

She couldn't get enough of him and how he made her feel.

"Patience, princess," his wicked voice said into the darkness.

She could barely see him. Only when lightning struck, could she see the outline of his wide shoulders and a hint of his face. But she knew he could see her clearly whenever lightning struck the sky.

The cloak of darkness intensified her feelings.

He caught her face in both hands and kissed her. His tongue conquered her mouth deeply before pulling away, making her feel drugged with passion.

"The first time I saw you in the cab..." he spoke against her lips. "...I wanted to kiss you to see if your kiss was as fiery as you." His lips began to move along her cheeks and jaw. They left a trail of fire. "The second time I saw you standing near the door of my apartment glaring at me, I wanted to carry you away to see if I could make you shout in passion instead of anger."

His wicked words made her shiver. "Pervert," she whispered.

She gasped and clutched his hair when he bit into her neck. Shivers racked her body in both intense pleasure and a hint of pain.

There was a wicked chuckle. "When it comes to you, princess. I guess I am a very big pervert."

Her stomach quivered in anticipation.

His lips moved from her neck to between her breasts and then lower. The hot, wet tongue on her quivering stomach made her restless. Need built up inside her, and she wanted something only he could give her. She dug her nails into his shoulders.

The bastard chuckled.

"I know what you want, princess. Only I can give it to you."

Even though she had the same thoughts a moment ago, she was annoyed by his arrogance. She opened her mouth to snap at him with a sharp remark, but only a gasp escaped.

He had moved even lower. His hot breath fell on the most intimate part of her through her thin cotton panties.

"Arju—" Her voice broke before she could call his name, and a shocked sound escaped her throat instead.

Once again, he kissed her. His tongue moving up and down at first before going deep into her. But this time it wasn't her mouth he was conquering.

"Oh God!"

Her entire body felt as though it caught on fire. Tight pressure built inside her. With each flick of his wicked tongue, the pressure became more intense.

"I can't," she gasped, wanting him to stop.

But her fingers dug into his hair and kept him close in case he would listen to her and stop.

She felt conflicted. Insane and wild.

And moments later, pleasure exploded.

She screamed and clutched at his wide shoulders, which were the only things anchoring her as she blew apart. She shuddered hard for a long time, and it took even longer to catch her breath.

When she could finally return to her senses, she saw his outline standing next to her as he scooped her up into his arms and carried her somewhere. Her back landed on something soft. It was his bed.

She wanted more. Her heart thudded in anticipation for what was to come. Her fingers and lips trembled eagerly to explore his hard muscles. But she was shocked when he got into the bed without removing his clothes and held her.

She tried to turn towards him, but his grip remained firm.

"I want to touch you," she said.

He let out a groan, and she could feel his hardness behind her. "No. Not tonight."

She frowned. "Why not?"

"Because you might regret it in the morning. And also because I want you to properly agree to our deal."

She tried to turn again. "No. I won't regret it. I want to—"

"Sleep, princess. It's late."

She was annoyed by his refusal. She opened her mouth to give him a piece of her mind, but a yawn escaped her. Thanks to the mind-numbing pleasure and a mind-numbing orgasm, she was pulled into a deep sleep within minutes.

CHAPTER TWENTY

Tanvi woke up to a hot furnace. She shifted, trying to get comfortable, but her bed was still too hard.

She frowned.

When did my mattress get rock hard?

She shifted a little more to get comfortable, but a deep rumbling groan followed by a tight grip on her hips made her freeze.

"Stop moving, princess."

Shocked, she opened her eyes, only to realize she was lying on top of her arrogant neighbor. Naked. She could feel her bare skin brushing against his hard body.

Oh my God.

She had sex with her arrogant neighbor. No, not sex. The previous night's events flashed through her mind, making her feel shocked and embarrassed.

They kissed again. But it didn't stop with the lips. He kissed her everywhere—on her neck, her breasts, her stomach and in between her legs. She recalled moaning out loudly, begging him to stop one moment and then demanding more the next moment. The jerk hadn't listened to her and did what he pleased.

Despite her desperate pleas, he hadn't finished what he had started. He put a stop to it saying she would regret it in the morning if they had sex.

He was right.

Her face heated knowing he was the one to put a stop to their make-out session. She scrambled away from him and got up from the bed. Her face heated all the more when she couldn't find her clothes.

Wrapping her arms around her chest to hide her bare breasts, she glared at him. While she was nearly naked, he was fully dressed in jeans and a t-shirt.

"Where are my clothes?" she demanded.

He smirked. "In the living room, princess. Where you threw them."

She recalled pulling up her t-shirt and throwing it away.

Oh God. How could I! What was I thinking?

That was the problem. When it came to her arrogant neighbor, she seemed to lose her bloody mind.

Even now, she couldn't take her eyes off him. He looked utterly sexy with his deep stubble and sleep-hooded eyes. He was watching her with an amused dimpled smirk.

"I have to go," she said. "I'm meeting my friends in a while."

His expression didn't change. Amusement grew in his eyes as it was obvious she was trying to run away.

"I'm scared of the storms," she added. "Whatever happened between us last night was because I was seeking comfort. You just... happened to be there."

The last part made the amusement vanish on his face. She opened her mouth to add more excuses to her previous night's behavior, but she gasped when he got up.

He got out of the bed, came towards her and then towered over her. "Are you saying it could have been anyone?" he drawled.

Her stomach fluttered at his nearness, and the subtle hint of his cologne made her want to bury her nose into his soft t-shirt.

"Yes," she lied instead. "It could have been anyone."

"Liar," he said. He stepped closer until there was barely an inch between them. "You wanted me, princess."

She wanted to deny it. But she couldn't. Not when her heart began to race at his nearness.

He seemed to be similarly impacted because he sucked in a deep breath.

"Fuck," he cursed. "You look so damn beautiful in the morning."

She didn't know who moved first. But her heart thundered when their mouths crashed together and met in a deep kiss. She dug her fingers into his hair and kissed him back greedily.

Their mouths parted when her back fell on the soft mattress. She realized he had pushed her towards the bed. He lay on top of her, and buried his nose into her neck while he took in a deep breath.

"You smell so damn good too," he rasped.

Her stomach quivered, and heat pooled between her legs. Her face heated when he raised his head, and their eyes met. She recalled his hot and wet mouth on her intimate places.

His dimple flashed, making it obvious the jerk was recalling those moments too. "Do you recall agreeing to the deal, princess?" he asked.

"Yes," she whispered. She did recall, although she had no idea what it meant.

She had been too busy floating in a passionate gaze. Even right then, all she wanted was to keep on kissing him.

"Do you know what that means?" he asked.

"Uh. What?"

"It means we are going to eat meals together. Spend time together talking. Of course, all of that with some mind-blowing orgasms thrown into the mix."

Her mind focused only on the mind-blowing part. She had never had an affair before. But having an affair with her arrogant neighbor sounded quite thrilling.

"Fine. I agree."

He grinned. "Good. So I guess that makes you my girlfriend from now on."

Her heart jerked. "What! No. I'm not your—" Before she could protest the term, his mouth sealed their deal with a hot kiss.

Soon, she forgot what she was arguing about and wrapped her arms around his neck.

***

"You are late," Rashmi scolded.

Tanvi was meeting Rashmi and Kavita at Rashmi's place for lunch.

"Sorry, got caught up in some work and lost track of time."

Her friend Kavita frowned. "Are you falling sick? Your throat seems sore."

Tanvi's cheeks heated. Since last night and until a while ago, she had been screaming and begging and threatening at the arrogant man so much that her throat became slightly hoarse.

"I... uh... got caught up in the rain last night. Must be because of that. I feel fine now."

She sat down at the dining table next to her friends while lunch was served. Rashmi and Kavita kept talking, but she barely spoke and enjoyed the home-cooked meal.

She realized she was starving since she hadn't eaten her dinner properly the previous night, and she had skipped her breakfast that morning as she had been too busy with her arrogant neighbor. Arjun had offered to make her breakfast later, but she had to rush and get ready to meet her friends.

Her face heated, still feeling shocked and excited about the sudden turn of events with Arjun.

Pushing away the memories, she focused on her lunch with friends. But Rashmi must have caught her blushing.

"What's with you?" Rashmi asked.

"What?"

Rashmi narrowed her eyes. "You are practically glowing, and you have looked very distracted since you arrived. If I didn't know you very well and hadn't been your friend for long, I would think you had sex."

Tanvi controlled her blush at her friend's accurate guess. Although Arjun hadn't gone all the way to technically term it as sex.

"Nothing is going on," she said. "I just didn't get enough sleep last night because... I was working late at the office and also because of the storm."

Kavita frowned. "You still haven't found any information on the Prism chairman?"

"Not yet."

Rashmi looked thoughtful. "Arjun!"

Tanvi's heart jerked. "What?" she asked in shock.

Rashmi grinned. "Arjun is the solution for your sleepless nights. You should take his help in tracking down the information about the chairman. Sameer can probably help you too. But Arjun is definitely smart enough not to be caught."

Tanvi fought another blush. Arjun was hardly the solution for her sleepless nights. He was the biggest cause. But her friend was right about Arjun being smart enough not to be caught in case she took his help for snooping.

He was a security analyst and had access to the entire building. But she didn't know whether or not he would have access to the files that she needed.

Somehow, it didn't feel right dragging him into it. He might even think that she had agreed to their deal just so she could take advantage of him.

Ugh. Gross.

Even though she still thought he was an arrogant ass, she didn't want him to think poorly of her.

"No. I don't want to involve anyone else," she said. "They could lose their jobs if there is an investigation."

Rashmi frowned but nodded in understanding. "Yes. That might be true." Her friend's frown melted away, and she grinned. "By the way, I spoke to Sameer a couple of times. The guy is so shy, but I find him sweet and amusing."

Tanvi shook her head. "I happen to like Sameer as a good friend. Be nice to him. Don't scare him."

Rashmi grinned. "I promise I'll be nice to him."

Tanvi laughed.

She spent the afternoon with her friends, and they spoke about everything under the sun. She told them about agreeing to attend her father's high-profile event.

"Oh wow. So you think the guy your father wants to host for is the Prism chairman?"

Tanvi was very sure. "I feel it is the guy. If not the Prism chairman, then at least it is someone who has a huge stake in the mall construction. My father mentioned the man is a billionaire from the United States."

"So when is that party?" Kavita asked.

Tanvi shrugged. "I expected it to be this week, but my father didn't call me. I'm hoping it's sooner rather than later."

Her father seemed desperate to impress that man. Desperate enough to risk her attendance and confront the billionaire. She knew her father was racing against the time due to the upcoming elections.

"I'm starting my wedding shopping next month," Kavita said with a smile. "Rashmi and you better join me whenever I call you to destress. My mother and aunts are already driving me crazy with their suggestions."

"Anytime!" Tanvi said with a laugh. She didn't have a mother or a big family to drive her crazy.

But she could understand her friend. She was also happy and excited for Kavita, who was getting married at the end of the year.

It was late afternoon when Tanvi got up to leave. "All right. I'll get going. I have to stop by Mr. Munshi's office to drop off some paperwork."

"Are you free later tonight?" Rashmi asked.

Tanvi's heart jerked. "I... uh... have to prepare for my office work next week."

Rashmi looked at her suspiciously, but she eventually nodded. "See you next weekend then. We'll drop by to meet Arjun again."

"Sure." Fighting a blush, Tanvi nodded before waving goodbye to her friends.

While she left, her heart thudded in excitement. That morning, she had more or less run away from Arjun. She had felt overwhelmed by how she felt and how quickly their relationship had changed.

She didn't hate him. But she didn't love him either. She couldn't define how she felt towards her cocky, arrogant neighbor.

Lust. Desire.

Yes. That must be it. What she felt towards her handsome arrogant neighbor was desire. All she had to do was be careful not to feel anything beyond it.

Feeling slightly better at the self-talk, she hurried to her lawyer's office so she could head home sooner that evening.

CHAPTER TWENTY-ONE

Tanvi rushed home with anticipation fluttering in her heart.

But when she reached her apartment, she noticed that Arjun wasn't home yet. The door to his apartment was closed, and the lights in the living room appeared to be turned off.

Biting her lip in disappointment, she went into her apartment.

Stop getting disappointed. He'll know you are too eager and excited to be with him. He might think you are desperate.

She frowned.

She definitely didn't want him to think she was desperate.

Taking a deep breath, she decided to play it cool.

Taking a quick shower and changing into comfortable clothing, she settled down in her living room and worked on one of her articles.

As usual, she got lost in her work.

It was dark outside when she heard the sound of the opposite door opening. Her heart jerked with excitement. Putting her laptop aside, she sprang up, ran to her door and pulled it open.

Arjun turned to look at her.

"Good evening, princess. You are back early. Were you waiting for me?"

Belatedly, she recalled that she was supposed to play it cool. Pushing away her eager excitement from her face, she shrugged casually.

"I wasn't waiting. I was just about to go down to check the mail. I forgot you weren't home."

"Is that so?" he drawled.

She fought a blush and glared. "Yes! Why would I lie?"

There was a slow smile on his face. Her stomach flipped at his smile.

"Why indeed," he drawled. "Well, I know I might not interest you as much as the mail, but you agreed to the deal. So you need to fulfill your part."

She blushed. "Fulfill what part?" she challenged.

Her mind threw visuals of him asking for something dirty and inappropriate. But instead of feeling offended, she couldn't contain the excited thrill running through her body.

"I want you to invite me over for dinner," he said.

She was stunned. "Oh." She hadn't expected him to say that. Feeling slightly disappointed that he didn't ask for something dirty, she looked at him with a frown. "I don't know how to cook."

He looked amused. "Then treat me for a dinner, princess," he suggested. "After all the dinners I cooked for you and the orgasms I gave you since last night, I think I deserve at least a dinner from you."

She blushed hard once again. "You are such a shameless ass," she scolded, looking at the empty corridor.

He grinned. "Yes. But I'm also right."

She knew he was right. But she couldn't go out with him. After the recent conversation with her father, she was sure her father would keep a close eye on her. Her father would definitely think Arjun was the boyfriend she had mentioned. With the upcoming elections and the billionaire her father was trying to set her up with, she knew it would be risky for Arjun to be seen with her.

"How about I order from outside, and we can eat at my place?" she suggested in return.

"Sure."

She frowned at his easy acceptance. "And I... uh... have to talk to you about our deal. We need to set up... uh... some rules." She had to tell him about her father without scaring him away.

He looked amused. "Can't wait to hear those rules, princess. Let me freshen up. I'll see you in a few minutes."

She blushed as once again excitement and anticipation grew. She turned about to run back to her apartment to order dinner and set the table. But a strong arm wrapped around her waist and yanked her back. She crashed against a hard chest and before she could draw in a breath, her lips were caught in a scorching kiss.

Heat flared, and she clutched the soft material of Arjun's t-shirt and returned the kiss.

But it was a short kiss and he pulled away.

"Can't wait for tonight, princess," he murmured deeply with a sexy smile. And then, he turned away and disappeared inside his apartment.

She stood near her door, her lips tingling and mind racing with excitement but also with doubts. The man could make her lose her mind. She wasn't sure about whether or not she had made a mistake agreeing to the deal to spend time with him.

She didn't know much about him. She didn't even know his last name yet. What if he were some sort of conman? He knew her father was a rich, powerful politician.

She frowned at the thought.

If he wanted to trap you, he wouldn't have behaved like an arrogant ass with you.

He would have behaved as most men who knew about her behaved. They were overly nice and sucked up to her. They weren't at ease as Arjun was.

With that reassuring thought, she went into her apartment and prepared to receive her arrogant neighbor as her dinner guest while also setting up some rules to their deal.

***

The doorbell rang exactly thirty minutes later.

With her heart racing with excitement, she answered the door. Her heart skipped a beat seeing him freshly showered with slightly wet hair. He wore jeans and a t-shirt as usual. But the cologne he usually wore was more intense right then.

"I brought dessert," he said, handing her a small box.

Knowing it would be yet another scrumptious dish he made, she took it from him.

"Come on in," she murmured.

Strangely, she felt nervous. It was the first time she was allowing a man into her personal space. Apart from her small circle of friends, she hadn't invited anyone into her apartment.

"Nice décor, princess. Suits you."

"Thank you," she said.

She took the dessert dish and set it up along with the takeout dishes on her small table in the kitchen. Meanwhile, Arjun continued to explore her small living room.

All apartments in the building were identical. But her décor was different from others. She knew most people might find it strange that she had expensive antiques in her living room that cost more than the apartment.

"The antique show pieces belonged to my mother," she explained.

"I see." He was looking at the pictures on the walls. Most of them were of her mother. Only one picture had her father standing next to her and her mother. There were a few pictures of her with her friends.

Despite what she let him do to her the previous night and earlier that morning, allowing him to look at her personal pictures felt way too intimate.

"Let's have dinner," she said hurriedly.

He smirked at her. "You seem to be in a hurry, princess. You want to get rid of me? Or are you in a hurry to get started on the next part of our date?"

She blushed. "I'm more worried about eating the food while it's still hot."

He looked amused as he joined her at the small table. "Just so you know, you can't get rid of me easily, princess."

She raised an eyebrow at him. "I have known that since our first meeting."

He threw his head back and laughed at her remark. Her stomach fluttered watching him laugh.

Soon, they began eating.

"Not bad," he said after having a few bites of the food.

"It's from the restaurant at the end of our street," she said. As someone who knew how to cook delicious food, the takeout food must be just tolerable to him.

"Where did you learn cooking?" she asked.

"My mother taught me," he replied.

She was surprised.

His mouth twisted. "Why do you look so shocked?"

"You don't look like the kind to listen to your mother's instructions," she replied.

He laughed. "I did give her a hard time in many things, but cooking is something I did to help out while she was working and studying to be a teacher. I cooked as a necessity at first, but soon I began to enjoy it."

She was touched that he helped his mother while his mother was busy working and studying. He might be an arrogant ass, but he was also a *considerate* arrogant ass.

"What about you?" he asked, reading her mind easily.

"Well... I can't cook. But I do want to learn." She didn't want to mention anything about her mother or father. She already regretted mentioning her mother the previous night.

He picked up on her omission but didn't prod her.

"I can teach you cooking if you want to learn," he offered.

That excited her. "Really?"

"Yes, really." His eyes danced with amusement while a smirk formed. "The preferred uniform for the lessons is an apron and nothing else."

She threw a paper napkin at him. "Pervert!"

He grinned. "Most definitely, princess. Very perverted. You'll discover it soon."

She fought a blush even as her heart raced. Immediately, she changed the topic. "Have you met the Prism chairman?" she asked.

His eyebrow rose at her question.

"I mean... I was wondering if he is young or middle-aged or maybe old." According to her father, the man was an eligible billionaire. But it could mean any age group.

"Why are you so interested in the Prism chairman?" he asked, sounding amused.

"I'm not." At least not in the way he was imagining. She despised the Prism chairman because the man was a ruthless bastard whether or not he was young or accomplished.

"Then let's talk about us, princess."

She didn't want to talk about anything personal. But she did want to ask him something.

"What's your name?" Her face was on fire as she asked that question.

"Arjun."

"Arjun what?"

His mouth twisted. "Does it matter?"

Ugh.

She felt a déjà vu recalling a similar conversation. But he was right. She didn't need to know his name during their temporary fling. So she brought up the topic which would set the boundaries.

"About the rules..." she began. "We can't go out on dates."

He looked amused. "I thought you would set rules about wanting something kinky."

She blushed. "I'm being serious! I can't be seen with any guy alone. My father... wouldn't like it. Other people can't know either that we are... together."

He grinned. "Fine. No dates outside."

"And... this... this... fling that we are going to have... it is temporary. I'm not promising anything in the future."

He placed a hand on his heart with a dramatic expression. "I'm hurt, princess. How can you call it a fling when I thought ours was going to be true love based on how we met and our interactions so far."

She shook her head at his comment. "Arrogant jerk," she scolded.

He continued to grin. "What else?"

"That's it for now. Do you... uh... have any rules as well?"

He nodded. "We are going to spend every free moment we have together."

Her heart jerked. "Why?"

He smirked. "You are hot, princess. I want access to that hot body of yours."

"Pervert," she said once again.

He grinned.

Soon, they finished their meal, and it was time for dessert. She got up to bring two small bowls, but he stopped her. "You can eat it from the container."

"What about you?"

His smile was slow with a heavy sexual undercurrent. "I'll watch you eat."

With her heart racing, she opened the box. It was one of his sticky pudding desserts. When she dug into it and ate from a spoon, she felt too self-conscious.

Her skin sizzled at his raw, intense look at her. His amusement was gone, and his eyes now held a sexy, hooded look.

"It's... it's... good," she whispered, her voice getting stuck in her throat. The dessert was rich and delicious, but the way he watched her made her feel as though she were removing her clothes seductively for him rather than just simply having dessert.

His gaze fell over her lips around the spoon and then on her tongue as she licked it clean. Her cheeks heated when she saw the familiar fire in his gaze. He wasn't touching her, but the electricity coursing through her body was similar to when he kissed and touched her intimately.

"Finish it all," he ordered softly.

Gulping in nervousness and anticipation, she ate a few more spoonfuls under his intense watchful stare. When there was none left, he slowly smiled.

"I think I'll have some dessert too, after all."

She frowned and wanted to say there wasn't any left, but her voice remained stuck in her throat. He was watching her lips. Suddenly, his fingers caught her face in a firm grip, and he leaned towards her. His mouth met hers in a slow kiss. His tongue licked the dessert's sweetness from her lips and then from inside her mouth.

Fire spread through her body and turned into an inferno.

"You are right," he murmured huskily. "It is good. But you know what tastes even better? You."

She shuddered hard at the wickedness in his tone.

"Dinner is not done, princess. I'm hungry for a feast."

Oh God.

Her clothes disappeared. And then, her back was against the cool, hard surface of her table.

"Oh God!" she screamed as he kissed her, and tasted her and drove her crazy.

He paused briefly, and there was a satisfied smirk. "I'm glad you think I'm God."

Annoyance flared along with arousal. "You are an arrogant ass!" she snapped even as she dug her fingers and clutched his shoulders.

Laughing wickedly, he once again made her completely lose her mind. Much later, he carried her boneless body to her bed. Before she could touch him properly, he turned her the other way and held her.

"Sleep, princess. You didn't get enough rest last night."

She opened her mouth to argue that she was not sleepy and wanted to explore him. But the soft stroking of his fingers on her hip made her eyes droop. Soon, she was pulled into a deep sleep.

And just before she slept, she heard his deep murmur.

"My name is Arjun Vardhaman."

CHAPTER TWENTY-TWO

"Mr. Varma. The documents show that the transfer of funds began the day after the loans to the lower-income homes project were approved."

Aryan was seated in the boardroom while a private investigator updated him with information he had specifically asked for. Aryan flipped through the folder.

The name on the account to whom the funds were being diverted belonged to Girish Shetty's wife. Whether or not she was aware of her husband's doings, Aryan didn't know. But a large portion of the money that belonged to his father had been siphoned off by the bastard Girish Shetty.

"Find out information on Girish Shetty's wife. I know she died fifteen years ago, but I want to know everything about her."

The private investigator nodded. "Sure, Mr. Varma."

As soon as the private investigator left, Aryan got up from the chair and went to the window overlooking outside the Prism building.

Aryan knew Girish Shetty's wife came from a well-to-do family. She had practically opened doors to Girish Shetty, who until then had been a struggling lawyer. According to the records, her death was an accidental fall from the stairs when she was nearly nine months pregnant.

According to the newspaper articles he briefly saw during the initial investigation, the woman left behind a grieving husband and daughter.

Aryan knew Tanvi loved her mother and missed her a lot. Her apartment was filled with memories of her mother. But what took him by surprise was that she didn't seem to share the same bond with her father. As the only parent alive and with a shared loss of a loved one, he expected her to be closer to her father. The fact that she didn't live with her father and barely communicated meant that Girish Shetty was a cold bastard even to his daughter.

Everything about Girish Shetty made his blood boil with anger and hatred. And yet, when it came to the man's daughter, he couldn't seem to find the middle ground.

Aryan knew he was supposed to hate his father's murderer's daughter. Each time he looked at her, he was supposed to recall his devastating loss and his mother's inconsolable tears.

And yet, when he saw Tanvi Shetty, he saw something beyond a pawn to his revenge.

He had made the deal as a means to get closer to her. But he shouldn't have touched her intimately. And now that he did, it was hard to stay away.

The problem wasn't about giving in to their attraction. The problem was it felt beyond that.

On the night of the storm when he discovered that the demons that haunted him also haunted her, he felt connected to her in a way he had never been able to connect to another woman. Instead of just being his father's murderer's daughter, he thought of her as the beautiful woman he had been instantly drawn to and slowly began obsessing over.

Kissing her, touching her and tasting her only made that obsession grow. Even though he vowed not to take her completely, her mere presence challenged his control.

No. This is only a part of the trap. Nothing more.

Tanvi Shetty is going to be like any other woman I've dated. Once the mission is accomplished, I'm going to forget her

CHAPTER TWENTY-THREE

Having an affair was exciting. And having a secret affair with her arrogant neighbor was exciting and exasperating.

Although they spent every free moment together, they pretended not to know each other well when others were nearby.

"Arjun. When are you inviting us over for dinner again?"

Tanvi was near the mail boxes when the group of college girls who lived downstairs surrounded Arjun once again. Although she was not looking towards him, she could hear the conversation.

"Are you still with that possessive girlfriend of yours, Arjun?"

He spoke to his ardent fans. "Yes, I'm still with her," he replied in amusement.

"Why?"

"I like her fiery nature. And I have never met anyone like her."

There were dreamy sighs.

"Aww. Your girlfriend is so lucky, Arjun."

"Yes, she is very lucky," the arrogant ass drawled. "She says that to me all the time."

"Does she visit you here?"

"Yes. She enjoys my cooking and my... uh... company."

There were several knowing giggles.

Tanvi decided to kill the arrogant ass later.

"All right, ladies. My girlfriend ordered me to make her a special meal tonight. I need to get going to slave in the kitchen before she arrives."

"Please tell her again that she is the luckiest woman on earth."

"Oh, I definitely will." The arrogant ass sounded amused.

Tanvi shut her mail box. The sound was louder than usual and drew attention to her.

"Oh hi, Tanvi," one of the girls greeted.

"Hello."

"Have you seen Arjun's girlfriend?"

Her eyes fell on him. His dimples flashed, and the jerk looked beyond amused.

"No. I haven't seen her," she replied.

She realized her voice came out slightly annoyed.

"Excuse me," she said and walked to the lifts with her mail, most of which was junk that she needed to trash.

She stepped into the lifts and immediately pressed the button to shut the doors. There was one more person inside the lift, an old woman who lived on the second floor.

"Hello, Mrs. Murlidhar," she greeted and continued to press the button to shut the lift doors. But just before the doors closed, a masculine hand held it open at the last moment.

With an amused smirk, Arjun stepped inside the lift and greeted the old woman.

The woman greeted him back with a smile. "Hello, Arjun."

Tanvi ignored him and pretended to sort her mail.

There was silence in the lift until Mrs. Murlidhar got out on the next floor. As soon as the lift doors closed, the arrogant ass pounced.

"You look tensed, princess," he said, pinning her to the lift walls and trapping her by placing both his arms on either side of her. "I thought after earlier this morning when you kept calling God multiple times, you would be much more relaxed."

Her face heated, and she glared. "Stop it, you jerk. Someone might see us or hear us."

He grinned. She wanted to slap the cocky smirk on his face, but her body heated at his nearness.

She shook her head, trying to ward away his spell. "Arjun, I'm serious about not letting anyone know about us. It's not safe."

He frowned at her statement. "Not safe? What does that mean, princess?"

She didn't want to tell him about her father or the threat her father would pose against a man he thought was her boyfriend.

Taking a deep breath, she pasted an identical smirk on her face. "It means your demanding, short-tempered girlfriend is hungry. Time to slave away in the kitchen, lover boy."

He slowly grinned. "Oh yeah? I hope my girlfriend remembers that her cooking lessons are not over."

He had been teaching her how to cook, and she was quite excited to eat what she made with his help.

"I'm sure your girlfriend remembers, although she is still going to refuse to follow the dress code her perverted teacher demands each time." The perverted ass had wanted her to cook wearing just an apron.

He threw his head back and laughed.

Her stomach fluttered watching him laugh. In the few days since they began their affair, she discovered that he wasn't reserved like most men. He infuriated her, teased her, was playful and was also beyond passionate. Whatever he did, he gave it his all.

She was strongly drawn to every aspect of him.

He caught her staring at him, and his laughter slowly faded. His eyes turned heated with a familiar look that she now recognized. It made her stomach flutter more and her heart race with anticipation.

"The cooking lessons will have to wait, princess," he said huskily, lowering his head until his lips met her cheeks. "Your instructor demands prior payment."

She blushed.

***

"No. Don't stir it yet," Arjun's deep voice instructed from behind her. "Let the chicken brown."

They were inside her apartment, and the aromas drifting in the air were delicious. She still couldn't believe that she was cooking. She was super excited each time she made something, and it genuinely tasted amazing.

She turned to see Arjun leaning against her refrigerator while sipping a beer. He had stocked her refrigerator with lots of groceries, including his beer.

He smiled in amusement at her excitement.

"The chicken will be browned in a couple of minutes, princess. Start getting ready to add the rest of the ingredients."

She followed his instructions and kept the vegetables and spices close to her. A couple of minutes later, she added them in the sequence he mentioned.

When everything came together, he came closer for a taste. "Hmm... you are a fast learner, princess. I think I'm going to have you slaving away in the kitchen more often."

She laughed and hit him on his shoulder. "Jerk."

He grinned. When she tasted the dish she had made, she was shocked too. It came out well, almost as good as his.

She was still touched by the fact that he had learned cooking at a young age as a way to help his busy working mother. Not many children were as considerate, especially little boys.

Although she was the one to establish the rules, she was curious about his life. "Does your mother work still?" she asked.

Something flashed in his eyes at her mention of his mother. Before she could analyze it, it disappeared. She wondered if she had imagined the reaction.

He nodded with a smile. "Yes. She is a teacher. She teaches kids in underprivileged neighborhoods."

"Oh. That's so awesome." She felt an immediate liking towards his mother. The older woman sounded sweet and wonderful for choosing to teach underprivileged children.

"What about your siblings?" she asked. "What do they do?"

He looked amused at her prodding. "They are in the construction and hospitality industry."

She assumed they must be a civil engineer and maybe a hotel manager.

"Do they live here in the city?"

He shook his head. "No, they don't live here."

She hadn't seen anyone visiting his place so far, which meant he probably went to his native place or some other place to visit his family.

"Do your brothers cook as well?"

He let out a laugh. "Unfortunately, no. I was the only one to learn from my mother. My brothers started working from a young age and weren't home much. It was mostly me and my mother."

That made her all the more curious about his life. She recalled the brief conversation on the night of the storm. He had mentioned that his family was forced to leave their home on the day of his father's funeral.

It was heartbreaking. But she admired that despite the circumstances, his family chose hard work and compassion. She also liked that he came from a humble background.

Although she wanted to know much more about him, she knew that the same would be expected from her in return. And she wasn't prepared to reveal much about her life. Not without putting his life under threat.

"What are you thinking, princess?" he asked.

She shook her head. "Nothing. I'm just hungry. Let's eat."

There was a knowing flash in his eyes, but he didn't call her out. With a small smile, he helped her serve the dish and set the table for dinner. They sat across from each other and began to eat.

She enjoyed eating with him each night. After a hectic day at work and when she scrambled her other commitments, she looked forward to spending the time with him.

"Rashmi plans on asking Sameer out on a date. I had to warn her not to scare him."

There was a flash in his eyes before he once again looked amused. "I thought you liked Sameer."

She smiled, recalling the times she tried to use Sameer as a shield to fight the attraction towards her arrogant neighbor. "I do like Sameer. He is very sweet. But I like him only as a friend."

There was a smirk. "And why is that, princess? Why just a friend?"

The arrogant ass knew what was missing. But he expected her to spell it out.

"Chemistry," she replied. "There's not enough chemistry between Sameer and me. We are good as friends."

When his eyes flashed in satisfaction, she narrowed hers. He was way too cocky, and she knew just the way to prod him.

She pretended to look thoughtful. "Although... they do say friends make the best life partners. So maybe Sameer and I might end up together in the future. And when we do, we might have the perfect chemistry. Maybe I should kiss him once to confirm if chemistry is just a myth."

She reveled in the possessive flash in his eyes.

"Sorry to break your fantasy, princess. You already agreed to our deal." His fingers wrapped around the back of her neck and pulled her close until his words fell hotly against her lips. "Which means you don't kiss anyone but me because you are my girlfriend."

"I'm not your girlfrien—" Before she could protest the term, her lips were caught in a scorching kiss.

By the time their mouths parted, they were breathing heavily.

"Are you still hungry?" he rasped.

She shook her head because her voice was stuck in her throat.

"Then let's get back to the dinner later."

She curled her arms around his neck when he pulled her up from the chair. Their mouths met once again, and passion took over. He carried her to her bedroom.

***

Tanvi was frustrated. Although her body lay boneless and content with pleasure, her mind was frustrated and restless.

Arjun had once again stopped as soon as she reached her pleasure. She rolled towards him and placed her hands under his t-shirt. His muscles immediately jumped under her palms, and she could hear his breaths increase.

"Why do you keep stopping midway?" she asked.

"You are not ready, princess."

It was the same answer he had been giving her for the last two weeks since they began their affair. It drove her crazy. And it also made the arrogant man in control of their relationship. He was the one to drive her pleasure, and he was the one who stopped midway.

No more.

She needed to take control of their affair. She didn't know how long it would last. But she wanted to experience the most of it with the most handsome, arrogant and exciting man she had met.

She narrowed her eyes as a plan began to form.

"What are you thinking, princess?" he asked in amusement. "You have that look in your eyes again."

"What look?"

He smirked. "The look of a battle cry that promises mayhem if you don't get what you are after."

He was right. She was determined.

She was determined to seduce her arrogant neighbor until he broke.

CHAPTER TWENTY-FOUR

Aryan was beyond frustrated.

"What's with you?" Bhargav asked. "You have been snapping and restless since the moment you arrived."

Aryan was meeting his brothers at Bhargav's penthouse to look at the restoration plans of the Vardhaman Estate. Looking at the 3-D images which were close to reality, he once again felt as though he were re-living the past. He hated it. He also felt deeply nostalgic, making the loss of his father all the more devastating.

"Anya shouldn't have been hired as the architect for the mansion restoration," Aryan gritted.

Bhargav didn't let anything show on his face. "She is the best person for the job."

Aryan knew his brother was right, but he couldn't let the fact go that the architect hired wasn't a part of their plans. "What if Anya finds out the truth in the middle of the restoration?" he demanded. "Kashyap will be alerted and all of our hard work will blow up in our faces."

"She won't know. I'm taking care of it."

Aryan frowned. He wasn't convinced by his brother's assurance.

He looked at Yash, who was seated next to them. "Narmada is getting a bit too close to discovering the truth," he said. "The investigator she hired is digging up information on us in New York."

Yash threw him a cool look. "She can dig as much as she wants," Yash replied. "But she will not be able to guess the truth either."

Aryan was frustrated by his brothers' calm assurances. "Even if Anya and Narmada don't guess the truths, I'm more worried about how our plans are impacted by your relationships with them."

Yash shrugged. "I'm more or less engaged to Mohan's daughter, and the wedding will go ahead as planned in a few weeks. Why do you think there is a threat to our plans?"

Aryan knew his brother was engaged to Divya Mohan, one of his enemies' daughters. But based on how obsessed Yash was when it came to the enemy's daughter-in-law, it was hard to picture his brother going ahead with the wedding as planned with the intended bride.

"You shouldn't underestimate Narmada," Aryan told his brother. "She is not going to let you marry her sister-in-law. She hates you for what you did to her in Milan and what followed after with her stocks."

Yash didn't say anything, but his silence spoke volumes. Aryan knew he hit on the truth.

He looked at Bhargav. "Don't underestimate Anya, bro. You can't deceive her for long. She will find out who ruined her father and brother."

Bhargav's pawn who was yet another enemy's daughter was sweet in nature. But Sukanya Kashyap aka Anya was also Bhargav's biggest weakness. The history between Bhargav and Anya would make it harder to execute their final plan.

Bhargav didn't respond as well to Aryan's deductions.

Aryan was frustrated that his normal cold and ruthless brothers were deviating from their original plans because of the women who were only meant to be pawns.

Deep inside, Aryan knew there was another root cause of his frustration. But he chose to ignore it and instead focused on his brothers.

But Bhargav gave him a knowing look.

"You keep warning Yash and me. But what is happening between you and Shetty's daughter?"

Aryan immediately closed up. Somehow, he wasn't ready to discuss Tanvi with his brothers.

He looked at his brothers and shrugged. "Shetty's daughter is different. We need her cooperation to sign the trust papers. She doesn't know our family history and isn't personally involved like Narmada or Anya."

Bhargav's mouth twisted. "Actually, Tanvi Shetty does know about our family," he stated. "She has even visited the estate once. I believe you recall one particular instance quite well, little bro."

Yash's poker expression melted away, and even he looked amused. "I recall it too. I was the one to pull you out of the water fountain before you ended up drowning."

Aryan clenched his teeth, once again cursing his brothers and their damn good memories.

He had tried to ignore the fact that he had known Tanvi briefly during their childhood. He didn't want that brief meeting to impact the revenge plans. But their first meeting was way too eventful for him to forget or ignore.

He recalled it clearly even though both he and Tanvi had barely been seven years old at that time. Tanvi and her parents were invited to stay for a weekend at the Vardhaman Estate.

He had an immediate crush on her. It was the first time he had liked any girl. And as any seven-year-old boy, he tried to attract the attention of his crush by pulling her long hair followed by a goofy grin.

Although it had only been one long yank, seven-year-old Tanvi had made a big stink of it. She punched him hard in his stomach and pushed him into the water fountain. And then, she immediately ran and complained to his mother about him being a bully.

He had only been seven at that time, but he had been equally pissed, scared and smitten of the girl who had punched him when he tried to get her attention. He reasoned that although the seven-year-old girl looked like an angel, she was actually a she-devil.

"I don't think you spoke to any girl for a long time after that incident." Bhargav sounded amused.

Aryan ignored his brothers' amusement. "Ha ha, laugh it up, big bros. At least I didn't fall in love with a girl when I was nine years old or accept a girl's proposal when I was twelve."

His two brothers had a more complicated history with their pawns. The kind that would make the deception and lies harder to implement.

"You should have listened to me when I said you should have switched your pawns. Yash should have gone after Kashyap and you after Mohan. Then you wouldn't have had the... distractions."

His brothers didn't say anything. But their silent, knowing looks spoke volumes.

He felt both annoyed and also like a hypocrite.

He had been putting off analyzing how things had changed between him and Tanvi. Two weeks had passed since the deal began, and in the meantime, he was slowly beginning to lose his mind and sleep.

He was more than distracted by his pawn. So much so that he couldn't wait to get back to his apartment each evening to spend every moment with her. Even now, when things in their plan were deviating and close to getting fucked up, all he wanted to do was spend time with his fiery pawn.

Fuck.

"Excuse me," he said, getting up from the couch. "I'll speak to you both later."

Bhargav watched him with a small amused smile. "Good night, little bro. And say hello to your beautiful neighbor."

Fuck.

***

Aryan frowned as he took the stairs to the apartment. He was deliberately returning to his place later than usual. He had spent the last couple of hours in his penthouse he still maintained in the city. He often caught up with his work during the day at the penthouse.

But after spending a couple of hours in his near-empty penthouse that evening, he had begun to feel restless. He felt a deep craving to look at a beautiful face with flashing fiery eyes ready to argue and banter with him. He also felt the craving to kiss the pouty lips and taste the smooth curves of her body until she lost control.

Fuck.

He was painfully aroused.

He had kissed many women over the years. To him, kissing was the preliminary to having sex. He kissed a woman to make his intentions clear. But until his fiery pawn, he had never kissed a woman knowing he wouldn't have sex right after.

He kissed Tanvi Shetty simply because he wanted to pleasure the woman who obsessed him in many ways. He wanted to drive her crazy like she drove him with her smiles and fiery nature.

Kissing her and arousing her excited him more than being with other women sexually.

Fuck.

No. I am not obsessed with her. My brothers are wrong. I can resist her easily.

He decided not to kiss her that night. Even though it would lead to more frustration, he was going to use the excuse of work and stay away from her.

With a frown, when he reached the top floor, he went to her apartment first. He was going to greet and make the excuse before leaving.

He rang the bell.

He heard the scrambling sounds from inside. "Come in!" she said.

Listening to her voice, his hands clenched into fists. He wanted to stop himself from pulling her into his arms and kissing the hell out of her.

He pushed open the apartment door and stepped inside. He wanted to greet her before leaving, but he stopped and blinked once. The lights were turned off and only a few candles were lit on the kitchen counter and the small dining table.

"What happened, princess?" he asked. "Did you lose power in the apartment?"

He saw her then.

"Fuck." The word escaped his mouth. She was wearing an apron as she held a dish in her hand and placed it on the small dining table. He noticed that she wasn't wearing anything else.

With a sultry smile that would make even a dead man come alive, she came towards him and threw her arms around his neck.

"You are late," she murmured, pulling his head down towards her. "I had to slave away in the kitchen all by myself."

"I had to attend to some work, princess. In fact, I still have to—" He broke off in a groan in the middle of the excuse because her soft lips brushed against his.

She didn't kiss him fully like he wanted her to. The little witch was trying to mess with his mind and make him desperate. She was succeeding.

Her soft breasts brushed against his chest. And knowing only the apron lay between his hand and her soft curves, his fingers itched to yank off the apron.

"Let's make tonight special," she murmured against his lips. "I want to know how it feels to have you inside me."

Had she been any other woman who came on to him like that, he would have had her under him within minutes and taken her right there on the kitchen floor until they both collapsed with pleasure and exhaustion.

But she was his enemy's daughter. And an innocent one at that. He dragged his mouth away from her.

"No, princess. You are not ready. I will let you know when you are."

She blinked her eyes through the sexual haze that surrounded them. And slowly, her eyes narrowed in determination. "We'll see," she challenged ominously.

He was once again amused and frustrated. Tanvi Shetty constantly challenged him. Even though he succeeded in getting close to her, she surprised him in many ways.

But suddenly, his amusement died.

She stepped away from him slightly, then put her hands behind her and untied the apron.

With her cheeks flushing, she let the apron drop and stood in front of him in just her tiny underwear.

Fuck.

He stared at the vision in front of him. The woman was determined to be the death of him.

His body screamed in agony.

"Well?" she challenged.

He knew her game plan. His little seductress was determined to break his control. She was almost succeeding.

Clenching his hands into fists, he forced out a smile.

"You put on a great show, princess," he deliberately drawled. "But you are still not ready."

She opened her mouth to argue, but only a gasp came out when he dragged her close and swung her up into his arms.

"Stop being a controlling ass!" she said with a glare. "We are doing it tonight."

He didn't say anything. He carried her to her small bedroom and threw her on the bed.

She gasped when her back hit the mattress. And then, she gasped even louder when she saw the look on his face. She tried to scramble back, but he caught her ankle and dragged her close.

And then, he punished her.

He punished her for captivating his mind and body. For being the most irresistible yet unattainable woman. For driving him to near madness and obsession.

He kissed her and tasted her everywhere—on her breasts, on her stomach, and then, he flipped her and kissed her smooth back, including the soft curve of her buttocks. He bit into them before he flipped her back again. Spreading her legs, he kissed her at his favorite place.

He drove her to fever pitch but drew away when she was about to climax.

She moaned. She cursed out loud. And she dug her sharp nails into his arms before begging him more. But he kept at it for a very long time.

When her cries turned hoarse and a sheen of damp sweat covered her soft skin, he relented.

Watching the object of his obsession scream in pleasure and climax was a sight that would forever be branded into his mind.

He then moved up her exhausted body and kissed her.

"When you are ready for me," he murmured against her mouth. "Nothing can stop me from taking you. Until then, I'm only going to enjoy your sweet taste."

Even though his body screamed and was in physical pain, he then dragged himself away from her forcibly.

His mouth twisted into a satisfied smile. "Come on, princess. Let's eat. I'm hungry for food now."

Despite her exhaustion and having lost the challenge to seduce him, he saw her eyes lighting up with a fight. "I'm going to get back at you soon, you cocky bastard," she said.

Fuck.

He definitely knew his fiery prey would be the death of him.

CHAPTER TWENTY-FIVE

"How do you seduce a guy?"

At Tanvi's question, both Rashmi and Kavita nearly choked on their drinks.

Tanvi was meeting her friends at a restaurant.

Rashmi got over her shock first and became excited. "Oh my God! Who are you trying to seduce? Arjun?"

"No one. I'm trying to get information for an article I'm working on."

Both Rashmi and Kavita looked disappointed. She knew her friends would be excited but worried if she told them about her affair with her arrogant neighbor. Despite wanting her to have a boyfriend, they were quite protective of her. They would want her to be with a guy who would declare his undying love for her.

Her arrogant neighbor would be the last man to do that. And neither would she expect or want him to do that. Their affair was temporary, and she didn't want their hearts to be involved.

"I guess you need to put on something sexy and find privacy."

Tanvi frowned at Rashmi's suggestion. She had already done that. She had literally stripped to her underwear. But the damn arrogant neighbor of hers still wasn't seduced. He even deliberately drove her crazy and made her beg.

She was determined to drive him similarly crazy and make him break.

"Hmm..." Kavita looked at her thoughtfully. "There is another way. Although it's manipulative, I heard that it is quite effective."

Tanvi was curious and also desperate. She was willing to try anything. "What? What is it?"

"Jealousy," her friend replied. "Apparently, letting the guy know he has serious competition will make him commit and not take you for granted."

"Oh." Tanvi's frown grew.

She didn't know if Arjun was the kind to ever be jealous of another guy. He was way too cocky and arrogant to believe she would be interested in anyone else.

She did use Sameer briefly to make him jealous. But the arrogant jerk would know immediately if she tried to pretend once again that she was interested in Sameer.

"What if there is no competition?" she asked.

Kavita smiled. "Then simply make up one."

Tanvi didn't think that would work, but it was worth a try. She opened her mouth to say that when her phone began ringing. It was from her father's office.

She answered the call right away, hoping it wasn't about documents related to the trust.

"Hello?"

"Miss Shetty. Your father has asked me to inform you that there is a party event being held on Sunday at home. He wants you to attend it."

Tanvi's heart jerked. "What event is this?" she demanded. "Who is the guest of honor?"

"Uh... I was told that the guest of honor is a business acquaintance of Mr. Girish."

"What's his name?"

"I'm not entirely sure, madam."

Tanvi frowned. "Does he happen to be from New York or America? Is he the chairman of Prism Corporation?"

There was a pause. The assistant seemed taken aback by her questions. She usually didn't bother asking questions about any of the parties or events her father invited her to because she had barely attended any of them.

"I'm not sure about that too, madam. I can check with your father and get back."

"Yes. Please do. And also tell him I will be attending the event."

The man murmured something polite and ended the call.

"What happened?" Rashmi asked. "Why do you look so excited?"

Tanvi smiled. She knew her smile was that of satisfaction. "I'm going to finally meet the chairman of Prism Corporation. He is attending the party my father is hosting."

Her friends looked surprised. "How do you know it is him?"

"My father revealed it. He also warned me that I shouldn't hound the Prism chairman at the event. I promised him that I wouldn't."

Rashmi laughed. "Are you going to keep up the promise?" she asked.

Tanvi smiled. "No," she replied. "I'm going to let that ruthless bastard know exactly what I think of him and his project."

***

Tanvi got back home and began planning while getting things ready to cook dinner. She had only two days to prepare for the party. Although she didn't care about what she would wear and the rest of the logistics, she had to plan on how she should be cornering the guest of honor so she could speak to him uninterrupted.

Maybe I should dress sexy.

Her stomach turned queasy at the thought of trying to catch the attention of the ruthless bastard who cared more about his profits than the fragile ecosystem or health of nearly a million people living in the city.

Ugh.

She knew she was racing against time. She couldn't afford to think about her sensibilities. She had to corner that bastard somehow and speak to him. And if she could do it only by catching his attention in skimpy clothes, then so be it.

"What are you scheming about, princess?"

She jumped and screamed loudly.

"Arjun! You scared me. When did you come?"

His mouth twisted. "I came in a couple of minutes ago. I did greet you, but you seem lost in scheming something."

She narrowed her eyes. "I was just thinking about what we should have for dinner."

He looked amused. "Really? That must have been a tough decision, considering you already took out last night's leftovers and dessert and placed it on the counter to reheat them."

The arrogant man was way too cocky. But even as she glared at him, her heart raced seeing him.

In a simple buttoned-up blue shirt, he looked heart-stopping sexy. He must have attended a meeting at work to dress up formally. Usually he went to work in casuals.

He came closer and wrapped an arm around her waist before capturing her lips in a mind-numbing passionate kiss. She kissed him back, once again missing him even though they had only been apart a few hours.

"Missed you, princess," he murmured, pulling away a little. He looked at her with a smile. "I was hoping to find you in the apron once again."

Her cheeks heated, recalling how her last seduction attempt had failed. The arrogant jerk had driven her crazy. Although she had reached her peak, she was still left wanting because she wanted it all.

Succeeding in seducing her arrogant neighbor now became her top obsession, along with meeting the ruthless chairman and stopping the construction of the mall in the park.

Suddenly, an idea struck her. Her heart jerked and once again raced in excitement.

"What are you thinking about, princess," he asked, smiling at her excitement.

She twisted her mouth into a smirk. "Actually, I was thinking about the party I have to attend at my father's place on Sunday."

"Sounds boring, princess. Why don't you ditch the event? We can go on a long bike ride. You will be wearing a helmet, so no one will know it's you."

His plan sounded more thrilling and exciting than attending her father's boring event. But she wasn't attending the event for entertainment. She was on an important mission to meet the Prism chairman.

And she also had the perfect opportunity to use that event to drive the man in front of her crazy.

"Actually, it's not just a mere party," she said. "My father wants me to meet someone."

"Who?"

She tried to put on a casual demeanor. "A man who does business with my father. My father wants me to meet him."

There was no spark of jealousy on Arjun's face. "Still sounds very boring, princess. The bike ride I'm planning is to a beautiful river a couple of hours away from the city. It's inside an estate where no one lives currently. You can even swim naked in the river if you want. No one will hear us or disturb us."

Her cheeks heated as she was tempted by the visual put into her mind by the arrogant devil in front of her. "Umm... maybe we can go next week if I won't have to go out with that other man."

He raised an eyebrow. "Other man?"

"Yes. The man my father wants me to meet is actually a prospective groom."

He froze.

She tried not to smile victoriously. "My father is insisting I consider the proposal. The man is apparently some hot shot young billionaire from New

York."

His eyes flashed. "I didn't know you were a gold-digger, princess."

She stopped herself from grinning. Instead, she shrugged. "I'm practical. What girl doesn't dream of a hot billionaire as a husband?"

"How do you know the man is hot? Most billionaires have a pot belly and double chin."

She smirked. "With his billions, he can easily buy hot looks if he wants. Maybe I can even convince him to look like you."

She could see Arjun's jaw clench.

"According to our deal, you don't date any other damn guy," he gritted.

She batted her eyelashes. "Oh. I'm not going to date him. I'm considering him as my marriage prospect."

"You are lying. I know you have no interest in that guy as a marriage prospect."

"Am I?"

He gritted his teeth again. "You won't be happy marrying a man you don't like or care about."

She twisted her mouth into a smirk. "I didn't like you at first either. But now, we get along just fine. In fact, I'm very touched that you are preparing me for my married life without taking what belongs to another man."

He growled before dragging her close. "You don't belong to another man. You are mine!"

She opened her mouth to protest. But her mouth was caught in a kiss. The kiss was punishing and possessive, but she reveled in it. Grabbing him close, she kissed him back equally passionately.

"I know you are manipulating me, princess," he growled against her lips before swinging her up and carrying her to the bedroom. "I know you don't want that other bastard."

Her heart thundered. "How do you know that?" she asked.

He looked at her with a heated, possessive gaze. "Because you want me as much as I want you. Which is a damn fucking lot."

She did want him. She craved him like a drug. He filled her mind constantly with thoughts of him. He annoyed her. He made her laugh. And he fascinated her like no other man.

He was the only man she wanted and needed.

When he placed her on the bed, she somehow knew he wouldn't stop midway. He was going to possess her completely. Her heart raced in anticipation.

He lay next to her and kissed her again. "I have wanted you for so damn long. It damn near kills me each time I leave without taking you the way I want."

"Then take me," she urged. "I want it too."

He groaned at her words. When she slid her hands under his shirt, she felt his heart race.

She slowly slid her hand lower and went past his hard stomach and to the blatant masculine arousal. A tortured sound escaped his throat.

"You will be the death of me, princess," he groaned.

"Then let's die together tonight," she whispered. "Show me everything."

One moment, she was cupping his arousal, and the next moment, she was lying flat on her back with his hot, aroused body covering hers. He stripped her bare. And unlike the previous times, he shed his clothes, stripping down to nothing as well. His heated skin lay bare against hers, and she could feel his hard arousal lying against her stomach.

Desire coursed through her like liquid fire. She ran her fingers over his broad back, loving the feel of his muscles jumping and leaping with her touch. She wanted to touch him everywhere and taste him like he had done to her many times.

But the raw urgency that gripped them didn't allow for leisurely exploring. She cried out when his arousal brushed against her core. She raised her hips, wanting to feel more.

He groaned. "Fuck. I can't wait," he said.

Her body shook in anticipation. "Then don't wait. I want you now."

The heated intensity in his eyes turned darker with passion. He lowered his head and kissed her deeply even as his hands gripped her hips and raised them. He slid into her.

Despite the blazing passion, she wasn't entirely prepared for his entry. He was too big and she felt stretched and too full.

She cried out with her back arching and her fingers digging into his shoulders. She felt overwhelmed with the feeling and sensations.

It felt as though he was everywhere—in her mind, in her body and inside her heart.

She couldn't escape him. Feeling panicked, she tried wiggling under him, trying to get him to ease out a bit. He groaned and held her hips still. He pulled back slightly, only to thrust even deeper than before, which she didn't think was possible. She cried out as hot pleasurable sensations overwhelmed her along with hints of pain.

He placed his forehead against hers. "You are so damn perfect," he rasped. "Everything I imagined and craved."

Even as he spoke, he continued to pull out and thrust in deeper. The impact of each thrust made her body tremble. She felt possessed.

Knowing there was no escape from him, she embraced the overwhelming sensations. She raised her head and kissed his rough jaw. She kissed his chin and then bit his neck. She deliberately avoided his lips.

He groaned, and his movements turned harsher. He didn't let her escape. He caught the back of her head and gripped her hair to kiss her deeply while his body possessed hers.

It was raw. It was wild. And it was all-consuming.

He drove into her as though he was determined to fuse them into one being. He was deep inside her and she felt consumed.

When the climax hit her, it came without warning. She screamed as her body convulsed and shook as the tidal wave of pleasure hit her.

He didn't stop. He continued to possess her until a similar wave hit him. Throwing his head back, he roared out his release. Along with his seed that spilled deep inside her, she felt a flood of emotions that shook her from the inside out.

Shockingly, she burst out crying. Tears spilled out of her eyes as she clung to him.

He held her as their bodies continued to tremble with the powerful aftermath. Later, when the trembles began to lessen in intensity, she still felt overwhelmed by her emotions.

"I-I don't know what is wrong with me," she said, feeling embarrassed about her crying bout.

He raised his head higher to look at her clearly. "Nothing is wrong with you, princess," he said, pushing her hair away from her face. "You are beautiful and perfect."

He was perfect too. So much that the act that began purely as desire felt as though it meant so much more. "Is it always like this?" she asked.

He didn't reply. Instead, he kissed her again, a sweet kiss that was the complete opposite of the raw, passionate and intense act between them just moments ago. The sweetness of his kiss pushed away her fears and reduced the overwhelming feeling. It reminded her of the sweet bond and friendship that had begun to develop between them.

She kissed him back, enjoying the simple brushing of lips.

But soon the kiss caught fire. Her heart raced, and she could feel his heart thumping harder along with his hard arousal once again jumping against her stomach.

He groaned. "We should stop, princess."

"Why?" she asked even as her sore, exhausted body started to come alive.

"You won't be able to walk for the next few days."

She blushed at his bluntness. She knew what he meant because she already felt the soreness in between her legs. "I don't care," she whispered.

He gritted his teeth as he watched her. She returned his stare, and then she knew the exact moment he lost the fight with himself.

"Fuck it. I want you too damn much." His mouth crashed on top of hers.

Once again, the raw intensity and magic gripped her. Even as the arrogant devil possessed her body and mind, she knew he was equally possessed.

CHAPTER TWENTY-SIX

Aryan looked outside the small window at the rising sun.

He knew he had fucked up royally.

The woman who had captivated him right from the beginning with her fieriness was now sleeping peacefully in his arms after having stolen his peace of mind.

"Is it always like this?"

When Tanvi asked him that question, he knew exactly what she had meant.

Was sex always sweet, passionate, uncontrollable and overwhelming?

No. It wasn't always that way. And though he was experienced, he didn't feel all those things with the same woman.

Despite fighting hard for many days not to possess his enemy's daughter, he finally broke and gave in. He wasn't the possessive kind. He didn't care if any of the women he had slept with dated someone else. But when it came to Tanvi Shetty, he turned into a damn caveman.

Her deliberate taunt about a billionaire from New York as a prospective groom made him realize how close he was to losing the woman he wanted more than anything. He knew she was deliberately egging him on. But still, his mind screamed to make her his completely.

And he did.

The feel of her, the sweet smell of her, her taste and her sassy fierceness finally broke him. He had already been obsessed with her. But now, he became addicted. He became addicted to how her eyes turned soft and glazed while her face twisted with ecstasy before she climaxed.

She might be his enemy's daughter, and she might hate him soon. But she was the only woman he needed more than anything.

Yes, I'm completely and royally fucked.

"Good evening, Miss Shetty."

Tanvi's father's assistant greeted her outside her father's home. "Good evening, Mr. Prasad."

The older man looked tensed and worried. "Your father is waiting for you inside, madam."

She knew her father would blast her for arriving late to the party. She hadn't picked up his calls from a while ago as well. Her face heated as she recalled the reason why she couldn't attend the calls and also why she was running late to the party. An arrogant devil had deliberately kept her busy.

"Has the guest of honor arrived yet?" she asked. She could hear faint music coming from inside.

"No, madam."

"Do you happen to know the name of the man?" she asked.

"No, madam."

Tanvi frowned. She expected her father's assistant to know the name of the guest of honor.

"Your father is in the lawns, Miss Shetty. He is a bit... upset."

Tanvi wondered if the reason for her father's upset was because she hadn't picked up his calls or that the guest of honor hadn't arrived yet.

"Thank you, Mr. Prasad."

She knew she would face her father's anger regardless of whether she was late or not. She also knew her father wouldn't reveal his upset in front of others. She smiled at the thought.

Her smile turned into a small grimace as she walked to the lawns where the party was being held. The place between her legs was quite sore. She blushed and cursed the arrogant devil responsible.

It had been two days since she had goaded Arjun into taking her completely. Since then, they had barely spent a moment apart. She had reveled in his possession and also in the power she felt for making a man like him lose control with a simple kiss or touch.

But earlier that evening when she explained to him that it was important for her to attend her father's party so she could meet the Prism chairman, Arjun behaved as though he was very understanding.

But the arrogant ass deliberately delayed her by cornering her right after she got ready and was about to step out for the party.

"When you are talking to the hot-shot billionaire or any other man tonight, remember that no one else can make you feel this way except for me."

Her cheeks heated even more at the memories. She had wanted to resist him, but the arrogant devil knew exactly how to kiss her and what to do in order to make her lose her mind. And once he was done with her, it took her nearly an hour to redo her hair and makeup. The arrogant ass simply watched her with a smirk even as she cursed him while getting ready in a hurry.

Pushing away the thoughts of her distracting lover, she focused on the mission at hand.

The music grew louder as she neared the lawn area. When she entered it, she was taken aback.

She had expected it to be a small garden party with an exclusive set of people. But her father seemed to have gone all out and invited everyone he knew.

How am I to find the damn chairman in this crowd when he arrives?

And even if she did find him, it would be quite a task to corner him and find time to speak to him uninterrupted.

Frowning, she walked into the lawn area and tried to find her father.

Her father hadn't spared any expense for the event. The house was lit up and decorated inside and out. Dozens of uniformed men and women were hired for the event to serve the guests. Drinks seem to flow generously while live music played in a corner.

She was barely there for a few minutes, but she was once again reminded of why she hated attending her father's parties. The place was filled with noted politicians, bureaucrats and businessmen. The politicians and bureaucrats got on her nerves right away. With their fake smiles and deliberate modest clothes that hid their corruption, they canvassed the place extracting campaign funds and bribes from rich businessmen. In return, the businessmen showed off their wealth in expensive suits, shoes and watches while they sealed investment deals and future favors from the influential people.

The women who attended the party were mostly wives of the politicians, bureaucrats and businessmen. They were rich socialites showing off their clothes and jewellery. She could hear the buzz of conversation which was mostly gossip.

Her mother had taught her to be kind and not to judge people. But the current company made it very hard for her not to.

She wanted to go up to the stage where the live music was playing and take the mike and scream into it saying, '**Don't you all care about City Central Park! The ruthless bastard who is the guest of honor wants to destroy it!**'

But she knew that before she could finish her speech about conserving the ecosystem and the health of the people living in the city, her father would have her escorted out of his home right away.

So she kept her instincts under control and decided to suffer through the party until she met the Prism chairman.

Her dress shimmered in the soft yellow lighting. Her father had the dress and matching accessories delivered to her earlier that morning. The woman who had dropped it off was also told to stay and help her get ready. But Tanvi sent the woman away insisting she could get ready on her own.

The dress was traditional yet modern. It was a long red gown with heavy ethnic embroidery. The sleeves of the dress were thin straps with a plunging neck that bared her back and a generous amount of cleavage. The long, sheer gold duppatta with embedded pearls was the only thing covering her nearly exposed cleavage.

It was the dress that had driven Arjun crazy. It was obvious to him and to anyone that her father wanted her to attract the attention of the billionaire businessman.

Normally, she would have ignored the dress her father had sent and chosen to wear something much simpler and sober. But since she had to attract the attention of the ruthless billionaire, she went ahead with the low-cut dress.

She pulled up her sheer duppatta as it began slipping. Her face heated since there was an obvious love bite right on top of her left breast where her arrogant devil had deliberately left his mark for the night.

Caveman.

"Hi, Tanvi."

Tanvi turned and was surprised to see her friend, Divya.

"Hello, Divya. What a pleasant surprise. How are you?"

Divya looked tensed and worried. Although Tanvi knew that Divya was always anxious, she sensed something was wrong.

"Are you okay?" she asked.

Divya shook her head. "C-can we talk somewhere?"

Although Tanvi wanted to find her father to let him know she had arrived, seeing her friend's anxious face, she nodded.

"Let's go into the house. We won't be disturbed there."

Divya nodded. Tanvi led her friend into the house and into the sitting room that had some privacy.

"What happened?" she asked.

Divya looked close to tears. "I-I got engaged recently. My father brought me here because m-my fiancé is attending the party."

Tanvi frowned. "Fiancé? I hope you mean Rahul."

Divya's face fell. "N-no. It's some other man. I'm getting married in two weeks."

"What?" Tanvi asked in shock. "How can you agree to marry some other man? Don't you love Rahul?"

Divya looked heartbroken. "I-I didn't exactly agree to marry the man. But I don't have a choice, Tanvi."

"Of course, you have a choice! This is ridiculous. Let me speak to your father and mother. Are they both here at the party?"

Divya shook her head vigorously and held Tanvi's hand tightly. "No! They will get angry with me for telling you. And it might be okay because m-my sister-in-law promised to help me break off the alliance. I-I trust her."

Tanvi frowned. She hadn't met Divya's sister-in-law. But she had heard about her from Divya and admired the other woman who was a self-made businesswoman. When Divya's brother had died in an accident, Divya's father had humiliated his daughter-in-law publicly during the funeral. Tanvi was proud of how Divya's sister-in-law had stood strong without falling apart.

"Are you sure you don't want me to speak to your parents?" Tanvi asked Divya.

Divya nodded again.

Tanvi had a bad feeling. "Why don't you talk to the guy your father is forcing you to marry?" Tanvi suggested. "Tell him that you don't want to marry him."

"I already did."

Tanvi frowned. "And yet, he still wants to marry you?"

Divya nodded hopelessly.

"Who is that man?" Tanvi wondered what kind of guy was willing to marry a woman who loved someone else or wasn't interested in marrying him.

Divya shook her head. "H-his name is Yash Varma. He is from New York."

Tanvi's heart jerked. *Oh my God. Is he the Prism chairman?*

No. He can't be. If Divya was engaged to the Prism chairman, why would my father try to pimp me out to the man as well?

Something was off.

"Is he the chairman of a company?" she asked.

Her friend nodded. "Yes."

Tanvi frowned. "Does he own the company that is destroying City Central Park to build a mall?"

Divya looked confused. "I-I don't think so. He owns a company that recently acquired my sister-in-law's software company. I'm not sure about the mall construction."

Tanvi continued to frown. If the man had acquired a software company, then he most likely owned a software enterprise as well.

But how many rich men could there be from New York who were investing in the city and hobnobbing with the city's elite?

It was odd.

Even though she knew the man Divya was engaged to wasn't the Prism chairman, she wanted to eliminate all possibilities.

"How does the man look?" she asked Divya.

Divya blushed despite her anxiousness. "He... is very good-looking, but in an intimidating way with a scar on his cheek. I couldn't stop looking at him even though I was scared of him."

Tanvi frowned. She made a note to look out for a good-looking man with a visible scar on his cheek.

"I don't know why he wants to marry me," Divya said in both confusion and quite a bit of awe. "I love Rahul, and I can't live without him. But... a part of me feels flattered that Yash Varma who is so... so... good-looking and a rich billionaire wants to marry me. Even I know that a man like him would never be interested in me under normal circumstances."

Tanvi didn't like her friend putting herself down. But from what she was hearing, it was quite strange that a billionaire from New York would want to marry someone in an arranged marriage.

Divya's father was modestly rich. But the older man wasn't influential or active in politics or the business circuit. Unless the man who got engaged to Divya was some sort of conman pretending to be a billionaire, there was no reason why he would want to marry a woman he had never met before.

"Be careful, Divya," she warned. "Don't spend time alone with that man. Something definitely seems off."

Divya nodded. "Narmada warned me as well not to talk or spend time with Yash Varma."

Divya's sister-in-law must have excellent instincts. Tanvi hoped the other woman would successfully stop Divya's marriage to the other man.

"All right," she said. "If you are sure your sister-in-law can help, I will not get involved. But if you need my help, don't hesitate to call me."

Divya nodded. Her friend thankfully looked slightly less anxious, knowing she had people who cared and could help.

"And you can meet Rahul at my place," she offered.

Divya's eyes grew big. "What! If my father finds out, he will kill Rahul and then me."

"I will be there with you, Divya. And if your father or anyone asks, tell them that Rahul is my boyfriend and you just came to visit me. You don't have to meet him right away. Meet him when things settle down. Your father might not even know."

Her friend bit her lip in nervousness and nodded.

"Let's get back to the party. My father and your parents might be looking for us."

They hurried back to the party. Like Tanvi had predicted, Divya's mother was looking for her. Greeting the older woman politely, Tanvi went in search of her father.

She spotted her father talking to someone in a business suit. Hoping that the man was the Prism chairman, she hurried towards them.

"Hello, Papa."

Her father turned and looked at her. A flash of annoyance passed through his eyes, but he immediately hid it with a forced smile. "You are late, Tanvi."

She put on an equally fake smile. "I came here a while ago, Papa. I was speaking to someone."

He frowned. "Who?"

"To my friend, Divya."

Her father's frown melted away, and he had a look of dismissal. "Oh. You mean Rajesh Mohan's daughter?"

She nodded. "She was telling me about her engagement."

Her father shrugged. "Yes, I heard."

Seeing her father look unbothered, she could confirm that Divya's fiancé wasn't the Prism chairman.

"Has the guest of honor arrived?" she asked.

Her father immediately frowned and looked upset. "Not yet. But we are hoping he will be here soon. He must have been caught up with some urgent work."

Tanvi hoped that the man would show up soon.

Her father dismissed her and returned to his conversation with the man in a suit. Meanwhile, she wandered around the party feeling strangely anxious.

She wanted to speak to the Prism chairman and get whatever information she could from him. But she also wanted to return home to Arjun because she was missing him desperately.

She wasn't hungry, and she decided not to drink alcohol that night. She needed all her senses alert to be able to speak coherently to the chairman and state her purpose clearly. So, she wandered away from the food and chose to wait inside the house.

Maybe I should call Arjun and let him know I'm still here.

She and Arjun didn't call or text each other. She had wanted to maintain distance from him outside their apartments. But she missed him deeply even though it had barely been a few hours since they were apart. She wanted to desperately speak to him.

At some point she knew she needed to acknowledge that the man she had barely known for a few weeks was beginning to mean so much to her.

It was only a matter of time when she and Arjun would have to part and go their separate ways. Arjun would find some other woman, and she would continue with her causes. But she knew that even if years passed by and they would end up with other people, Arjun would always remain in a special place in her heart. She would cherish the memories with him.

Letting out a deep sigh, she walked into the house and went towards her father's office wing. Thankfully, the place was empty since most guests only wandered in the living areas where the guest bathrooms were.

She slipped into the room next to her father's office which was thankfully unlocked. She knew her father was obsessively careful, and his office room would always be locked if he wasn't around.

She turned on the small table lamp in the room. The room was used as a waiting area by the people who had appointments with her father.

Closing the curtains to block the view outside, she dialed Arjun's number.

He didn't pick up.

She frowned and tried calling him again. But he still didn't pick up. It was close to ten in the night, and he was usually home around that time. Maybe he chose to go out because he knew she wouldn't be home until much later.

Feeling disappointed, she left a brief text message.

T: Getting bored. Wish you were here.

Letting out a sigh, she sat on one of the couches. She looked at the pictures and show pieces on the wall in the small room. When her mother was alive, they had used the room as a crafts room. Her mother was good at making beautiful crafts from reclaimed wood. But none of those pieces were on display. Strangely, paintings and artwork collected by the family who used to own the house before were on display.

A memory flashed in her mind. It was of her father getting upset with her mother when her mother had wanted to change something in the house.

Why did her father insist things remain as it is in the house? Yes, the décor was beautiful. But it felt like they were living with the ghosts of the family who had lived there before.

A small shiver racked through her body as she recalled what had happened to the other family. She hadn't known them well and had met them only once when she and her mother were invited to their estate along with her father.

"I told you the party would be boring, princess."

Tanvi shrieked out aloud, but she cut off the sound by placing her hand on her mouth.

She was shocked and nearly had a heart attack seeing Arjun standing next to the couch with an amused smirk. "Arjun! What are you doing here!"

He didn't say anything. He simply looked at her as she sat on the couch. Shock subsided quickly while panic began to take over.

"Arjun, you are in my father's house!"

The arrogant devil barely looked bothered. He simply grinned. "Thanks for letting me know, princess."

She sprang up from the couch. "Are you crazy! You have to leave before someone sees you! My father cannot know about you!"

"Aww, princess. I came this far to see you." He came closer and pulled her towards him. "I missed you too," he murmured against her lips.

She melted against him, but her panic didn't subside. "I will be back home in a couple of hours, you ass! You have to leave now!"

"Nope. Not before I lay claim to my woman once again."

She wanted to yell at the stubborn man and slap some sense into him. But she couldn't risk someone hearing them or seeing him. Her father would freak out and have a major meltdown if he found out about Arjun, especially on the night she was supposed to be introduced to an eligible billionaire who would help fund the elections.

"Arjun! I'm serious. You have to leave! I—" She broke off in a gasp when she was suddenly picked up and pushed back on the couch. Arjun lay on top of her.

"I'm serious too, princess," he growled. "I don't like it that some other man is going to enjoy your company and imagine you naked while you are trying to impress him."

She blushed at his words. "I already told you why I have to meet that man."

"Yes. I understand the reason perfectly. But that doesn't make me any less pissed off."

She stared at his handsome face as he scowled. Her arrogant devil was possessive. She knew she would feel the same about him. She would hate it if some other woman was trying to impress him.

"I want just you," she murmured.

And then, she held his face and kissed him. She had meant it to be a sweet kiss. But the moment their lips touched, they ignited like always. He caught the back of her head and kissed her passionately. She kissed him back, her hands clutching his broad shoulders while their tongues tangled.

He dragged his mouth away and groaned against her mouth. "I missed you. I want to be inside you."

A thrill ran inside her, and she desperately wanted the same. "Someone might come, Arjun." She panted even as he held the bottom of her long dress and began yanking it up.

"I locked the door. No one can come in."

She knew it was risky for him to stay. But her body was on fire. Her mind was filled with the thoughts of the man above her. Her body remembered the taste of him, the scent of his cologne and the feel of him deep inside her.

With trembling hands, she reached for his belt and began unbuckling it. That's when she realized he was wearing a suit and not his usual jeans and t-shirt. It was semi-dark in the room with light from only a small table lamp. And she had been in too much of a shock to register his clothes a while ago.

He must have snuck into the party wearing a suit so that no one would suspect his presence. Another thrill ran through her at his deviousness.

"Help me!" she said in frustration because she found it hard to unbuckle his belt. She didn't have the necessary experience or the skill to undress others.

The arrogant devil grinned because he already had her long skirt pushed up with her legs bare and exposed. His wicked fingers pushed her panties aside and slid in.

She groaned. "Arjun!" she cried out in desperation.

His fingers disappeared, and with a few quick movements, he unbuckled his belt and then pulled down the zipper of his trousers. Meanwhile, she wrapped her legs around his hips.

Her heart pounded in anticipation.

He grabbed her thighs and widened them before he thrust deep into her.

She cried out loud at the addicting sensation—the rough stretch of her internal muscles, the slight burn and the hot rush of pleasure.

"You feel so damn good, princess," he groaned against her ear, pulling out before thrusting again deeply. His teeth bit the sensitive lobe of her ear, making her body tremble.

Her head fell back, and she bit her bottom lip to stop from moaning loudly in pleasure. But the arrogant devil didn't allow her to hold back. His grip on her hips tightened before he possessed her. Faster and harder he pounded into her until harsh sounds escaped her throat.

She couldn't hold back the sounds.

He watched her while he claimed her. "You are mine, princess," he growled. His hand grabbed her breast in a rough possessive way. "Every part of you belongs to me just like I belong to you."

He leaned down and caught her lips in a rough kiss. "Don't ever forget it," he rasped.

His rough, possessive touch, his words and the way his body claimed her pushed her to the edge. She came hard. And when her body squeezed him with her internal muscles, he came hard as well, letting out a harsh cry. She clung to him as they trembled together.

Sounds of their heavy breaths filled the room as they tried to draw air into their lungs.

Sudden laughter from right outside the window jerked her back to reality.

Oh my God.

She realized she was in her father's house attending a party. And she just had sex with her arrogant lover who had crashed her father's party.

"Arjun! Get off!"

Panic filled her, and she tried to push him away. But the arrogant devil looked at her lazily.

"Give me a minute, princess. Don't wiggle so much unless you want round two."

"Stop it, you jerk! We might get caught. I'm sure my father must be looking for me."

With a groan, he moved away from her. He stood up and simply tucked himself in and zipped up his pants before he adjusted his belt.

He looked just like he was when he walked into the room. But she was a mess. She sprang up from the sofa and adjusted her dress which was wrinkled. Her hair luckily was left loose, so she only had to finger-comb it.

"How does my face look?" she asked, hoping her makeup hadn't smeared.

"You look damn sizzling hot, princess," he said huskily.

He lowered his head to kiss her, but she put her palm on his mouth and glared at him.

"Don't you dare! You need to leave now before you are discovered!"

Seeing her panic, his eyes softened. "Fine. I'll leave. But come home soon. I'll be waiting for you."

Her heart melted when he referred to their two apartments as home. She did consider them as home too. "Yes. I'll come home soon. Let me finish what I came here for."

He nodded. And then, giving her a sweet kiss on her palm, he stepped away. "See you later, princess," he said.

Then flashing his dimples, giving her a flying kiss with his two fingers, he slipped out of the room. Her heart thudded, and she waited anxiously, hoping no one stopped him on his way out.

Five minutes later, she slipped out of the small room. Brushing her hands over her long skirt, she went back to the party.

Everything seemed to be the same as before. The live music continued to play, and the guests continued to converse while drinks and food were served.

She caught the sight of her father's assistant and approached him. "Hello, Mr. Prasad. Has the guest of honor arrived yet?"

He shook his head. "Not yet, Miss Shetty."

Tanvi frowned. She was annoyed that the Prism chairman was ditching the event thrown in his honor. She knew her father must be beyond upset by the missing guest of honor as well.

"Thank you, Mr. Prasad," she said before walking away.

She decided to get herself a drink. Her cheeks heated when she realized that her recent bout of passionate sex in the small room made her feel thirsty.

What was Arjun thinking coming here!

And what was I thinking allowing the arrogant devil to get his way?

Her face heated, recalling their stolen moments.

"Tanvi?"

She turned and saw that it was Divya. "Oh, hi, Divya."

Her friend stared. "Are you feeling okay?" Divya asked. "You look flushed."

Controlling her blush, Tanvi nodded. "Yes. I'm fine. Just a little overheated with the crowd."

She knew the excuse sounded ridiculous, considering the party was held outdoors. But her friend simply nodded.

"Come on. Let's get some drinks and food. I am starving."

If she didn't get to meet the damn chairman, then at least she could have a drink and eat the expensive food her father must have ordered to impress the billionaire.

She picked up a drink and then sat down with Divya at one of the tables and let the uniformed men serve food on her plate. Since they were seated in public, she spoke to Divya about general topics, mostly about their common college friends.

It was midnight when Tanvi decided to leave.

"I'll see you later, Divya. Please don't hesitate to call me if you need anything."

Her friend nodded. "Thanks, Tanvi."

Waving her friend goodnight, she went in search of her father. She couldn't spot him anywhere in the lawn area. She saw his assistant waiting by the back entrance to the house.

"Hello, Mr. Prasad. I can't find my father anywhere. Please tell him I'm leaving."

The man nodded anxiously. "Sure, Miss Shetty. Your father is having a meeting and had asked not to let anyone disturb him."

She frowned, wondering who her father was meeting.

"Thanks, Mr. Prasad. Have a good night."

Her father's assistant followed her outside. "Narendar will drop you home, Miss Shetty," he said.

Since it was late at night, she agreed to have her father's driver drop her home.

She got into the back seat of the car. When the car began to move, she leaned back her head and closed her eyes.

She was angry and disappointed that she couldn't meet the chairman. But she was also looking forward to returning home to Arjun and falling asleep curled in his arms.

The thought made her smile.

CHAPTER TWENTY-EIGHT

"Mr. Varma. Thanks a lot for coming. I was hoping you'd come earlier so we could spend more time together."

Aryan was seated across from Girish Shetty in the older man's office room. The party hosted in Aryan's honor was continuing outside.

"I got tied up with another commitment, Mr. Shetty."

The older man nodded. "Yes, I understand. I'm simply glad that you were able to make it."

Aryan didn't say anything. He hadn't intended on attending the party that night. He had wanted the older man to be anxious about the large party funding that was promised at the beginning of the construction of the mall.

But knowing that Tanvi was attending the party, hoping to meet the Prism Corporation chairman, he decided to come. It was a huge risk. But he wanted to ensure she wasn't disappointed.

He knew it was flawed thinking because she would be disappointed for not meeting the chairman. But he wanted to distract her and fill her mind with thoughts of him to be able to forget the other disappointment.

He hoped it worked. The passionate moments in that small room were still branded in his mind.

"Mr. Varma. The construction of the mall is going to start in six weeks as planned. They will be cutting down trees in three weeks. All the politicians, officers and the contractors involved are here attending the party. They can vouch for the same."

Aryan sat back in the chair. "And your daughter?"

Something flashed in the older man's eyes. "My daughter promised not to intervene, Mr. Varma. She is here at the party, and she is very eager to meet you."

Aryan knew Tanvi had left the place fifteen minutes ago. He had received a notification that she was headed home. He was glad that she agreed to take one of her father's cars instead of choosing to call a taxi. He had asked Girish Shetty's assistant to follow her outside and personally put her in the car.

"This is my daughter's picture," the man said, pointing to a photo frame placed on the office desk. It hadn't been there during the previous visits. The photo seemed to be taken a couple of years ago. "She resembles my late wife."

"I know how your daughter looks, Mr. Shetty. Yes, she is beautiful. I've seen the videos of her protesting in front of the Prism building."

The older man's face reddened with embarrassment and anger. "Yes. She deeply regrets those moments as I had mentioned before."

Aryan kept quiet.

The older man fidgeted. "You see, Mr.Varma, my beautiful daughter is... available."

Something about the older man's tone made Aryan's skin crawl. He wasn't entirely sure if the man was trying to arrange a marriage alliance for his daughter.

"I'm not interested in marrying, Mr. Shetty," he said.

There was no disappointment in the older man's face. "Of course. You are still too young. But you see, my daughter is still available. She is ready to meet you and... please you."

That's when Aryan knew. The man in front of him was a sick bastard devoid of any morals. If the bastard could pimp his daughter to the highest bidder, he wouldn't shy away from murdering an innocent man for money and power.

Aryan wanted to punch the bastard's face. But he clenched his hands into fists and controlled himself. He was getting close to destroying the bastard in front of him. And he also needed to unearth the truth of what happened with his father all those years ago.

He got up from the chair. "I'll keep that in mind, Mr. Shetty," he said.

The old man looked satisfied. "Would you like to meet her now? I will send her to you."

Before Aryan was tempted to knock the old man unconscious, he stepped away. "Not tonight. It's already late, and I have to be somewhere else."

Girish Shetty nodded. "Yes, yes, of course." He gave a knowing smile as though he knew Aryan was going to another beautiful woman with whom he would be spending the night.

"Have a good night, Mr.Varma. It's a pleasure doing business with you."

Aryan nodded curtly before walking away from the sick bastard.

His heart raced due to uncontrollable anger. He couldn't believe that Girish Shetty had pimped his innocent daughter.

How the hell had Tanvi lived with that sick bastard?

He was glad she had left her childhood home and chose to live separately.

Clenching his jaw, he tried to bring his anger under control. He called his brother. Although it was midnight, he knew both his brothers would be awake.

Bhargav answered in the second ring. "What happened?" he asked.

"Girish Shetty. I am one hundred percent sure he is the mastermind behind Dad's murder. I'm going to get the bastard soon."

He ended the call and looked out of the darkly tinted car window.

The car stopped in front of the apartment complex. He got out and instructed his driver to go back to the penthouse.

With his mind still racing with anger and other dark emotions, he took the stairs to the fourth floor and went to his apartment. When he stepped inside, he didn't turn on the lights.

He went into his bedroom. His heart ached at the sight of the beautiful woman curled up on his bed.

He quickly shed his clothes and lay next to her before pulling her into his arms. She let out a small sigh and continued to sleep.

He took a deep breath of her fragrant hair and kissed her gently on the top of her head.

Tanvi Shetty.

He still couldn't define what she meant to him or what would happen to them when the truth came out. But he vowed he would protect her and keep her safe until his last breath.

CHAPTER TWENTY-NINE

Tanvi woke up to loud shouts.

Rubbing her groggy eyes, she sat up in her bed. It was dark and raining heavily outside. Her mother said there was a storm expected that night.

Although Tanvi was scared of the loud noises of the storms, her mother comforted her by saying storms were natural, and there was nothing to be scared about.

"Shh, you are safe, my love," her mother soothed her often.

Why isn't Mamma sleeping next to me?

Tanvi's mother always slept next to her during nights when there was a storm. But during the past week, her mother slept next to her instead of with her father. Tanvi loved holding her mother's big stomach where there was a baby inside. Tanvi's little brother or sister was expected to come out in one month.

Tanvi was excited because she would then have someone to play with.

But she didn't know why her mother was suddenly sad and angry. She saw her mother crying a few days ago and shouting at her father. Her father tried to console her mother, but her mother still seemed upset.

Tanvi frowned when she once again heard shouts coming from outside the bedroom.

"How could you have done that to innocent children, Girish!" her mother shouted. "Just because Parvathi didn't want you, you destroyed her entire family!"

"You are overreacting. I'm not responsible for anything. The fire was an accident."

"No, I'm not overreacting, and the fire wasn't an accident! You are a greedy, selfish and jealous man. I was stupid to ever trust you because you were Ganesh's best friend. I thought I could love you as much as I loved Ganesh, but your obsession with Parvathi consumes your life."

"You are my wife, and you are carrying my child. Forget whatever happened in the past."

"I can't forget! Not when I know you are capable of hurting even innocent children!"

Tanvi frowned, wondering who got hurt and why her mother was shouting. Her sweet, beautiful mother always smiled and laughed. The only time Tanvi saw her mother sad was when her mother looked at some man's picture. The man's name was Ganesh. Tanvi's mother called out the man's name when she cried, looking at the picture sometimes.

Suddenly, there was a loud scream.

Tanvi's heart thudded. Apart from the loud thunder outside, it was utterly calm outside her bedroom.

"Mamma?" she called out.

Pushing her blankets away, she got down from her bed. She opened the bedroom door, and it was dark in the hallway. The only light came from the lightning flashing outside the windows.

"Mamma?" she called again.

There was no response either from her mother or her father. Holding the railing of the staircase, she carefully went down the steps. She jumped as the thunder continued to rumble loudly in the sky.

When she reached the last step, her foot touched something. She didn't know what it was.

It was only when lightning flashed and the living room lit up, she saw what she had stumbled on. It was her mother lying in a pool of blood.

She screamed. "Mamma! Oh God. Mamma!"

She cried and tried to shake her mother awake, but her mother lay still and continued to bleed.

"Mamma, please get up. Don't leave me, Mamma! Mamma! Come back!"

Her mother didn't get up. But someone hugged her from behind. "Princess. I'm right here."

Tanvi got up with a jerk. She realized she was once again dreaming. The room was dark, and she felt warmth enveloping her from behind even as her body was covered with chills.

"You are okay, princess. I'm right here."

Arjun's deep voice comforted her while stroking her hair.

She realized she must have spoken out loud in her dream. She must have cried too as she could feel the wetness of her tears soaking her t-shirt.

Slowly, she felt the warmth of Arjun's embrace spreading within her, and her body stopped trembling violently. Only small chills shook her.

She felt embarrassed.

"Sorry, I woke you up with my nightmare."

She knew her nightmare was triggered after having spent hours at her father's home during the party.

"It's okay, princess." He pulled her into a tighter embrace until the chills subsided completely.

They lay like that silently.

Her heart continued to race due to the remnants of her dream. She hated that even though she had serious doubts about her mother's death, she hadn't told anyone. She hadn't trusted anyone.

Until now.

She didn't know much about Arjun, but she began to trust him. Her gut instincts told her that he did care for her the way she had begun caring for him. It wasn't just lust and attraction. She was now seeing the man behind the cocky attitude and began to fall for that man too.

"I-I dreamed about my mother," she whispered.

"You often dream of her. You had the same dream during the night of the storm too."

She nodded. "Yes. I had the same dream." She then took a deep breath. "B-but this time, I also recalled the conversation between my mother and father before she... fell down the stairs."

She felt Arjun's body tense. "Your father was there on the night of your mother's death?"

"Yes," she whispered. "They were arguing. I-I don't know if her fall was accidental, or if he deliberately pushed her down the stairs. But I know he wanted her to keep quiet about something."

Tanvi knew she shouldn't involve Arjun with what had happened in the past. Her father was powerful and dangerous. Arjun would not be able to challenge or do anything to a man like her father.

But she felt protected in Arjun's embrace.

"I'm sorry, princess. I'm sorry you had to go through your grief alone and hide the truth for so long."

Tanvi closed her eyes, and tears of relief leaked down her cheeks. Her chest felt slightly less burdened that someone other than her knew the truth of what happened on the night of her mother's death and believed her.

She took a deep breath. For the first time, she didn't feel utterly alone. Although she knew whatever she had with Arjun wouldn't last long, she felt cherished and protected by his presence.

"Thank you," she whispered.

"For what, princess?"

"For listening to me. And for being here. I loved every moment we spent together."

Suddenly, he turned her. He watched her with an intense look before his mouth twisted into a smile. "Don't thank me so soon, princess. Our deal won't end anytime soon. I'm going to stick around you for quite a long while."

Her cheeks heated in pleasure while warmth radiated inside her heart.

"I guess that makes you my boyfriend then," she said.

He smirked, flashing his dimples. "Yes, princess. You are my girlfriend."

She laughed, and held his face before she kissed him. He held the back of her head and returned the kiss. Although it started as a sweet, tender moment, soon passion ignited and spread like fire.

Lips clung. Hands reached out and touched each other everywhere. Their joining was raw and intense as always. But with their hearts thumping together and the way he looked at her while moving deep inside her, it made her feel it was more than lust-fueled desire.

It felt like lovemaking.

CHAPTER THIRTY

"Did you get abducted by the aliens and get dropped back with a different brain?"

Tanvi blinked at her friend's statement. Slowly, she focused and realized Rashmi was watching her with an amused look.

"Sorry, what?"

Rashmi laughed. "What's going on? For the past two hours, Kavita and I have been talking our heads off, and you barely said a word. You keep gazing in the distance with a dreamy smile. Who are you, and what have you done with our spitfire friend Tanvi?"

Tanvi blushed. "Nothing. I was just thinking about my work."

"Really?" Kavita asked. "You look more love-struck than anything else."

Tanvi's heart jerked. "No, I don't!"

"Yes, you do. It's the same look you and Rashmi accuse me of having from time to time."

It was true. Kavita often zoned out with a dreamy look whenever she spoke to or spent time with her fiancé.

"Okay, spill!" Rashmi demanded. "Who is that man who put a dreamy smile on your face."

Tanvi blushed. "No one."

"Oh, please. Kavita and I guessed it a while ago. But we want you to be the one to tell us."

Tanvi was surprised. "What?"

Rashmi grinned. "It was obvious when you spoke of seducing a man and showing up to our lunches with love bites on your neck."

Oh God.

Her face heated even as she cursed the arrogant devil who put those marks on her.

Rashmi laughed. "Kavita and I knew it was inevitable when we saw the way sparks flew between you and Arjun the night we went to the restaurant. We knew you both would end up with one another."

Tanvi was shocked. Even she hadn't known at that time.

She shook her head. "I didn't want to tell you both because you would worry. Arjun and I struck a temporary deal. It is only meant to be an affair."

Rashmi frowned. "But it's obvious that you are falling for him. And we saw that he couldn't take his eyes off you when we met. Why can't you both be together?"

Tanvi fell quiet. She couldn't tell her friends the entire truth about her father. It might endanger their lives or put them in trouble.

"My father won't approve of Arjun."

Her friends looked shocked.

"Since when do you do what your father asks you to?" Rashmi demanded with a disbelieving laugh.

Her friend was right. She had always opposed her father in almost all things. But when she fought for her causes, she wasn't putting anyone else in danger. If her father came to know about Arjun, he would immediately ensure Arjun was warned off. Arjun might even lose his job, and his family might be threatened.

After hearing so much about Arjun's mother and a little about his brothers, she hated the thought of that sweet family being harassed because of her.

But her heart ached at the thought of leaving him.

She looked at her friends who have always rooted for her happiness. They had always given her moral support during any fight with her father or an outsider, and they would continue doing the same.

She took a deep breath. "I'm going to tell my father about Arjun just before the elections."

Her friends smiled with joy. "Yes! That's our girl!" Rashmi said with an excited squeal.

Tanvi smiled even as she began to plan.

She was hoping to gain complete control of her trust before the elections. Without the money from her trust and the source of his campaign funding being cut off, her father would be left powerless.

The source of her father's campaign funding was the ruthless Prism chairman. The same man was also the main cause of the destruction of City Central Park.

If she could bring down that ruthless bastard on time, she would win over her cause and fight for the man she was falling in love with.

***

Tanvi was forming a list of the top real estate companies in New York.

It had taken her several hours to compile the list. And seeing the sheer number of companies, her mind spun. It was ridiculous and frustrating because all the damn companies looked the same.

She was about to throw her hands up in disgust when the door to her apartment opened.

Her stomach fluttered. Excitement and happiness bloomed, pushing away her frustration.

It was Arjun. He was wearing one of his bike jackets and sun glasses while holding his helmet.

"All right, princess. Let's go."

She frowned. "Go where?"

He grinned. "I'm kidnapping you for the day to an unknown place where no one is going to hear your screams."

She blushed and laughed. "Oh. How fun. Just so you know, your roars are louder than my screams. Especially last night."

He pulled her close. "Evil witch," he murmured against her lips. She knew he was referring to how she had deliberately driven him crazy to get back for the times he had prolonged her release.

She grinned.

His eyes flashed. "If I didn't plan a day picnic today, I would carry you into the bedroom to spank you and make you scream."

She blushed at his passionate threat.

"But we have to leave," he said. He kissed her noisily on the mouth before dragging her towards the door. "Come on. Let's go before we lose the daylight."

"Wait. Let me change first."

He turned and gave her a sweeping glance. "You look perfect as always, princess. Let's go."

She laughed. She was about to adjust her long ponytail, but she stopped. If they were going on his bike, her hair was going to be a mess anyway.

Feeling excited, she followed him.

They took the stairs. He wore the helmet so no one would recognize him.

He put on the spare helmet hanging from the bike on her. With her heart thumping excitedly, she sat behind him and wrapped her arms around his torso.

"Ready, princess?"

She nodded.

With a powerful kick, he started the bike, and they sped through the familiar streets.

Soon, the landscape changed. From being surrounded by the city buildings, the bike zipped through the highway with open areas and trees.

They drove for nearly two hours with Arjun occasionally asking her if she wanted a break, but she shook her head. She enjoyed the wind on her face and hair.

The bike began to slow down when they took a road off the highway. They passed by green fields surrounded by coconut trees. They then drove through an open gate which seemed like an entrance to someone's land. When the bike finally stopped, she got down and let out a gasp.

"Where are we?" she asked in awe.

There was a beautiful river surrounded by trees and vivid-colored flowering bushes.

He put both their helmets on the bike and smiled. "We are on a private estate. It belongs to an acquaintance."

"Oh. This place is beautiful."

It also looked somewhat familiar too. Maybe because it looked like picture-perfect scenery a child would draw or one found in paintings.

"The family who owns this place is having the house restored," he said. "But since it's a Sunday, the workers are not going to be here."

"Oh."

She was excited to spend their day in the beautiful private paradise. He opened the bike seat and drew out a takeout box along with a couple of bottles of water and soft drinks.

"Sandwiches and beverages," he said. "A royal picnic for the princess."

She giggled.

Smiling, he pulled her close and kissed her at the beautiful scenic spot. Throwing her hands around his neck, she kissed him back.

He groaned. "I always want to kiss you and touch you."

"Me, too," she whispered.

"Fuck. I'm going to miss you, princess."

Her heart jerked. "What?"

He had a regretful look on his face. "I have to go home tonight for two weeks. My brother is getting married. I'll be back as soon as I can."

Her heart felt heavy at the thought of him leaving, even if it was for only two weeks. But she knew she couldn't make him feel bad for going to his own brother's wedding.

She looked at him with a smirk. "Well, then I suppose I have to make the best use of our time. I need to make sure you don't hook up with some hot girl at your brother's wedding."

He laughed. "You are the hottest girl I know, princess. There's never going to be anyone like you."

Her heart melted. They kissed again. But this time, there was desperation because of not being with each other for the next two weeks. Her hands fell on his jacket to push it away from his shoulders. Meanwhile, he tugged on her t-shirt. They stripped each other while continuing to kiss desperately. And even before they were both completely naked, he had her pinned on the soft grass by the river and drove into her.

Her cries of ecstasy filled the air along with his harsh grunts as they made love. In between, they took brief breaks and fed each other picnic sandwiches. The weather was perfect, not too sunny and not too windy. A cool, pleasant breeze blew over their sweat-slicked skin as they sat on the grass by the river.

"Who is your brother marrying?" she asked.

A shadow passed by his eyes. But he smiled. "Someone he knew during childhood and met again recently."

She frowned at his tone. "Don't you like her?"

He laughed. "She's fine. It's just that my brother was supposed to marry someone else in two weeks. But he changed his mind about the bride."

"Oh."

She wasn't a romantic person. Until a few weeks ago, she would have found switching brides in the last minute to be irrational and dramatic. But after knowing how it feels to be with the person who makes you feel alive and touches your heart, she understood why Arjun's brother chose to marry a different woman.

"Is your mother okay with it?" she asked.

He nodded. "My mother would always want us to be happy regardless of who we marry."

His mother truly sounded wonderful.

I can't wait to meet her.

She blushed at the thought of having to meet Arjun's mother.

"What are you thinking, princess?"

"Nothing. So this is your oldest brother's wedding?" she asked.

He nodded. "Yeah. Although I sense that my other brother is not that far away from getting hitched as well."

She smiled. "You seem annoyed by your brothers' choices in brides. Are you jealous that no beautiful woman has proposed to you?" she teased.

She shrieked out loud when he pushed her back on the grass and fell on top of her. He tickled her, making her laugh uncontrollably.

"Take your words back," he said.

She shook her head, and he tickled her more, making her laugh with tears rolling down her eyes.

"Fine!" she said, laughing. "I'm sure there's a silly woman somewhere out there who wants an arrogant jerk as her husband."

She shrieked as he continued to tickle her. But soon, her laughter turned into a moan when his fingers slid in between her legs and into her intimate place.

"Don't you dare!" she said breathlessly, knowing what he was planning. He wanted to punish her by driving her crazy with arousal and prolonging her release.

The arrogant devil smirked. "I am going to dare, princess. I will keep you hanging until you say I'm the greatest man on earth and beg me to marry you."

He drove her crazy. But she drove him crazy back too. She gripped his arousal and squeezed while she bit his jaw and throat.

"Fuck," he groaned. "I shouldn't have taught you so damn well."

Laughing and groaning, they drove each other crazy until they both couldn't wait anymore.

He pushed into her, making them both groan. He held her face and looked into her eyes while he joined them together.

"You are all I want, princess."

Her heart melted as his words resonated deep inside her. He was the only one she wanted too.

They spent the rest of the day together, sharing laughter and making love. He spoke briefly about his childhood and told her that his father had loved nature too. His father had planted hundreds of trees and grew the best fruits and vegetables.

There was a shadow of darkness in his eyes whenever he spoke about his father. Her heart ached, and she felt a shared loss because she knew how it was to have a loving parent snatched away at a young age.

Soon, the sun began to set. They cleared up their small picnic, and he placed the bag back into the bike. Straightening their clothes, they got onto the bike and headed back home.

It was dark by the time they reached the apartment complex. They went to her flat.

He pulled her inside her small bathroom, where they washed away the dust and dirt from the long drive. She briefly thought he would be tired after driving for four hours, but she was wrong.

Her arrogant devil continued to make love to her. Against the bathroom wall. And then in her small kitchen. And then in her bedroom. By midnight, she was exhausted even though she clung to him and reveled in his possession.

"I'm going to miss you, princess. I'm going to miss you so damn much."

She would miss him too. Before she could say the words, she fell into an exhausted sleep in his arms.

CHAPTER THIRTY-ONE

Aryan looked at Tanvi. She had passed out in his arms.

She looked beautiful even though she had shadows under her eyes due to exhaustion. He had taken her to the Vardhaman Estate, and although she had visited it once during her childhood, she didn't recognize the place.

It somehow felt right to have her in his childhood home. Until then, he hated the place and the dark memories of the last two days he spent before being forced to flee the country.

But somehow, with Tanvi's company, all he recalled were the good memories spent during his childhood. He also made new memories that day with Tanvi, which he would carry with him for the two weeks apart from her.

"I'm going to miss you, princess."

Her eyes remained closed, and her breaths came out in soft puffs through her lips that were red and swollen from their kisses.

Two weeks wasn't long. But after getting used to seeing her each day, it would be hard to stay apart.

He had to go. He hadn't lied when he said his brother was getting married. Yash was not only getting married, he also wanted their mother to attend the wedding. The woman Yash was marrying was not Divya Mohan. It was the bride's sister-in-law, Narmada.

Aryan had a bad feeling about the wedding. But since Yash seemed determined to marry a woman who had hated him and vowed revenge, there was nothing Aryan could do.

Aryan knew he was being a hypocrite. He was obsessed with Tanvi despite her being his father's murderer's daughter. He desperately wanted a future with her and was willing to do anything to win her over when the truth came out.

In the last few days, he had wanted to tell her everything, but he had to stop and bide his time. He needed to put together the necessary proof first to convince her why he had to deceive and trap her.

He and his brothers were getting closer and closer to destroying their enemies and unraveling the truth. By telling Tanvi the truth without proof, he could risk the entire plan he and his brothers had put into motion.

He let out a sigh. "I'm sorry, princess. But I promise to tell you the truth soon."

Kissing her lips one last time and then brushing his lips on her forehead, he gently rolled her back on her pillow. Then covering her naked body with a blanket, he got out of bed.

He didn't pack anything for the trip. He and his brothers would be flying to New York, where most of their things were already in their penthouses.

He was both happy and wary about meeting his mother. After the confrontation on her birthday when she had slapped him, she hadn't spoken to him much. Mostly it was because she was on a holiday cruise and then busy with her school. He was determined to bring a smile to his mother's face again. He wanted to be there when his mother would be returning to her birth country after fifteen long years.

And most importantly, he couldn't wait to introduce the woman he loved to his mother.

"I'll be coming back for you, princess," he said softly, looking at Tanvi's sleeping form one last time.

Stepping out, he headed to the airport where a private jet was waiting to fly him and his brothers to New York.

CHAPTER THIRTY-TWO

Two weeks passed since Arjun went to his hometown to attend his brother's wedding.

Tanvi missed him, and to distract herself, she was on a cooking spree. She had been cooking huge batches of her favorite dishes and inviting her neighbors from the apartment complex over for dinner. That evening, she invited her friends, Rashmi and Kavita.

"My God, Tanvi," Rashmi remarked taking a bite of the chicken appetizer. "We never knew you cooked so well."

"Thanks," Tanvi said with a small smile. "I learned cooking recently."

"When is Arjun coming back?" Rashmi asked.

"I'm not sure. He should be returning from his hometown any day now."

She didn't know for sure. He had sent her text messages over the two weeks. But his last message was two days ago.

She had sent him a message the previous night, and she didn't want to send another one. She was sure he might have been tied up in the wedding festivities or other post-wedding events. Or maybe he was simply travelling and was on his way back.

"So how are you doing?" Kavita asked.

"I'm fine. Just missing him."

Missing him was an understatement.

Despite having lived alone for the last four years, she felt a huge emptiness with her arrogant neighbor gone.

During the weekdays, she stayed late in the office, still trying to dig up information on the Prism chairman and trace back to which real estate company from New York purchased Prism Corporation. When she came home, she cooked a simple meal and worked on her articles until she fell asleep with exhaustion.

The weekends were harder. She continued to work on the trust operations and getting the changes in the trust expedited. But later in the afternoon, since she didn't have much to do, she decided to cook and invite neighbors and friends over for dinner.

In just two weeks, she felt as though she and Arjun had been apart for a decade.

Her two friends exchanged knowing looks before they looked at her.

"You love him," Kavita said with a smile.

Tanvi opened her mouth to deny it, but she couldn't. She had fallen in love with her arrogant neighbor.

Rashmi shook her head with a laugh. "Aww. Kavita is already engaged. And now you have a steady hot boyfriend. I need to buck up and find someone before I become the fifth wheel."

Tanvi smiled. "What about Sameer?"

Her friend grinned. "He said we both are better off as friends. I think I agree too. I need someone who finds my talkativeness quirky and isn't overwhelmed by my awesomeness."

Tanvi laughed. "I agree."

Her friends cheered her up for the rest of the evening. They stayed until late. Rashmi even offered to sleep over.

"Guys, I'm fine. Yes, I miss him, but I'm okay. He might come back tonight since it's the fourteenth day."

Her friends seemed convinced by the last part. They didn't want to intrude in what they thought would be a passionate reunion.

"Fine. Call us if you need anything.

She hugged Rashmi and Kavita and waved them good bye.

She then cleared up the rest of the dishes in the kitchen and freshened up for the night. But she didn't sleep in her bed. Locking her apartment door, she went to the neighboring flat. She went into the bedroom and pulled out one of Arjun's shirts from his closet. Slipping it on, she slid into his bed.

She held his pillow that smelled like him. Taking a deep whiff of it, she slid into a deep sleep.

Come back soon, Arjun. I miss you. I love you.

***

A phone was ringing somewhere.

Tanvi groaned and wanted to ignore it for a moment. But she jerked and sat up and reached for it quickly. She hoped it was Arjun.

"Hello?"

"Hi, Tanvi."

It was Divya. Tanvi frowned. It was still dark outside which meant it was well after midnight.

"Divya, is everything okay?"

There were sounds in the background when Divya spoke, which meant either Divya was at some late party or she was travelling.

"Yes, I am okay, Tanvi. I called to let you know I got married."

Tanvi was shocked. "When? And to whom?"

Divya laughed. She sounded happy. "I got married two days ago to Rahul. We are in London now."

Tanvi was happy for her friend. "That's great news, Divya! Congratulations."

"Thank you. Rahul and I are very happy. My sister-in-law, Narmada, helped us get married and fly to London. Rahul even has a job here, and I am going to find one soon."

Tanvi was glad.

"My father is furious, but there is nothing he can do. He was already angry that Yash Varma dropped the alliance with me and chose Narmada instead."

Tanvi frowned. Something about it was oddly familiar. But her sleep-deprived mind couldn't place it.

"Thanks for offering to help me, Tanvi. You are one of my few friends who understood me."

Tanvi smiled. "You are welcome, Divya. Although I didn't do much."

"Oh no. You did. Your words gave me a lot of courage. I was able to be brave and fight for my love."

"I'm glad you took the step, Divya. I wish you all the best."

"Thank you. I will keep in touch. And I wish you all the best in finding a perfect man soon."

Tanvi smiled. "Thank you."

The call ended, and Tanvi continued to smile. She had already found her perfect man. Handsome, cocky and arrogant, Arjun did drive her crazy most of the time. But he was perfect for her.

She hoped that, like Divya, she would find a way to be with him without risking him in anyway because of her father.

She let out a sigh and hugged herself. Something jingled in the pocket of the shirt she was wearing. She had been too tired and put on the first shirt she saw in Arjun's closet. She realized it was a formal shirt.

She reached inside the pocket to remove whatever it was and place it on the nightstand. Her hand touched a cold metallic clip. She pulled it out and saw that it was a badge.

Arjun's access badge to Prism Corporation.

CHAPTER THIRTY-THREE

It took a week to find the perfect opportunity.

Tanvi's heart thudded as she headed to the Prism Corporation stairways. Every cell in her body told her to stop what she was planning and get back to her office desk. But another part, the part that felt passionate about her mission to save the City Central Park and to do everything to have a safe future with Arjun, urged her to go on.

She knew Arjun might be in huge trouble because of her. She would, of course, take the entire blame on herself and ensure Arjun didn't lose his job. But still, there was a big risk of him losing trust in her.

Her heart ached at the thought.

She loved Arjun. She would do anything to convince him of that fact.

This might be her only chance to meet the Prism chairman. She knew there was a board meeting scheduled for that morning. She was the one who had done the scheduling and booked the room.

Taking a deep breath and filling her mind with determination, she slipped into the stairway.

She headed up to the topmost floor.

Luckily, no one was using the stairs right then. Most likely because the few people who were allowed to the top floor always took the elevator.

She reached the top flight of the stairs. Biting her lip, she scanned Arjun's card. She held her breath and waited. Her breath released only when the green light started flickering, indicating the door had unlocked.

She pushed it open quickly and slipped inside the floor.

She waited near the door for a few moments. Then taking a deep breath, she began walking purposefully. The floor was big, and the conference room where the chairman was located could be anywhere.

She looked at the names of the rooms. The doors to the rooms near the stairway were closed. But those were most likely individual rooms. The chairman would have a corner office overlooking the financial district and lake. She hurried towards that area.

Her heart beat faster when she saw a big reception desk right in front of the lifts. There was a man seated there talking on the phone. Putting her head down and pretending as though she were meant to be there, she walked past the desk and went towards the other side.

"Excuse me, madam," the man at the reception desk called out.

Shit.

Pretending not to hear him, she continued walking purposefully. She knew it was a matter of time that the man at the reception would follow her to ask where she was going.

Before that happened, thankfully, she came across a hallway that had directions written to a board room.

This is it.

"Excuse me, madam. You are not allowed in there."

She heard the man's voice and began to run.

"Hey, stop!" the man said in a panic.

She stopped in front of the board room and pushed the door open before slipping inside. There was a presentation going on and men dressed in suits sat around a large oval table. The room was semi-dark, and the men in the room were focusing on the presentation.

"This is an excellent proposition, Mr. Varma. I agree that despite the tight timelines, we should proceed with the mall construction."

Her heart thudded, knowing she was in the right room. Without further delay, she turned on the lights.

"You can't be here, madam!" the receptionist burst into the room, joining her.

But as soon as the lights turned on and the panicked voice of the receptionist could be heard, everyone turned to her.

Tanvi's eyes fell on the man seated at the head of the table giving the presentation. Their eyes met, and her heart jerked to a stop as shock ripped through her.

"Arjun..." she whispered.

For a moment, she thought her mind was playing tricks on her because she missed the man she loved. But when she saw the expression on the man's face followed by the soft 'fuck' he uttered, she knew it was Arjun.

"Excuse me, gentlemen," he said before further confirming his identity. "I need to speak with my assistant."

Tanvi didn't wait to let him explain. She turned and ran out of the board room.

***

Fuck! Bloody fuck!

Aryan didn't expect things to blow up at the most inconvenient of the times. He was in an urgent meeting with the board members to settle the issue of the construction of the mall when Tanvi burst in.

How the hell did she get in?

He let out a frustrated breath before calling the head of his security.

"Seal all the stairway doors immediately," he instructed before striding towards the stairs.

Things were going to change drastically now that he could no longer pretend to be her neighbor turned lover. It wasn't the reunion he had been envisioning when he thought he would surprise Tanvi that night.

Regret pierced him at the thought.

***

Tanvi's heart thudded as she ran down the stairs. Her vision turned blurry due to tears, but she blinked them away.

He is one of them.

Her mind was numb with shock. She couldn't think of a single reason why someone would go to the extent of such an elaborate plan to trap her.

Pushing away the shock and hurt that threatened to overpower her, she focused on escaping the place. She stopped at the floor below and scanned her card before trying to pull the door open. But it didn't work. With trembling hands, she scanned Arjun's card. It didn't unlock with that either.

His name is not Arjun.

The thought threw her into further shock. She heard footsteps approaching on the stairs. Her heart thudded, and she continued running down the stairs.

There were fifteen floors in the building. She desperately tried to run down to the ground floor when she heard a familiar voice.

"Tanvi. Stop."

Her heart jerked hearing Arjun's voice. But she didn't stop. She continued running down the stairs.

She was panting hard when she reached the ground floor. And when she tried to open the door, once again, it was locked. She kept tugging it hard, hoping it would open or that the lock would break. But it stayed closed.

The footsteps turned louder. Feeling cornered, with her back against the door, she turned.

She saw the familiar face of Arjun. But he looked entirely different. He was wearing an expensive suit, but the cocky arrogant smirk on his face was missing. He held a determined look.

"Stop!" she shouted when he came purposefully towards her.

When he was just a couple of feet away, she tried to attack him with her nails. He caught her wrists and pinned her against the door with her hands on top of her head.

It reminded her of the time when he fake attacked her to prove she didn't know self-defense.

She struggled. But he held her captive with one hand. And then, using another, he made a phone call.

"Are you here yet?" he asked someone.

Listening to the reply, he ended the call.

She opened her mouth to shout at him, but he held out a hand, and a light mist covered her face. She coughed trying to avoid it. But soon, darkness covered the ends of her vision.

"Let me go, you bastard!" she tried to yell, but her voice came out slurred.

There was a grim look on his face. "Never, princess," he said. "I'm never letting you go."

At his reply, darkness took over completely.

CHAPTER THIRTY-FOUR

Tanvi groaned softly as she slowly awakened. Her head throbbed dully.

I must have overslept.

She stretched on the bed and loved how soft and plush it felt. She knew she was once again on Arjun's bed because it smelled of him. Smiling, she burrowed even deeper into the bedding, taking a deep inhale. Slowly, she opened her eyes to see if Arjun had returned, only to blink in confusion when she saw unfamiliar curtains.

She frowned. Arjun's bedroom didn't have curtains, and neither did hers. Their apartments only had window shades. And the windows weren't massive wall-to-wall extending from the ceiling to the floor.

Her heart began to pound as cobwebs in her mind began to disappear.

And then, it all rushed in—she using Arjun's access badge, barging into the boardroom and finding out that Arjun was the owner of Prism Corporation. She recalled trying to run away, but all exits were barred. Arjun then cornered her, and then there was darkness.

Oh God.

Her stomach turned queasy. She pushed away the plush bedding and got down from the bed hurriedly. She looked around quickly and ran towards what looked like the door to a bathroom. She ran towards it. And then, yanking the door open, she rushed to the toilet just in time to throw up.

There wasn't much in her stomach, but after it emptied, it stopped churning.

Flushing the toilet, she slowly got up. She was shocked to see a huge bathroom suite, nearly ten times the size of her apartment bathroom. There was a bathtub, a shower stall and a long countertop with dual sinks. Glossy marble and high-end fixtures screamed luxury.

Who the hell is he? Why did he go through such deception to trap me?

Her heart began thudding in fear.

In her experience, rich and powerful men often went to any extent to achieve what they wanted at the cost of others. She had seen her father being similarly ruthless.

How far would the man who trapped her go?

She shuddered.

But she took a deep breath. *No. I can't let fear overcome me.* She had been in dangerous situations before when she took on industrialists and other businessmen against whom she protested.

So what if the man who lay an elaborate trap for her and made her fall in love was more powerful and dangerous? She was going to fight him and escape.

She would not let him win.

She went to the sink and rinsed her mouth. Using her finger and toothpaste, she scrubbed her teeth and inside of her mouth. She refused to use the toothbrush that most likely belonged to him.

Splashing her face with cold water, she dried it with a towel. And then, with slightly trembling hands, she stepped out of the massive bathroom.

Her heart nearly stopped when she saw him waiting in the bedroom. He was standing by the bed.

"How are you feeling?" he asked.

A tidal wave of emotions overwhelmed her seeing him properly after nearly three weeks.

Anger. Happiness. Shock. Fear.

She clung to the anger. The fact that her heart raced with happiness for a few moments made her all the more angry.

He watched her quietly. Although her stupid heart continued to melt seeing the familiar face, her mind absorbed the fact that he wasn't the man she fell in love with. He wore an expensive suit, and it was the same one he had been wearing while attending the board meeting when she had barged in.

She wondered how much time had passed since he kidnapped her. If he hadn't changed his suit, it probably meant only a few hours had passed.

"Why am I here?" she demanded.

He didn't respond and continued to watch her.

A trickle of fear crept into her heart. "Are you going to kill me?"

His eyes flashed. "I'm not going to harm you in any way."

She shook her head. "I don't believe you. I know you are a ruthless bastard who came into my life and deliberately trapped me. And I also know I'm the only thing standing between you and what you want."

"What I want is to have you in my life," he said calmly.

Her heart jerked before anger filled it again. "Stop it! I'm not going to fall for your lies again!"

He continued to watch her silently.

"If you don't plan on killing me, what do you plan to do to me?" she demanded. "It will take weeks for the trees to be cut in the City Central Park and lay the foundation of the mall. You can't keep me here that long. People will know I'm missing."

His eyes flashed. "I don't care about the fucking mall. I never had any intention to cut down the trees to build a mall in the park. But I have to keep you here until things settle down."

She looked at him in disbelief. He was a billionaire with a real estate company who had come to India with the sole purpose to expand his company's presence in the city.

"I don't believe you," she snapped.

He let out a sigh. "I know it's hard to believe me right now. But I will reveal the truth when the time comes. Until then, you have to trust me—"

Before he could finish the sentence, she slapped him hard. It was involuntary as rage and hurt filled her at the word. "Don't ever ask me to trust you!" she yelled. "I don't care about your so-called truth. You are a ruthless bastard, and I want you to let me go!"

His eyes flashed darkly, and his nostrils flared. He clenched his palms into fists as though he was controlling himself from touching her. Whether to hurt her or something else, she didn't know.

At that instant, she didn't care.

"I know you are still in shock," he gritted. "So, I'll give you time to adjust. But know this, princess. I'm not letting you go."

CHAPTER THIRTY-FIVE

Aryan was quite pissed, worried and frustrated.

He was still in his bloody penthouse when he should have been with his brothers and mother, where there was an ongoing family crisis.

His brother was supposed to get married a week ago. But instead, Yash was not only ditched at the wedding, he got shot by their enemy.

Chaos had ensued, and he had been tied up for two straight weeks in putting out fires and ensuring nothing got out of hand. His brother was doing fine and was even planning a wedding in a couple of days. But with one enemy dead and the time to strike the remaining two enemies getting closer, Aryan had to stay back and finish what they started.

If only Tanvi hadn't found out the truth at the most inconvenient time.

He had miscalculated by thinking she would stop trying to unearth the truth about the new Prism owner after having tried for two months. But his fiery pawn was stubborn as always.

It hadn't struck him that she would go through his things and find his damn access badge.

Had she found it accidentally? Or was she deliberately searching through my things?

The shock on her face inside the boardroom seemed genuine. Until then, she hadn't known or suspected him.

Although he understood her anger and feeling of betrayal, he had no fucking idea how to fix it right then. He had to wait until he could tell her the truth because he couldn't risk her warning or confronting her father with the information she had.

That bastard would immediately be on alert if he knew the owner of Prism had been wooing his daughter under false pretenses. Girish Shetty would also find it too suspicious if that news coincided with the mall construction and other projects put on indefinite hold.

Fuck.

There was a knock on the door.

"Come in," he called out.

It was his housekeeper. The old man looked worried.

"Sir... madam is not opening the door. I have her dinner readied."

Aryan frowned. He knew Tanvi was going to give him trouble. But he needed her to stay put and be safe until things got sorted. He needed a few more days' time. And until then, he needed to let her know she has no choice but to remain in his penthouse as his guest.

"I'll take the dinner to her room. You can leave now."

The old man nodded and left.

Frowning, Aryan left the guest bedroom and went to the master bedroom where Tanvi was going to stay. The dinner cart was left right outside.

He entered the bedroom code and pushed the door open before taking the dinner cart inside. It was dark inside the room.

"I want to be left alone!" an angry feminine voice growled.

He turned on the lights. Tanvi was seated on the bed. She blinked with the sudden lighting, but her face went back to the original glare.

"I have to leave tonight," he said. "I won't be back until a while. I want you to stay put and not trouble my housekeeper or the maids. I know you are angry. But you have to trust me on this. When I come back, we'll talk again."

She was quiet.

He pushed the cart towards the bed and opened the covers on the dishes. Serving a little of everything on the plate, he handed it to her.

She looked at the plate and then at him. With a sudden move, she swung her hand on the plate and knocked it out of his hand. The plate fell and crashed into pieces, the contents spilling all over his new suit.

She tried to run towards the open bedroom door. But before she could take a few steps, he wrapped a hand around her waist and threw her on the bed.

She hissed and fought him. "Let me go, you bastard!"

Anger shot through him.

The lack of sleep for the last two weeks also caused his patience to run thin. "Don't bloody push me, princess," he growled.

She looked at him and glared. "Fuck you, you ruthless bastard!"

He knew she had a reason for being more than upset. But weeks of being apart from her and missing her every damn moment, and the stress from the anger, fear and worry for his brother over the last two weeks took a toll on him. He snapped.

He caught her jaw in a firm grip and crashed his mouth on top of hers. A shocked sound escaped her throat. And then she was angry. She bit down on his bottom lip hard until he could taste the slight metallic tang of his blood.

He didn't care for the slice of pain. He thrust his tongue deep into her mouth and groaned at her sweet, familiar taste which felt like homecoming after so damn long. He kissed her with a rough intensity, wanting and seeking what only she could give.

Her nails dug into his arms, hurting him even as her tongue tangled with his. The sounds of her anger turned into a moan while he deepened the kiss. He continued to kiss her and touch her. He cupped her breast and brushed the hardened bud on the top with his thumb. His hands were starving for the feel of her body, which he badly missed in the weeks they had been apart.

He wanted to kiss her, taste her and touch her everywhere like before and let her fill his senses.

"I missed you so damn much, princess," he groaned, pushing his hard arousal against her softness. He wanted to lose himself in her body and claim her until they both collapsed with exhaustion.

She suddenly stiffened under him. He knew the exact moment she got back to hating him again.

She turned her head to the side. "Get off me!" she hissed.

Fuck. He shouldn't have spoken out loud. He should have continued to kiss her until she forgot everything. But his fiery pawn wasn't willing to forget or forgive anytime soon.

She tried to shove him off her. "I said get off!"

Groaning internally, he dragged his painfully aroused body away from her and stood up.

"Don't ever touch me!" she yelled, scrambling up from the bed.

The tips of her breasts were hardened against the soft material of her t-shirt, and her face was flushed. He knew if he slid his fingers into her soft core, she would be dripping wet with arousal.

But she was also angry and hurt.

So taking a deep breath, he took a step away from her while trying to bring his body under control. "I'll send a maid to clean up. There are cameras in every room, and the doors are automatically locked from outside. Don't try to escape."

With those instructions, he turned away and walked out the door.

"I hate you!" she screamed. "I won't let you get away with this, you bastard!"

He had barely stepped out of the bedroom suite when something crashed against the door, a split moment after it closed. It must have been either a book or the digital clock placed on the nightstand.

He let out a sigh. His fiery pawn was definitely going to be the death of him.

CHAPTER THIRTY-SIX

Tanvi's mind was in huge turmoil.

She hadn't slept the entire night. She was angry.

How could I respond to his kiss!

For a moment, her heart and mind had become confused thinking she was kissing Arjun, the man she fell in love with and had missed so much. The familiar touch of his lips along with his demanding tongue made her melt against him.

But it was only much later she realized that Arjun was only an illusion. And the man kissing her was a fraud who had deceived her into falling in love with him.

Her eyes took in the large luxurious bedroom suite with a stunning view of the city. She compared it with Arjun's small apartment across from hers where she had spent most of her time with him.

The contrast of it made her beyond pissed. He had known exactly how to trap her. With his simple lifestyle, delicious food and a sexy, arrogant smirk, the ruthless bastard knew exactly what he was doing.

And she had fallen into his trap easily.

I hate him!

She had to escape him somehow.

***

She was prepared for yet another blowout when Arjun, or rather Aryan Varma, came back. But the ruthless bastard didn't come the next day. Instead, someone else came.

She knew it wasn't Arjun. There was a tentative knock on the door. Even when she had known Arjun as her arrogant neighbor, he was never hesitant.

"Tanvi?" a familiar man's voice called out. "May I come in?"

Tanvi was shocked.

"Come in," she said.

The door to the bedroom opened, and she saw Sameer entering.

"Uh... hello, Tanvi. How are you? Mr. Varma... I mean... Arjun has sent me here to speak with you."

Tanvi stared at Sameer in shock while he shifted uncomfortably with a guilt-ridden expression.

"My God," she said. "You are a part of the ruthless bastard's deception too?"

The guilt on his face grew. "I'm so sorry, Tanvi. I know you must be shocked and angry. But Mr. Varma did all this for a reason. He and his brothers had to—"

"Stop!" she cut him off. "I don't care why the ruthless bastard deceived me. I want to know your role in it."

Sameer's face fell, and he became suddenly silent.

"Tell me, Sameer!" she demanded. "What was your role in this?"

He looked like he was about to throw up. "I-I... I had to trap you. Become close to you, and then... make you fall in love with me."

She was stunned.

"But you moved into the apartments two months before he did. Did he ask you to trap me when he came into the apartment complex?"

Sameer shook his head. "No. I was sent there before. But when I couldn't catch your attention for two months, Mr. Varma purchased the entire apartment complex and moved in as your immediate neighbor."

The sheer length to which that ruthless bastard went to for trapping her shocked her.

All of this for a bloody mall and a few construction projects?

He was despicable.

"Why did he send you to me now?" she demanded. "Does he expect you to trap me even now too?"

"No. He sent me to keep you company until he returns."

Where the hell did he go?

She was sure he was moving things at a faster pace for the mall construction. She didn't believe him when he said he had no intention of destroying the City Central Park to build his mall.

He was a player who used lies and deception to lay a trap for her.

No more. Even though he had the upper hand at the moment because he kidnapped her and held her captive, she was determined to trap the player in his own wicked games.

CHAPTER THIRTY-SEVEN

The ruthless bastard returned ten days later.

Tanvi was on the balcony of the penthouse by a huge swimming pool. She and Sameer were playing a game of chess.

Sameer came in each morning and stayed until dinner before he left the penthouse to return the next day. The place was maintained with heavy security, and she couldn't open the main door to escape. And when she tried to talk Sameer into helping her escape, he looked guilty and helpless.

Although she hated that Sameer was a part of the deception too, she knew he was genuinely nice. She believed him when he said he agreed to the deceit for the sake of his family.

"By no means did Mr. Varma exploit me. He did give me a choice many times to walk away, and he would still compensate for what he had agreed to pay me. He had already given me a job at Prism and paid for my sister's college education. Walking away would have been easy for me, but I wanted to stay because I wanted to make sure you are fine. I knew Mr. Varma wouldn't hurt you and genuinely liked you. But I was concerned about what would happen when you discovered the truth..."

She did believe Sameer about everything. But Sameer was wrong when he thought Arjun genuinely liked her. The ruthless bastard was just a very good actor, that's all.

"Oh, hello, Mr. Varma!" Sameer greeted when Aryan Varma walked into the outdoor pool area.

Tanvi threw him a glare before focusing on her chess game.

But the brief glare was enough to take in everything about him. He was wearing yet another expensive suit. He looked slightly leaner in the face and a little tired.

She wondered what had happened to make him look tired and tensed and lose a bit of weight. Was he worried about what she would do when he released her?

He should worry, the ruthless bastard.

But despite her anger, there was a strange hollow feeling inside her stomach at the thought of him suffering.

"Good evening," he greeted in a deep voice. He walked towards the bar area by the pool. "Drinks?" he asked.

Sameer shook his head. "Just some sparkling water for me, Mr. Varma. I have to drive back home."

There was a sound of a bottle opening and small clinks of ice. A crystal glass with sparkling water and ice was placed next to the chess board in front of Sameer.

"And you, Miss Shetty. What would you like to have?"

Her cheeks heated at his deep voice calling by her last name. Flashes of what they had done to each other during their passionate affair filled her mind like some B-grade movie reel.

Controlling the heat in her cheeks, she glared at him. "Nothing except for my freedom," she snapped.

He was watching her closely. His eyes passing on every feature of her face as though he missed her for so long.

Liar. Bastard.

"When will I get my freedom, you lying bastard?" she demanded.

His eyes flashed. "You'll have to wait a while for that," he replied.

"Then there is nothing else I want from you, you deceiving creep!"

His mouth twisted slightly. "Your language seems to have gotten worse while I was away, Miss Shetty."

She narrowed her eyes. "No, it hasn't. Had it gotten worse, I would call you a son-of-a-bitch. But I happen to respect women and your mom. That is if she exists."

His eyes flashed again. "She does exist and everything I told you about her is true. She is a teacher who teaches kids in underprivileged neighborhood."

Her heart jerked. How much of what he had said was the truth?

No! Don't trust him.

Before she once again fell for his lies, she turned away from him. "Your move," she told Sameer, focusing on their chess game.

Sameer looked uncomfortable, but he stayed as though to ensure things between her and Aryan Varma didn't get worse. He moved a chess piece.

"You have to be careful, Sameer," she said. "Even a small pawn can kill the ruthless bastard enemy king. Check."

Sameer looked at the board where his king was trapped by a pawn. He looked like he was about to concede the game, but a masculine hand picked up the king and moved it away from being captured.

Annoyed, she wanted to stop the game. But her ego wanted to win over the ruthless bastard, even if it was a chess game. So she played, systematically deciding to surround the enemy king.

But a few moves later, the ruthless bastard had her king cornered.

"You are right," he drawled. "You never know when a pawn could become the queen and capture the heart of the king."

He had moved one of Sameer's pawns to her side to the spot of the queen. And then, placed a checkmate.

She glared at him. "Queens don't capture the heart of the enemy king. They kill them."

His mouth twisted. "We don't know what happens once the war is won, Miss Shetty. A pawn can turn into a queen and capture the heart of the enemy king."

Annoyed, she got up from her chair to walk away. But she suddenly stopped.

Aryan Varma had pretended to like her to make her fall in love with him. But the ruthless bastard had genuinely been pretty possessive. She wanted to test that theory and get back at him in every way possible.

She turned to him. "You mean nothing to me," she said. "What happened between us also meant nothing. It was only an affair. A means to satisfy an itch. You are the last man I would fall for."

Aryan's Varma's eyes intensified scarily, but she was determined to poke the bull.

She looked away from him and turned to Sameer. "You are the one I have always liked, Sameer," she said. "I was silly not to act on it at that time."

Sameer looked shocked and uncomfortable. She smiled, and then with an exaggerated sultry swing of her hips, she took a step closer to him.

She placed her hands on Sameer's chest. "You know. These last few days spent together, especially away from the cameras, meant a lot to me."

Sameer's eyes grew wider at her implication of having had a torrid affair under the nose of Aryan Varma. "Tanvi, please," he said, looking shocked and worried.

"Kiss me, Sameer. Let's not care about anyone else. We should elope and marry right away as we planned..."

There was an angry growl. A moment later, it was followed by her gasp when she was dragged against a hard body.

Outraged, she tried to escape by kicking back hard. Her feet made contact a few times, but the hard muscled arm around her waist didn't move.

"Let me go, you ruthless, lying, deceiving bastard! I hate you! I'm going to ruin you! I'll make sure you will not be allowed to do business anywhere in the world. You will rot in prison and beg for my mercy."

She continued to kick and struggle while cursing and threatening him, but the grip around the waist remained unmoved.

"I'll speak to you later, Sameer," Aryan Varma's voice rumbled from behind her.

"Uh... okay, Mr. Varma." Sameer looked at her with a concerned yet guilty look before he turned and left.

A hard kick of hers landed on the shin. Aryan Varma let out a grunt. Before she could plan another kick at the same spot, he picked her up and flung her on top of his shoulder. And like a caveman that he was, he carried her away.

"Let me down, you crooked bastard! How dare you!"

He let her down, but it was in the dining area where dinner was set up on the table along with candle lights. Each day, she had her meals with Sameer, but the table was never set up in a romantic way.

"I don't want to have dinner with you!"

He looked at her. "Then what else do want us to do?" he asked. His heated gaze slowly slid over her, leaving a trail of fire on her skin.

She was pissed by her body's reaction. "Never!" she spat. "You will never get to touch me again. What happened between us before was a terrible mistake."

His mouth twisted into a small, scorching smile. "Never say never, princess."

Heat exploded in her stomach and spread to her body. "Don't call me princess! You are not the man I thought you were! I hate you!"

She turned and ran from him. She went into the bedroom and banged the door shut, locking it.

Taking a deep breath, she decided to take a cold shower to snap back to her senses. The ruthless bastard still had the ability to heat her body with a mere look.

Ugh.

She went into the bathroom and took a quick cold shower. With great effort she kept her mind off the ruthless man. Instead, she thought about what her next steps needed to be. She couldn't afford to stall any longer. She had to escape. There were too many critical things going on that had to be done on time. The cutting down of trees at the City Central Park had to be stopped and also things in her trust had to be set in motion.

Shivering due to the cold water and also the heavy tasks set before her, she stepped out of the shower. And then, wrapping a towel around her body, she stepped out of the bathroom.

She nearly screamed when she saw Aryan Varma in the walk-in closet area in just his underwear. He was taking out a fresh pair of clothes from his closet.

"What the hell are you doing here!" she shouted, even as her eyes moved over his bare chest.

"This is my bedroom, princess. My clothes are here."

She knew that already after having been stuck in his bedroom for nearly ten days. She didn't know why she hadn't slept in a different room when she discovered it was his. His familiar cologne, even though it angered her, had made her feel safer.

"I locked the bedroom for a reason. Get out!"

At her order, he began to walk. But instead of moving towards the bedroom door, he walked towards her. He stopped right in front of her and placed both his hands on either side of her, trapping her in between.

Her heart thudded. Whether it was anger or excitement or maybe even both, she couldn't tell. But she latched on to the anger.

"I told you not to touch me!" she said.

"I'm not touching you," he replied.

He was right. He wasn't technically touching her. But the buzzing electricity due to his nearness made it seem like he was touching her everywhere.

She still missed the ruthless bastard. Missed his touch. Missed his arrogant smiles. Missed his smirks. Her eyes fell on his familiar features and then his body, recalling all the times when she had touched and kissed him everywhere, exploring the fascinating taste and texture of him.

"I don't want you near me," she whispered, even as her breaths turned faster.

His eyes turned intensely dark, and his chest rose and fell with deeper breaths.

"Why?" he asked before lowering his head.

She held her breath when his nose neared the knot tied right above her cleavage. He didn't touch her, but the deep inhale he took made her skin break into goosebumps. The cold shower became useless when her body heated up dangerously.

He raised his head and took another deep whiff, this time right behind her ear.

She shivered. "Because I hate you," she said belatedly. Her voice didn't hold much conviction either.

The arrogant bastard knew that as well because he smiled wickedly. "Just because you say it out loud many times or think it, doesn't make it true, princess. You don't hate me. The opposite of it is true."

She once again became pissed because he was right.

"I do hate you!" she said, this time with more conviction. "I hate how you made me fall for you. I hate how made me believe we had something special between us. I will never forgive you for that!"

Hurling those statements, she pushed him away from her. When he took a small step back, she stormed back into the bathroom and shut the door. Leaning against it, she closed her eyes.

Deep inside, she knew why she didn't want to listen to what he had to say. Because she knew she would once again believe his lies and fall for his trap.

Because everything inside her badly wanted to believe the man she still loved.

CHAPTER THIRTY-EIGHT

Fuck.

Aryan was beyond frustrated.

After the initial two weeks of hell had extended to two more weeks because his other brother, Bhargav, was shot and injured as well, like Yash, things turned chaotic once again.

Even though two enemies out of three were trapped, the most dangerous enemy was still out there. Girish Shetty had recently found out the construction of the mall project had been halted. The older man had also found out he was being cut out of the rest of the projects.

Bankrupt along with his goodwill destroyed, the old bastard was downright dangerous.

Aryan was determined to have Tanvi stay in the penthouse until the old score with her father was settled.

But Aryan discovered that holding the woman he loved captive in his penthouse was like trying to trap a storm. Tanvi Shetty unleashed her fury on him and let her presence be known each and every moment. Not that he could ever forget her, even for a moment. Even when he was physically away from her over the last few weeks, she had been a constant presence in his mind.

Both his brothers were now married, and the women they chose as their wives were sweet and friendly. He couldn't wait for his extended family to meet Tanvi, but that moment seemed quite far away.

If only his fiery she-devil didn't glare at him with equal parts of fury and hurt.

"Mr. Varma, are you sure you don't want me to come tomorrow?"

Aryan was on a call with Sameer. "Yes. I will be here from now on. I appreciate you agreeing to keep her company while I was gone."

"You are welcome, Mr. Varma. I do consider Tanvi as a good friend, and I do hope things between the two of you get resolved soon."

Aryan didn't say anything. He knew Sameer meant well and did consider Tanvi as a friend. But Tanvi's deliberate showdown where she tried to hint she was having an affair with Sameer was still annoying. The she-devil knew exactly how to push his buttons.

Thanking the other man again, Aryan ended the call. He then went to the master bedroom to ask Tanvi to join him for dinner when he noticed she wasn't inside. He looked for her in the other bedrooms, and she wasn't there as well.

Frowning, he went to the living room, half expecting the door to be open and her being gone. But he was taken aback when he saw her seated at the dining table.

She was already eating.

With a slight shake of his head and suppressing a smile, he joined her at the table.

She threw him a cold look that would freeze any other man. It made him all the more determined to break through her cold anger.

He placed a thin folder on the table next to her.

"Official order to stop the construction of the mall in the City Central Park. The mall has been relocated to an alternate place that does not involve disturbing the ecosystem."

She froze, but a few moments later, she resumed eating.

He knew it wasn't going to be easy for him to make her believe him. But nothing with Tanvi Shetty ever was. The woman was fiery, passionate and stubborn as a mule.

"It was never about the mall," he once again told her. "The reason I came into your life was very personal. It involves our families."

She glared at him then. "I looked you up. You are from New York. You became a billionaire at the age of twenty with your software company. Your brothers had their own businesses and were billionaires when you studied at Harvard at the age of sixteen. My father had never been to New York. Neither did my mother or I."

He fell silent. He couldn't tell her about what had transpired between their families fifteen years ago, not without risking everything.

Although he trusted her, the circumstances were too volatile to risk Girish Shetty finding out that the family he thought was dead was responsible for his complete ruination.

He looked at her. "When you know my brothers and I are already billionaires, why do you think I'd go to an extreme length to trap you for just the construction of a mall?"

There was a small frown on her face as though she had been having similar doubts. But her frown cleared, and she threw him a cool look. "Greed. For most corporates, nothing is ever enough."

"Then why do you think I got the mall construction at the City Central Park halted?"

She shrugged. "Because you don't want to risk a bad reputation for you or your company. Because I discovered your deception."

He laughed. "Princess, I have never given a damn about my reputation or my company's. And if it ever comes to a showdown, it's my word against yours. I could easily say I don't know who you are and that you are deliberately accusing me because of your cause."

There was a small pause as doubt filled her mind.

"Yes, I deliberately trapped you. But it wasn't for a mall or anything to do with money. It was personal. But after having met you and what we had between us, it was no longer pretense for me. What we have between us is real."

She shook her head as though warding off his words. "I don't believe you. You are a playboy. I saw your pictures with hundreds of women. This is just some kind of elaborate game you are playing for cheap thrills."

He knew she was justified to feel that way because of his playboy reputation, but still anger shot up inside him. "Cheap thrills?" he asked. "So you think I stopped myself from sleeping with you at the beginning of our deal for cheap thrills? Even though I fucking craved you every damn second, I didn't want to have sex under false pretenses. I wanted to wait until the truth came out. It was you who broke me."

Her cheeks reddened at his reminder of her relentless seduction.

"I had a shit-ton of things going on in my bloody life for the past month. Both my brothers' lives were in danger, and I had to see to them and my mother while also following up with things my brothers and I set into motion. But all the while, each and every moment, I thought about you. Whether you hated me and whether you would ever forgive me or whether I would lose you. Why would I think of you if it was only a cheap thrill for me?"

She looked shocked and uncertain.

"Yes, ours is not a conventional boy-meets-girl cute love story. Deception and lies were involved, and I had laid out a trap for you. It was wrong. But at the end of the day, we both did fall in love with each other.

Outside of my family, you are the only one who matters to me and who I would sacrifice my life for. I love you and am willing to do anything to have you in my life."

Her lips wobbled, and her eyes glazed with tears. But she quickly blinked them away.

She stared at him. "I can't trust you," she said.

It felt like a punch to his stomach. "I know, princess. But give us a chance. Give me time to win over your trust."

She was quiet. And then, she took a deep breath and looked at him. "Then trust me too. Remove the security guarding me. Let me be free to go in and out of the penthouse."

This time he fell quiet. He knew it was a huge risk to lower his guard right then. But it seemed to be the only way to win her trust.

"All right. I will remove the guards outside the penthouse starting tonight. But I prefer that you don't go out until I say it is safe."

She frowned. "Who would try to harm me?"

He looked at her. "Your father."

There was a look of shock on her face. But surprisingly, she didn't say anything.

"I know you might find it hard to believe it. But in time, I will tell you everything."

The rest of the dinner continued in silence. Once again, he felt a pang of regret for losing her trust. He recalled their laughter-filled meals where he teased her often and she always had a sassy remark in return. He knew it would take time to get there once again.

"Leave them," he said when they finished their meal, and she got up to clear the dishes.

She nodded.

He led her towards the master bedroom. As they walked together, he could sense her nervousness. She bit her bottom lip and avoided looking at him.

He wanted to push her against the wall, kiss her until all her doubts vanished and they would once again lose themselves in hot passion. But he clenched his fists. Taking a deep breath, he controlled himself as they reached the bedroom.

"Good night, princess," he said. "I'll see you in the morning. Let's cook breakfast together."

She looked shocked that he was leaving her. "Okay," she whispered. "Good night."

His body screamed when he walked away from her and went into one of the guest bedrooms.

He stared into the night through the glass wall before pulling out his phone and calling the head of security.

"Discharge men from outside my penthouse starting tonight. I'll call and give further instructions." With that order, he ended the call.

It was a huge risk he was taking. But he wasn't lying when he told Tanvi he was willing to do anything to win back her trust.

He continued to stare into the night unable to sleep knowing that the woman he loved and desired was in the same house, but he couldn't touch her.

Five damn weeks was a long time being away from her. Even though thoughts of her and memories of their time together helped him blow off steam, he craved to hold her in his arms.

He didn't know how long he had been staring into the night when the bedroom door clicked open. Frowning, he turned. The housekeeper or anyone else always knocked before entering.

But it wasn't any of his household help. It was Tanvi.

With soft light falling on her face, she looked otherworldly and dreamlike as she walked towards him. He wondered if he had been craving her so much that he was imagining things. But she stopped in front of him and touched him, proving she was real.

She placed her palm on his chest. "I still think you are an arrogant, deceiving bastard," she said. "I won't forgive you anytime soon and plan to make your life miserable. But... I don't want to sleep alone tonight."

CHAPTER THIRTY-NINE

Tanvi's heart raced. The heat in Arjun's eyes stripped away the thin material of her night clothes.

She gasped when his arm wrapped around her waist and pulled her close until her chest was pressed against his hard one. "I'll do anything to win back your trust, princess. Just anything. I already ordered the security outside the penthouse to leave tonight. Tell me what else you want?"

Her heart thudded. She wanted to ask him who he really was and why he had laid out an elaborate trap for her. She wanted to ask him what he had been doing during the weeks he had disappeared, leaving her alone. And she also wanted to ask him why he wanted to keep her safe from her father.

But all those questions would have to wait. Right then, she wanted the man in front of her way too much. She missed him. She missed his cocky, arrogant smirks. She missed the sounds of his deep groans. And she missed his sweet, tender smiles when he held her and they fell asleep in each other's arms.

She stared at him with her heart thudding hard inside her chest. "You," she replied to his earlier question. "I want you."

His eyes flared, and the grip on her waist increased as he stared into her eyes. Then, letting out a harsh sound, his lips crashed against hers.

She moaned as her body caught fire. Throwing her arms around his neck, she kissed him back greedily. But touching him and kissing him wasn't enough. Weeks of being apart made her insane for him.

Dragging her lips away from his ravaging mouth, she whispered. "Now. I want you now. I don't want to wait."

He groaned. And then, letting out a rough animal-like sound, he picked her up by the waist and carried her to the bed. A gasp escaped her mouth when he dropped her on the mattress. He didn't move away.

He tugged at her clothes frantically, baring her legs. He groaned when her hands cupped his hardness through the material of his trousers.

"We should slow down, princess," he said in a tortured voice. "I don't want to hurt you."

"Don't stop! I want you now."

With another rough sound, he bent towards her and kissed her deeply while adjusting his clothes. Then yanking off her panties and widening her legs, he thrust deep into her.

She gasped, her back arching off the bed. She was tight, and he felt too big. Even though it burned and the pressure felt too much because it had been a while, she clutched him close.

"You have no idea how much I missed you," he rasped.

Despite the urgency she felt, her eyes prickled with tears. "I missed you too," she whispered.

Their lips met once more, and then both of them let go. He drove into her like a wild storm while she clung to him.

"I'm never letting you go, princess," he vowed. "You are mine. My heart belongs to you."

He possessed her—body, heart and soul.

His fingers dug into her hair at the back of her head and kissed her hard. "I love you, princess," he said.

I love you too.

She couldn't say those words aloud as her throat seized with ecstasy and emotion. The only sound that came out was a choked cry.

Her body trembled as pleasure built like a wave and then exploded. She clung to him, her grip becoming tighter inside and out. Letting out a harsh roar, he joined her in climax.

But once wasn't enough. Their breaths had barely slowed down when he made his need for her known once again. He stripped her clothes before removing his. And then, he kissed her damp throat. They made slow love to each other until urgency caught on again.

She wanted to possess him the way he always possessed her. She wanted to claim his body, heart and soul.

She pushed at his shoulders. "Let me," she demanded.

Staring at her intensely for a moment, he rolled them and adjusted her until she was seated on top of him. Keeping her eyes locked on his, she placed her palms on his muscled chest and moved on top of him.

He cupped her breasts and brushed his thumbs against her hardened tips, making her stomach tremble. Before she lost control again, she caught his wrists and pushed them on the bed on either side of his head before leaning against him to keep him trapped under her.

But the arrogant devil didn't stop making her lose control.

He raised his head and caught the tip of her breasts with his hot mouth and sucked hard. She moaned, unable to control the rush of pleasure that rose as a wave. She took him deeper and harder inside her, aided by his powerful thrust of his hips.

She dug her nails into his wrists to stop him from driving her insane, but his hips continued to rise and he drove into her. Just when she thought she could take no more, he bit the top of her breast, the sting of pain combined with pleasure pushing her to the edge.

She screamed his name as release ripped through her. He groaned and his movements turned even harsher before he climaxed with violent shuddering of his body. She collapsed against him and they rode the waves together, their bodies trembling with the aftershocks.

She didn't know how long they lay still, absorbing the pleasure of the familiar embrace when they had been together. He stroked her back.

"Are you hungry?" he asked.

She nodded. Surprisingly, she was even though she had her dinner.

He kissed her forehead and rolled her to the side. "Let's go," he said, getting out of the bed.

He pulled up his boxers. Blushing, she sat up and reached for his formal shirt and pulled it on. It covered her until her knees.

He led her to the kitchen and began fixing her an omelet.

Her heart felt tight, and her stomach flipped as she watched him cook. It reminded her of the simpler times when he used to cook for her in their small apartments. He had been her arrogant neighbor Arjun, then. But in the massive, sleek kitchen of the penthouse, he was Aryan Varma, the billionaire from New York.

"What are you thinking, princess?" he asked.

She shook her head. "Nothing. I was wondering if I could ever get used to your actual name."

He looked at her for a few moments. He then came closer and held her face in both his hands.

"You can call me whatever you want. I'm still the same guy, princess. Nothing has changed between us. I promise that when things settle down, I'll tell you everything."

She didn't say anything. She nodded.

They fed the omelet to each other. And as soon as they were done, she held his hand and pulled him towards the master bedroom.

"I missed you," she whispered.

His eyes flared. "I missed you too, princess."

It was close to dawn when they fell asleep in each other's arms.

***

Tanvi's heart thudded when she put on her clothes in a hurry. She kept looking at the bed where Arjun was fast asleep.

Her heart ached at the sight of him. He would be fast asleep for a few hours.

Even though she knew she was justified, a heavy feeling of guilt sat inside her stomach.

"Outside of my family, you are the only one who matters to me and who I would sacrifice my life for. I love you and am willing to do anything to have you in my life."

Those words touched her as nothing else ever could.

She closed her eyes.

No. You have to escape.

Love couldn't change what was going on in her life and what she still had to do.

Taking a deep breath, she quietly slipped out of the master bedroom. And then, with her heart thudding, she opened the penthouse door and stepped out of Aryan Varma's life.

CHAPTER FORTY

It was early morning when Tanvi reached her apartment. She began packing right away.

She didn't pack any of her clothes. She just put in all the picture frames and antiques that belonged to her mother. She knew she should have left right away without them, but the pictures and antiques were the only things she had of her mother.

Zipping the bag close, she hurried out of her apartment. She had just pulled the door closed and locked it when she saw two large men approaching her.

"Miss Shetty. Your father wants to speak with you."

Her heart thudded in fear. For the first time, she wondered if she should have stayed with Arjun and asked for his help.

***

"Where are you taking me?" Tanvi asked as the car drove away from the city limits. They weren't going towards her father's home.

Her father's henchmen looked at each other. "Your father asked us to take you to a different place, Miss Shetty."

The bad feeling inside her grew into panic. But taking a deep breath, she put on a calm look on her face. "Oh, okay."

It was close to a two-hour drive. The car stopped, and she was led into the massive warehouse. She had never been to the place, so she knew it didn't belong to her father.

"Good evening, Papa." Her greeting came out slightly more cheerful than usual.

Her father was seated in the warehouse on a plastic chair with documents placed in front of him on a small table. She could see the trust logo on the top of the papers.

"Where the hell were you all these days?" he demanded.

She pasted a smile. "I went on a vacation with my friends, Papa. We went to Coorg. It's really lovely this time of the year."

His eyes narrowed. "Why didn't you pick up your calls?"

She put on a heavy frown. "There were no signals at the coffee plantation we were staying at for three weeks."

Her father looked at her face suspiciously. But a few moments later, there was only annoyance.

"Sign these trust papers. I'm dissolving the trust. I need the money for elections."

Her heart thudded. She had already started the initiation process of transferring all the trust money to the charitable organizations of her choice. She was only keeping a small portion which included the house that belonged to her mother's family. It was the house she had lived in with her mother until she was seven.

So far, she had kept the decision confidential, and the lawyer helping her had been working for her mother's family for several decades.

"What happened to the money from your primary donor, Papa?" she asked.

Her father's eyes flashed. "That bastard ruined me. It's all your fault because you protested and made a big stink out of it. He's building the mall at a different location. And all the other construction projects don't involve me anymore. He cut me off entirely!"

Tanvi's heart thudded. She now knew Arjun wasn't lying when he said she had to stay for her security. It was security from her own father.

"I'm sure there will be other donors."

Her father looked pissed. "All the donors combined wouldn't come close to what that bastard had offered me. Because of that, I had even made risky investments, hoping to double the money. Those blew up in my face too." He glared at her. "It's my hard work over the last fifteen years that helped grow the trust money. I need that money now."

She didn't know how to get out of the situation. If she signed the papers, the trust dissolution would be invalidated, or the trust money would be gone before its distribution.

"How much do you want, Papa. I can sign the checks."

He shook his head. "No! I don't want to keep begging for money that rightfully belongs to me. Sign the papers and transfer all the funds. When I win the elections, I will return the amount."

She knew the last part was a lie.

Her hands and legs trembled. She knew she had no choice but to sign the papers. But what terrified her more was what would happen as soon as she signed the papers.

Had it been the mere transferring of the trust, her father would have asked her to do it at his house or even in the legal offices. But the fact he did it in a faraway isolated place filled with his goons indicated to what he had been planning for a while.

He wanted her out of his way. Forever.

He had been planning that for the last year, arranging for it to appear like an accident or an unfortunate incident. She recalled the recent incidents when he had sent the goons to the protest, hoping to make it appear she died in a violent scuffle. The next incident was when he sent goons to wait outside her office building one stormy night.

She had managed to escape them all. Until now.

"Why were you packing up your things in the apartment?" he asked. "Were you planning to leave?"

Her heart thudded. She knew the goons must have told him about what she had been doing when they found her.

"I was planning to move back home," she said. She tried to force a smile. "You are right. I missed home. And I thought I should help you with your campaigning for the upcoming elections."

He looked at her suspiciously. "Fine. Yes, we'll talk about that later. First, sign the papers."

She knew she couldn't put it off any further. With trembling legs, she went towards the papers. She wasn't going to make it easy for her father. Everything inside her had been screaming for a long time to confront him and demand the truth.

It would be risky and would more or less seal her fate. But if she were to die, she would do it knowing the truth.

"I know what happened, Papa."

At her statement, he frowned. "What?"

She took a deep breath about to tell him what she had seen on the night of the storm and what she had discovered later. But before she could say anything, there were sounds of a scuffle.

There was shouting and footsteps of people running towards something or someone.

Her heart thudded in fear.

And then, her worst nightmare came true when she saw Arjun walking into the warehouse. He must have tracked her cell phone to know where exactly she was.

"You!" her father shouted.

Arjun appeared cool even though she could see the tick in his forehead that indicated his anger. Whether it was directed at her father or her, she didn't know.

Her father continued to shout. "How dare you come here after ruining me! You brought me to the streets! You even made me mortgage the house I'm living in!"

Arjun continued to appear calm while he spoke. "The house didn't belong to you," he said. "It is back to the rightful owners. The Vardhamans"

Tanvi saw shock on her father's face. She was confused for a moment until something clicked in her mind.

"My name is Arjun Vardhaman."

Shock ripped through her. When he had told her his last name, it hadn't registered in her mind. The family she knew with that last name had died fifteen years ago.

Or so she and everyone thought.

"Who are you!" her father shouted. "What are you talking about? How can that house go back to the rightful owner? The Vardhamans are dead! Did you ruin me because you confused me with someone else?"

Arjun's mouth twisted into a small smile. "The house would be registered in Parvathi Vardhaman's name."

This time, her father's face turned completely pale. He looked as though he were a moment away from getting a heart attack. "P-Parvathi..."

Her father's eyes roved over Arjun's face, taking in his features closely. "My God," he said in shock. "You are Parvathi's son. You and your mother escaped the fire..."

"Yes. We escaped your murder attempt."

Tanvi watched her father break out into rage. "It was all your mother's fault that your family had to go through those things. Hadn't she been a gold-digging whore and ditched me, I wouldn't have gone after your father."

Arjun's jaw clenched. "My mother wasn't a gold digger. She loved my father. You married a rich pregnant woman after having her fiancé murdered. You even killed your wife when she found out what you did to my family."

Girish Shetty panicked. He looked at Tanvi. "He's lying!"

Tanvi didn't say anything.

Her father looked cornered. Then suddenly, he pulled out a gun.

Tanvi's heart thudded in fear while Arjun remained calm.

"I'm going to kill you, you bastard," her father raged. "Yes, I had your father killed. I was the one who drugged him and hung him to death, making it appear like a suicide. But it was your mother's fault! She rejected me and my love. She chose a rich man instead. She got what she deserved when your father died. And she will suffer more when you do too. I want her to suffer until her dying day and repent that she rejected me."

He raised the gun and pointed at Arjun.

"Papa, wait!" Tanvi called out.

Her father threw her a dark look. "Don't come in between."

She shook her head. "I'm not coming in between, Papa. He deserves to die. But I want to shoot him."

Her father looked shocked. "What?"

"He deceived me too, Papa. He pretended to be someone else and... and... took advantage of me. He made me fall in love with him. He was the one who asked me to keep the trust fund away from you."

Her father's jaw clenched.

"Let me shoot him, Papa. I want him begging for his life and repent for what he did to me."

Her father hesitated a moment. But slowly, he handed her the gun.

"Shoot him dead like a dog. Everyone Parvathi loves deserves a dog's death."

Tanvi held the gun in her hand and slowly pointed it at Arjun. Arjun watched her calmly.

Her hands trembled as they locked eyes. Memories of their first meeting and the time they spent together flashed through her mind—his arrogant smirks, his wicked smiles and laughter, and the intense look when he declared his love for her.

Taking a deep breath, she pulled the trigger.

The loud sound of the gun resonated in the air while a bullet ripped through Arjun's chest. Her stomach shook, and she controlled herself from breaking down.

The impact knocked Arjun back against the wall. There was no shock on his face as blood pooled from his chest where the bullet hit him. His eyes began to glaze, and he staggered a little, sliding down against a wall.

"By God, I didn't think you would do it!" Her father's voice sounded proud and satisfied. "You proved yourself as my daughter for the first time."

Dragging her eyes away from Arjun, she looked at her father. "My friends think I'm at your house. If we leave now, we can prove we weren't involved in Aryan Varma's death."

Her father frowned.

"I'll sign the trust papers in Mr. Munshi's office. He can be the alibi too."

Her father's frown melted away, and he nodded. "Good idea. Then your signatures can't be contested as fraud."

She nodded.

She and her father, along with her father's henchmen, stepped out of the farmhouse, leaving Arjun behind. She got into an SUV with her father.

The ride was tense, and she could barely stop from bursting out crying and going to pieces. But she held herself in check.

Two hours later, they reached the lawyer's office. Mr. Munshi received them as she had called him from the SUV and let him know she and her father were coming. She had also asked for some of the trust board members to be present.

"Hello, Tanvi. Mr. Shetty. Please come in."

They went inside the lawyer's office. As soon as everyone was seated, her father handed her the documents to sign.

Tanvi barely glanced at them. Instead, she looked at the people in the room.

"I wanted everyone to come here to be witnesses to the decision I'm making regarding the trust."

She turned and locked her eyes with her father. "Girish Shetty will no longer be the trust enforcer. I'm dissolving the entire trust and donating the proceeds to charitable organizations that I have listed. Mr. Girish Shetty cannot contest it because he is not my biological father. There are DNA test results from two years ago that support my statements."

Shock ripped through her father's face.

She looked at the man who murdered her father and mother. "I'm also reopening the case of my mother's death because I am witness to the fact that Girish Shetty was home at the time of my mother's death. They had been arguing about the Vardhaman family's unnatural deaths before my mother fell down the stairs."

Her father erupted in a roar. "You little bitch! You deliberately framed me!"

He was about to get up and attack her, but the security Mr. Munshi had arranged beforehand stopped him.

Her heart thudded. She wanted to confront her father and seek answers, but her mind was on the man she loved—the one she had deliberately shot in the chest, injuring him.

She hurried out of the room and called Arjun's phone. The phone rang but no one answered. She badly hoped he had been taken to the hospital before he lost a lot of blood. Under ideal circumstances, the bullet she had shot into his chest should not harm him fatally. She had seen it pass through his chest and hit the wall behind him.

She also knew he must have come with backup enforcements. But because she was alone with her father who had a gun, Arjun must have chosen to come inside the warehouse alone.

Oh God. Please let him be okay.

Her eyes filled with tears as she rushed out of the building. On her way, she crashed into something solid. She looked up to see the blurred form of a man in a business suit. Wiping her tears, she opened her mouth to apologize, but when the man's face became clear, she was shocked. And confused.

She wondered if she was imagining things because she was worried about Arjun.

The man in front of her looked a lot like Arjun. But he clearly wasn't. Although the man had the same high cheekbones, hard jawline, bold masculine nose and piercing eyes, this man had a scar on his cheek. He didn't have hints of dimples either. Not that the man was remotely smiling. The expression on the man's face was completely opposite of the devil-may-care attitude of Arjun's.

Another man joined him who also looked similar yet with noted differences.

"Miss Shetty?" the first man spoke. "I'm Yash Varma."

"And I'm Bhargav," the other man added. "We are Aryan's brothers."

Her heart jerked. "Oh God. How is he?" she demanded. "Please take me to Arjun!"

Both men looked at her and must have thought she was becoming hysterical. But she didn't care. All she wanted to do was go to Arjun.

The man named Bhargav spoke. "He's still at the hospital—"

"Why! What happened! I thought the bullet went clean through his shoulder! Oh God! What happened! I shot him because there was no other way to keep him safe!"

"He's doing fine, Miss Shetty. He had called us to let us know he was going to you at the warehouse. We got to him on time. He's having the gunshot wound attended to at a hospital. And you did the right thing. In fact, you saved the life of our hotheaded brother."

"Please take me to him!"

The man named Yash nodded. "I'll take you." The man looked at his brother. "Secure Shetty. Make sure he doesn't get bail."

Bhargav nodded.

Tanvi knew they were talking about her father. She had dozens of questions to ask, but right then, her priority was Arjun.

"Come with me, Miss Shetty," Yash Varma said before leading her to a car parked outside.

But before they got in, Yash Varma stilled. And he began looking at the sky. A strange sound filled the air. Tanvi looked up to see a helicopter. She wondered why Yash Varma was watching it with a frown.

"Can we go right now?" she said. "I want to—" Her voice drowned when shockingly, the helicopter landed on the street.

Before the helicopter propellers even stopped rotating, the door to the chopper opened. Her heart jerked to a stop and began racing when she saw a man stepping out.

She ran towards him. Although her heart sang seeing that he was doing okay, anger fueled by worry bubbled over seeing his hand in a sling.

"You arrogant ass!" she yelled. "What were you thinking storming into that warehouse alone!"

She knew his actions had saved her life, but she was still upset that he risked his life for her.

"Don't ever do that, you jerk!" she shouted.

"Easy, princess," he said laughingly, wrapping his free arm around her waist and pulling her to him. "My girlfriend shot me a while ago. Be nice to me."

She was relieved, and her heart melted seeing his dimples flash with his broad grin.

Before she could say anything, another feminine voice spoke.

"You must be Tanvi," the woman said.

Tanvi turned to see a somewhat familiar-looking middle-aged woman. And even though there was a worried look on the older woman's face, the woman smiled.

"Yes, Ma. This is Tanvi. The woman who shot your favorite son earlier this afternoon." Arjun sounded amused.

Tanvi froze, and her face heated.

Oh God. It was Arjun's mother, the generous-hearted woman she had always wanted to meet.

Tanvi realized, she had already met Arjun's mother once. She had met Parvathi Vardhaman as a child at the Vardhaman Estate. She never thought she would be meeting the sweet woman again under such circumstances. Her face heated all the more at Arjun's introduction.

"Aryan!" his mother scolded with a laugh. "Stop teasing the poor girl. She's worried about you."

Tanvi's heart melted at Parvathi Vardhaman's words. But immediately, her heart began to ache remembering what the sweet woman had to go through. The man who was still Tanvi's father in the world's eyes had destroyed Parvathi Vardhaman's life due to his jealousy and greed.

Does she know who I am?

Parvathi Vardhaman smiled. "You look beautiful and sweet as you did when you visited the Vardhaman Estate."

She does remember me.

But there was no hate or anger or bitterness in the other woman's eyes. Parvathi Vardhaman must have read some of her thoughts.

"Your mother was a sweet and generous woman, Tanvi. She helped us when we needed help the most. She purchased tickets for us to New York and ensured I had a job and a place to live. You are just like her."

Tanvi didn't understand what that meant. But Parvathi Vardhaman smiled. "We'll talk later. Let's go back to the hospital. My stubborn son wouldn't listen and rest until he made sure you were doing well."

Tanvi's heart fluttered. Arjun's hand was still wrapped around her, and he was watching her with a smile.

Her eyes prickled with tears at his protectiveness. Although she was still upset that he risked his life for her, her heart felt safe that she loved a man who would put his own life at risk to save her.

"You can cry all over me at the hospital, princess. Let's get out of here."

She laughed at his arrogant statement. But she understood his need to get away. He didn't want his mother to come across the man who killed his father.

Police cars had arrived and were surrounding the law office right then.

Tanvi followed Arjun and his mother into the helicopter.

She held Arjun's hand. Even as the helicopter took off to the hospital where a team of doctors was waiting to monitor him, Tanvi didn't let go of his hand. And neither did he loosen the grip on hers.

"I'll never let you go, princess."
Those words resonated deep in her mind and filled her heart.

Epilogue

Five years later...

"Thank you all for helping us reach the goal of planting a thousand trees in two days. With this drive, we are not only protecting our future, but also our present."

Tanvi's statement was followed by claps and cheers. She was hosting a voluntary event at the Palki Foundation. The event was to plant trees in the city's parks and public areas. Volunteers consisted of not just environmentalists but also families living in the city, including many young children.

"Where were the saplings acquired, Miss Palki?" one of the reporters asked Tanvi.

Tanvi knew where the conversation was heading, but putting on a polite smile, she replied, "Most of our tree saplings are indigenous varieties from the Vardhaman Estate. We are grateful to the family for donating them and participating in the drive."

The reporter's eyes lit up. "Miss Palki, when will you be a part of that family? There are rumors that you and Mr. Aryan Varma have been engaged for the last five years. And that Parvathi Vardhaman is preparing for a wedding at the Vardhaman Mansion."

Tanvi suppressed the urge to sigh out loud. She knew that despite the scandal being five years old, news channels and many people were still curious about the Vardhaman family, who after being presumed dead for many years had returned to the estate.

Tanvi continued to smile politely. "Today is about the plantation drive. We are happy that children of all ages have volunteered and shown interest to learn more about the environment."

Games and fun activities had been organized during the plantation drive to make the event more exciting for the young ones.

"Miss Palki. You have often been spotted with Narmada and Sukanya Varma. Are they helping you shop for your wedding?"

The reporters stuck to the topic like a leech.

"They are my good friends who I meet often. They have helped me with the organization of the current drive. As you could see, their young ones have also participated in the event."

Tanvi waved at the little girl and boy who were Narmada's four-year-old daughter and Sukanya's three-year-old son.

Before the reporters could ask any other personal questions, she got up with a smile. "Thank you all for coming. All of us had a long day, especially the children who must be tired. We'll see you at the next event that is a month away. "

Using that excuse, she stepped down from the makeshift stage.

Although publicity for events with good causes was good, she drew a line at discussing her private life. Once again, she thanked the organizers and volunteers of the event before they all began to leave. She waved them goodbye, adding a few kisses to the little munchkins.

"Bye, auntee Tanvii!"

Tanvi smiled and blew a kiss at Narmada's four-year-old daughter, Netra. "Bye, sweetie."

Sukanya's three-year-old son, Rishaan, had already fallen asleep in his mother.

Tanvi smiled at her two friends who had been more like family for the last five years. "Thank you so much for coming," she said.

Narmada and Sukanya were quite busy running their software and interior design businesses while taking care of their little ones. Tanvi really admired them, especially because the two women were sweet and always ready to help.

"Oh, come on," Narmada said with a smile. "No need to thank us. We enjoyed the plantation drive, especially Netra and Rishaan."

Sukanya laughed. "I think Rishaan enjoyed it a bit too much." The three-year-old's clothes were covered in mud.

Tanvi smiled. "I'm glad."

"We'll see you next week, Tanvi." Narmada's voice lowered and she shook her head with a laugh. "I can't believe those reporters somehow sensed Ma is readying the mansion for the wedding."

"Must be one of the wedding vendors who leaked the information," Sukanya said.

Tanvi knew it was impossible to keep the wedding a secret. As long as people didn't gatecrash the intimate family event, she was fine. The Varma brothers would ensure there was enough security placed at the mansion and around the estate.

"I'll manage the reporters," she said with a smile.

Waving them goodbye, she walked towards the other side of the parking area where there was lone pickup truck waiting in the distance.

As soon as she opened the truck door and sat inside, it began to move. A deep voice spoke in the tone of a journalist. The man wore a blue checkered shirt and a cap.

"I want to know too, Miss Palki. Why haven't you married the hot hunk, Mr. Aryan Varma? Why did you reject the poor man's multiple proposals for five long years?"

Tanvi let out a laugh. She recalled the multiple proposals, most of which were made on a day-to-day basis. "Aryan Varma is an arrogant ass," she said in a mock, annoyed tone. "The only reason I finally agreed to marry him is because of his family who I happen to love."

"Huh," he said. "I thought it was because you are addicted and can't get enough of Aryan Varma's massively huge—"

She slapped his arm with a laugh. "Stop it, you jerk!"

"I was about to say huge heart, princess," he said.

"No, you weren't!"

He grinned, flashing his dimples.

Tanvi's stomach fluttered. Even after five years, the man next to her made her feel like how it had been during their initial days of meeting.

"So where are we going?" she asked.

He had come to pick her up from the volunteering event. But no one recognized him because he wasn't in his usual sports cars or fancy bikes. Instead, he arrived in a pickup truck and was wearing a cap and sunglasses.

"We are going to your place again. Ma has spies in the penthouse to ensure I'm not defiling her future daughter-in-law before the wedding."

Tanvi's cheeks heated. Parvathi Vardhaman wanted to follow the tradition of the bride and groom not meeting for a week before the wedding ceremony. But the older woman's arrogant son had already broken the tradition multiple times.

The pickup truck stopped in front of a big house. Five years ago, Tanvi had moved into the house that belonged to her mother's family. It was the same house she had spent her first seven years of childhood.

"Are your friends arriving tomorrow?" Arjun asked.

"Yes."

Rashmi and Kavitha were flying in from the United States and arriving the next day. Tanvi was looking forward to spending time with her friends who would be with her until the wedding. Her other friend, Divya, would be joining them a day before the wedding.

"So technically, we just have tonight then," Arjun said with a frown.

Tanvi laughed. "The wedding is only five days away," she reminded.

She knew she would miss him too, even though it would be just four days. They have been together for five years, and they slept together most nights in either his penthouse or her home. She even accompanied him sometimes on business trips to New York or elsewhere. It was only when she visited the Vardhaman Estate that she was given one of the guest rooms, but Arjun still managed to sneak in.

After the wedding, she would officially be able to share his bedroom suite at the estate.

She was very excited about the wedding. Not only would she be marrying the man she loved, but she would also be getting a family who loved her.

Despite what Girish Shetty, the man she grew up thinking was her father, had done to the Vardhaman family, every member of that family welcomed her with open arms. They didn't hold a grudge against her. If anything, they empathized with her because Girish Shetty was also responsible for the murder of her biological father and mother.

She pushed away those dark memories and instead focused on the happy ones that the man next to her gave.

She often spent her weekends at the Vardhaman Estate. With the restoration of the mansion completed along with the revamping of the estate grounds, the place was now breathtaking.

The first time Arjun had proposed to her had been by the river at the estate, five years ago. She had turned him down even though she loved him because of the heavy guilt she felt about the ongoing murder trial of Girish Shetty. And also because she felt that she and Arjun had fallen in love way too soon.

But five years after Arjun had crashed into her life like a storm, she still felt his strong love along with being cherished and desired.

"By the way, you looked quite hot on that podium," he said as he followed her into her bedroom. He pushed her into the bathroom and turned on the shower. "Did I tell you how much I love the hot and fiery activist vibe?"

He had told her that many times. In fact, he had even told her about the first time he had seen her on a video during one of her protests.

She laughed. "Pervert," she scolded.

"Only for you, princess," he said while rapidly stripping her clothes.

Her breath hitched, and her heart began racing in anticipation. After spending all day outside planting trees and hosting an event, she should feel exhausted. But as usual, a single touch and a heated look from the man she loved energized her.

Her hands fell on his checkered shirt, and she tried to unbutton it. But Arjun began kissing her throat, making her fingers tremble and become clumsy. He had stripped her naked while she was still struggling with the third button on his shirt.

"Five years, and you still haven't learned to unbutton my shirts, princess," he said with an arrogant smile. "I guess we aren't practicing enough."

She blushed at his teasing. But soon, she narrowed her eyes in determination. She knew exactly how to make the arrogant man's cocky smirk disappear.

She cupped his hard arousal and squeezed.

He sucked in a harsh breath while his eyes flared. "You always play dirty, princess."

She raised her chin. "I play to win, Mr. Varma."

With another arrogant grin, he stepped closer. "We'll see about that, Miss Palki."

The rest of the night was a passionate war.

Much later, during the early hours in the morning, she lay exhausted and content in Arjun's arms. She ran her fingers gently on his chest where there was a faded bullet wound from five years ago. Each time she saw it, her heart still clenched, recalling the terrible moments when she was forced to shoot him.

But the man she loved made it easy for her to forget it.

"I love you, princess," he said with a sweet kiss on the top of her head. "I can't wait to call you mine in front of the world."

"I love you too," she whispered. She couldn't wait either. She was excited to marry him and let everyone know that the handsome, arrogant man was all hers.

***

"Congratulations, little bro. You are now officially a family man."

"Welcome to the club."

Aryan laughed as his brothers teased him.

Tanvi was inside the mansion with his mother, his sisters-in-law and Tanvi's friends. She was getting ready to take off on their honeymoon. The other wedding guests, Mr. Rao, Sameer and Tanvi's friends' husbands were chatting at a distance.

The wedding ceremony had finished a while ago. The entire mansion was decorated from inside out. Although it had been five years, he was still surprised by how stunningly similar it looked to how it had been two decades ago. Bhargav's wife, Anya had done an excellent job at the restoration. Bhargav had been right when he said no one else could come close to getting the humongous task completed.

Nostalgia pierced Aryan's heart. Although everything remained the same, he missed his father. Each time he saw the beautiful gardens and orchards surrounding the mansion, he imagined his father laughing and working there. The long, polished marble corridors inside the mansion reminded him of the laughter when he and his brothers played hide and seek while his father and mother looked on with indulgent smiles on their faces.

With time, the loss of his father had simmered into nostalgia. He and his brothers often reminisced about the happy times spent with their father. So did their mother. Having their family grow in size helped in the healing process.

"Uncle Aryan, will Aunty Tanvi stay with us from now on?"

Aryan smiled at his four-year-old niece and ruffled her hair. "Yes, little monkey. She is going to stay here."

Aryan was close to his niece and nephew. He often took them on picnics on the estate and played with them whenever he visited them at their homes.

Bhargav and Anya lived at the estate with his mother. And Yash and Narmada shuttled between the city and the estate. Narmada's grandfather, Mr. Rao, who was now family, also lived with them. But no matter where they all lived, they often met and spent time together as a family. Tanvi was already close to his family, and now she was officially a part of it.

He had wanted to make her a part of his family five years ago, but she had turned down his marriage proposal several times. He knew she wasn't mentally ready because of what had been going on in their lives.

Girish Shetty was arrested, and the older man was proven guilty by law on all accounts. He was responsible for the murders of Ashok Vardhaman, Indira Palki and Ganesh Kumar who was Tanvi's biological father. Ganesh

Kumar was a lawyer activist who had been Girsh Shetty's good friend. Girish Shetty had his friend murdered so that he could marry his friend's rich, pregnant girlfriend. Girish Shetty confessed that he wanted to marry a rich woman to not just use her as a stepping stone, but also to get back at the woman who had rejected his love and marriage proposal to marry a rich man. Over the years, Girish Shetty systematically planned and got into the inner circle of Ashok Vardhaman and eventually had him murdered.

The court trial had lasted for only four months because of the readily available proof and the recorded confession obtained from the warehouse confrontation.

Aryan recalled how it had been a tough time for his mother, listening to the confessions. But with the love and support of her sons and her daughters-in-law, she stood strong. She had even said she felt vindicated because her husband's name was finally cleared.

The world now knew that Ashok Vardhaman was a kind and generous-hearted man who wanted to help the underprivileged by building lower-income homes. He was betrayed by his close friends and murdered by a greedy, jealous man.

Two months after the final verdict, Girish Shetty was found dead in the jail cell with a self-inflicted gunshot wound.

Although Aryan would have wanted the bastard to live longer and suffer, he was glad the old man was dead because he didn't want to risk the possibility of the older man using his influence and getting out of jail.

"By the way," said Bhargav. "Just so you know, Ma is going to drop several hints about wanting another grandchild."

Aryan shook his head with a smile. His mother headed charitable organizations under the Vardhaman trust. The stalled project of building lower income homes was now completed with over thousand homes being built across the estate and in the surrounding areas of the city. Aryan's mother built and personally ran several schools for the underprivileged children.

Although she was very busy, she still complained that her sons were yet to fulfill their familial duties. She had already been hinting to Aryan about wanting more grandchildren, saying Vardhaman Estate deserved to be filled with laughter from more children.

Even though Aryan had cleverly indicated that his brothers would be adding to the numbers, a part of him was excited at the thought of having a little girl who would look just like Tanvi and be equally sassy. He would most likely pamper his daughter, driving her fiery mother crazy.

He grinned at the thought.

"Take the entire month off," Yash said to him once again. "Bhargav and I will take care of things here."

Aryan knew his brothers wanted him to take a break. For the last five years, things had been quite busy at work as they moved their headquarters to India. He had been flying to New York and other locations to get things sorted, while his brothers took care of the new headquarters and the estate along with their growing families.

As a freelance writer, Tanvi's work wasn't dependent on a specific location. She only travelled occasionally to environmental conferences. Most of the time, they coordinated in a way where she could combine the trip with him by accompanying him to New York or other locations. They would continue doing that in the future until they decide to start a family.

"It's fine," he replied. "Tanvi wants us to spend time at the estate before I move into her place."

Tanvi's mother's home would be their primary residence. Like Yash and Narmada, they would visit the estate on the weekends and holidays. Personally, he didn't care where he lived as long as Tanvi was with him. She was his home.

There was a burst of feminine giggles. He smiled when he saw Tanvi stepping out of the mansion surrounded by family and friends. She looked beautiful in her bridal wear. But with her cheeks flushed and her eyes sparkling with happiness, she looked all the more breathtaking.

She's mine forever now.

He couldn't wait to pull her into his arms and declare that to her.

He heard her friends giggle as they neared.

"You are the first couple I know who are going to their honeymoon on a bike," Rashmi teased, pointing at the bike parked at a distance. "I envy you."

Aryan grinned. It was strange, but it was perfect for what he and Tanvi were planning. Their first honeymoon destination wasn't that far, and Tanvi enjoyed bike rides with him. They often went on long rides, mostly from the city to the estate.

"See you next month when you fly to London!" Divya Mohan hugged Tanvi.

Although the other girl was briefly engaged to Yash, and her father was killed during confrontation at the estate, Divya Mohan didn't have a grudge against the Vardhaman family. She was close to Narmada and Tanvi.

Tanvi's other friends hugged her too. "We can't wait to see you again." Since both her friends lived in New York, Tanvi often got to meet them when she accompanied him on business trips.

Aryan's mother hugged Tanvi. "You've already been a part of our family for the past five years," she said. "But welcome once again officially into our family."

Tears shone in Tanvi's eyes as she smiled with happiness. "Thanks, Ma. Thanks for everything."

Aryan's mother smiled.

Tanvi hugged Narmada and Anya who had become her close friends and were now officially her family. "See you two both soon."

The rest of the send off continued. Tanvi thanked her friends, including Sameer for attending the wedding. She hugged Mr. Rao who had become close to her and treated her like his granddaughter. She also hugged Yash and Bhargav who were now a part of her family and had been quite protective of her over the last five years. The time Tanvi often spent at the estate had increased the bonding between them.

"If your husband bothers you too much, don't hesitate to push him into the river this time," Yash advised with a small smile.

Tanvi laughed. "Yes, I will."

Aryan grinned as Yash reminded them all of the first meeting with Tanvi during their childhood. Aryan had tried to attract her attention by yanking her hair, only to be punched in the stomach and pushed into the water fountain in front of the mansion.

Aryan knew his fiery wife was capable of doing it again if he annoyed her too much.

His grin widened because he couldn't wait to tease her and watch the sparks fly.

"Ready?" he asked.

She blushed at his obvious impatience to get their honeymoon started.

Everyone laughed.

Waving to their family and friends once more, he finally led his wife to the bike. He put a helmet on her before putting on his and got on the bike.

Tanvi sat behind him and wrapped her arms around his hips.

"Ready?" he asked once again.

"Yes," she replied.

With a powerful kick, he took off.

Barely ten minutes later, he stopped the bike in front of a small wooden cottage by the river. The spot was often used by his brothers and their wives when they needed some time away to their busy lives. He had brought Tanvi a few times there as well. Everything remained the same at the scenic spot except for the small cottage that offered more privacy along with a few comforts of home.

"Finally," he said as he parked the bike in front of the cottage. "I thought our send-off party would last until tonight, and I might have to kidnap you again."

Tanvi giggled and whacked him playfully. "Jerk."

Grinning, he swung her up in his arms and carried her inside the small cottage, where a large bed was decorated with rose petals. As soon as they stepped inside, passion gripped them, five days of being apart making them desperate.

Her breath hitched as he stripped her bare of her wedding dress. Her hands fell on him, pulling at his wedding clothes, ripping a few buttons in the process.

Their mouths met hungrily, kissing and biting and touching. Soon, their joining was frantic and passionate. It felt like heaven being inside her. He pushed into her deeper and harder, wanting to be as close to her as possible. He didn't know how many times they made love. It was their honeymoon, and he was determined to claim his fiery wife.

But when initial desperation cooled a little, they finally took in their surroundings. The small cottage also had enough food stocked to last them a month.

"This looks like a baby trap," he said in amusement.

Tanvi blushed and buried her head into his chest. "Oh God, yes. Your mother not-so-subtly hinted she wants a grandchild. And that if we have a baby within a year, then Netra, Rishaan and our child can grow up being close to each other."

He laughed. "Doesn't sound like a bad plan, princess," he said, rolling on top of her again and watching her with a grin. "I think we should get started on it, especially if we are to have five kids."

He said the last part deliberately, knowing she would snap back at him. He loved it when she argued. It made their already passionate life even hotter.

Her eyes narrowed and she opened her mouth to argue, but seeing his heated gaze waiting in anticipation, she stopped. She had known him long enough to be able to read his intentions.

"Stop it, you arrogant jerk!" she said with a laugh. "I'm not giving you five kids. You are already a handful to me!"

He laughed, knowing it was true. And although he did want children, he was still too obsessed with his fiery pawn turned queen to share her with anyone yet. He wanted her all to himself for a while.

He smiled. "I love you, princess."

Her eyes softened, and she held his face before pulling him for a sweet kiss. "I love you too."

THE END.

Author's Note

Thank you for choosing *Wicked Trap*. I hope you enjoyed the Varma brothers family saga in the *Wicked* series.

After writing dark and brooding antiheroes in the 1st two parts, cocky, arrogant and charming, Aryan was a fun and exciting anti-hero to write. :) I hope you were able to escape into Aryan and Tanvi's passionate love story and their happily-ever-after.

If you haven't read already, do read the other Varma brothers Yash and Bhargav's love stories.

Thank you

MV Kasi

Email: manyavkasi@gmail.com

FB/Instagram: @mvkasi

Twitter: @author_mvkasi

M.v. Kasi's Book List

WICKED TRAP
WICKED LIES
WICKED DECEPTION
WILD IN LOVE
CRASH IN LOVE
DEVIL'S LOVE
DEVIL'S DESIRE
DEVIL'S KISS
UNTIL YOU
ACCIDENTAL HUSBAND
THE PROMISE
THAT SAME OLD LOVE
THE HOLIDAY AFFAIR
MISSION SUPERSTAR
UNTIL FOREVER
BOUND BY HATRED
THE CAPTIVE
SOULLESS
RUTHLESS
BREATHLESS

Short Stories (20-Minute Reads)
HIS CAPTIVE BRIDE
RECKLESS LOVE
THE ROYAL WEDDING
THE PROPOSAL
BOUND BY FOREVER
BILLIONAIRE ESCORT

www.ingramcontent.com/pod-product-compliance
Lightning Source LLC
Chambersburg PA
CBHW031253160726
47993CB00001B/133